# Marked For Murder

*A Matthew Diggerson Mystery*

by

D. G. Gillespie

This book is fiction. All characters, events, and organizations portrayed in this novel are the product of the author's imagination or are used fictitiously. Any resemblance to actual persons—living or dead—is entirely coincidental.



For information, email Cozy Cat Press,
cozycatpress@aol.com or visit our website at:
www.cozycatpress.com

ISBN: 978-1-946063-57-1

Printed in the United States of America

10 9 8 7 6 5 4 3 2 1

Dedicated to the inspiration and memory of J.R.R. Tolkien, who fostered the dream, and to dreamers everywhere.

## Chapter 1: To Introduce

Colons are marks that introduce information, such as lists, quotations, and explanations. To remember this mark, you can get help from the melody of a famous Rolling Stones' song.

Please allow me to introduce myself, I'm a mark that ends a thought.
Not a period, not a semicolon, to announce info, I am sought.
Students don't know what I'm called, they tend to say of me, "Those two dots."
You can put me before a list, or a quotation, a little explanation or a lot.
Pleased to serve you, a "c" begins my name.
I'm a colon, and introducing information is my game.

"You have such pretty eyes," she said, and Digger thought, *Anna used to say that* and then, *Why do I always go directly to Anna?* Even after sixteen years, Anna still surfaced so easily in his mind, morning vapor over a pond, a ghost. For the past eight years, his ex-wife had sent him a short greeting once a year, each Christmas, so in Digger's mind she had become the Ghost of Christmas Past, shining and beautiful, but intangible, touched by only the tattered tendrils of memory, except for that yearly smattering of letters, well wishes, plot with few details, words offering faint light and little warmth, no invitations, closed doors. *Oh, well!*

Digger mentally shook away his glimmering ex-wife, imagining Simba's and Snodo's (i.e., Snow Doe) shaking off a glistening spring rain on his back porch, and smiled at Johna Adams (pronounced "Joan-uh"), whom he had hired a week earlier to fill two open English 101 classes at Ocean View College. Johna was taller than Anna, less shiny but still attractive, and as she continued to look at his eyes, Digger felt a little foolish.

Should he thank her, tell her that her eyes were pretty, too? Digger was out of practice.

Then the third member of the standing trio, Bill Jacobs, still part-time, still a bit of a pain, eccentric, saved the scene: "I've always loved your eyes, Digger!" And then he batted his own beady brown orbs, a ludicrous image due to his heavily bearded façade, brown still but sprinkled lightly by Time. And Bill's eyes were bloodshot, too.

"Oh, and yours make me weep, Billy," said Digger to his old colleague, whom he had known for over twenty years now. After all, Digger was close to fifty, and Bill past that milestone years ago. Time had begun to assert itself.

Johna laughed at the two men and then said to Digger, "I'm not flirting, Digger." He had told her during the initial interview that everyone called him that (although his mother usually labeled him "Matthew" and Anna had always called him "Matt" and still did in those Christmas cards, which he kept in the kitchen's miscellaneous drawer and took out a couple times a month, reading the words, fingering what she had fingered). Then Johna, the un-flirter who definitely seemed to be flirting, added, "It's just that one minute they look blue, the next green."

"I'm a chameleon," said Digger while Bill Jacobs swiveled his bearded head and batted his little black eyes. Blocking out this sarcastic image, Digger thought of Anna's face instead. "Actually," he continued, "my ex-wife, Anna, had the same eye coloring, blue in the light, green in the shade. Mine are probably like that. People used to say that we looked like brother and sister."

"That's not so great for a romantic relationship," said Johna.

The statement made Digger feel defensive, but before he could respond, Lou Knightly, the last full-timer hired, a few years back, stepped between Johna and Digger and declared, “No time for romance, let’s get this meeting started, Digger!”

Lou’s tongue had a tendency to slip out and slide across his upper lip, right to left, as though searching for crumbs, and Digger looked at the man’s face, expecting the snake to emerge. Beneath his boxy dark-brown hair, Lou looked back, grinning, and then he said, “What are you three discussing about romance?”

“Digger’s eyes,” replied Bill before anyone else could speak, and then he continued, “We can’t decide if they’re sky blue or ocean green.” Digger groaned.

Lou’s tongue made its search. He was a tall and narrow fellow. Digger pictured him as the type of cartoon character who would vanish when he turned sideways, perhaps slipping through a crack in the floor. Looking down into Digger’s face, he announced, “They look gray to me,” and everybody laughed again. Of all the dozen or so full-time composition faculty, Louis Knightly, the lip licker, was the most sociable. Most of the others emerged from their narrow offices only to teach, and Digger was becoming more like that as the years passed. He thought of the Humanities corridor on the third floor of the Faculty Offices Building—the most famous of OVC’s edifices due to its history of murder!—as a cave where those little white eels would pop out of holes and then slide slowly back. Then he thought of electric eels, wondered if they could kill a man.

Digger wanted to end the conversation about his eyes. He had some news for his friends, his colleagues, and he wanted to get the meeting started. Having been elected Chair two years back, Digger had conducted this August meeting of all writing faculty twice before, but this year would be different because he was now an author and he wanted to share that news. Over the winter break, spring semester, and early summer, he had written a murder mystery loosely based on his experiences with Danny Jones, a sad student who had suffered from schizophrenia and just life, and who had jumped off the Bay Bridge, that towering presence to the south of OVC's campus. Digger still tried not to look at the looming structure, still never drove over it. Although the adjoining tourist town of Bayside beckoned on the other side of the bay, Digger had not set foot on its soil for over sixteen years.

His book, while based on reality, depicted fictional characters, an actual murder instead of a suicide, and a campus only hazily related to Ocean View College, but in Digger's mind his story was basically real—not far removed from reality, anyway. With the help of an editor for a scholarly publication that had displayed a handful of Digger's educational articles, Digger had found a publisher who built the book and put it on Amazon. Royalties were few and far between, but Matthew Diggerson had not written the story to make money. Doing so checked off a life goal, an objective for all writing instructors, most likely: to be read, to assert existence, to *join the conversation*, some would say. Thus, Digger knew that his colleagues would be interested, and he looked forward to telling them, to lifting up a copy of the book, to saying "See!" Today, unfortunately, he could only *tell* them since the printed book had not yet reached his mailbox, the one on a post outside his house, not the email kind.

Digger wanted to switch the "eye" talk, so he picked an easy subject, turning to his old colleague. "It's so damn early," Digger complained, "that everything looks gray! How do you teach in the morning every semester, Bill?"

"I like it when the students are asleep," said the bearded and sarcastic man. "They're less bothersome that way." Johna and Lou laughed, but Digger just smiled. He had heard this diatribe for decades.

"What about you, Johna," said the Chair. "Would an eight o'clock class in the future bother you?" He had actually given her a cushy spot, a noon Monday, Wednesday, Friday course, along with a Wednesday night class.

"I'm used to them," she answered, still chuckling a bit. "Along with my noon and night class here, I have eight o'clockers every day of the week at Sea View. I can still remember being in them in college, too, sort of."

"I can't," said Lou.

"I can't either," said Digger.

"I never went to college," said Bill. Everybody laughed at this.

"Okay," said Digger, still smiling. "I guess I'll get things started." And he moved from the little group toward the conference room on the third floor of the Faculty Offices Building, a room just barely large enough for the twenty or so teachers in attendance. Entering, Digger saw Diana Pell and was surprised yet pleased since she had often skipped this August meeting. Old and wise, Diana had taught creative writing and literature at OVC for half a century, it seemed—long before Digger arrived, anyway. Tobias Mann, of all people, had told Digger that Pell had once been State Poet, or as Mann had put it, "The old bag expects everyone to bow to the Poet Laureate." *Tobias!* Digger was not quite ready to write about those experiences—soon, though, for he had already begun taking notes for a second mystery. The new author looked forward to telling the former State Poet about his own literary achievement because he had never felt particularly friendly with the stern woman. He imagined that their shared writing experiences would forge a bond.

Surrounding Diana were all the full-time faculty, all closer to the window: Mary, getting old now (second only to the poetess in seniority), a nice woman, bit brainy (Digger always pictured her as floating a few inches above reality); Catherine, stuck firmly to the earth, stiff, upright (Digger always imagined her saying "Off with his head!" in another life); Jolie, thin yet substantial looking, short haired (looked machine cut), young but seeming older (Digger couldn't forget Bill's summation of Jolie: "Lesbo!"); Eliot, considerably gray now (thin, too!), a good-natured fellow (Digger liked Eliot but in his mind—never to a colleague—had nicknamed him the Breather because the poor old guy always seemed short of breath); Todd, a quick smiler, short, a slight Midwestern drawl (hired almost a decade ago but still "new" in Digger's mind); Jeff, quiet and scholarly, neither giving nor seeking (Digger rarely saw or thought of him at all!). The head of Tutorial Services, the Chair before Digger, Don Domberg was not present. *Must be out cutting his beard some more,* thought Digger, but not unkindly, because he had always liked the man, just not his beard so much.

On the other side of the room, divided in the middle by a rectangular table, slightly rounded on the edges, sat the part-timers, the adjunct faculty, and Digger wondered once again why the two sides didn't mix more, at least during these summer meetings. After all, both full- and part-time faculty had gone to graduate school, had read and read and hopefully learned how to teach, and both sides taught the same classes, the same students. Both understood the same triumphs and travails. Why the divide? Really, the only difference was the number of courses and money. And prestige. No doubt rebelling against the latter, Bill Jacobs would never sit with the full-timers, yet why didn't Johna follow Lou over toward the table's window side? Too full already, or was an unspoken aura present, one that hovered above the full-time faculty and announced, "Not so fast! Know your place"? The part-timers all seemed clustered around Bill, the dark nucleus. Digger was glad to see the newest adjunct, Jay Moore, whom he had hired to fill one last opening, a Wednesday night class. While he could have given the course to Johna, she already had a full adjunct schedule (three classes) at Sea View Community College, and chairpersons were wise to have one or two adjuncts who could take courses in emergencies. Moore was Digger's safety valve. Jay had sat himself in back, as though definitely knowing his place in the department, yet Digger could still see him blinking. *Must have some eye condition*. When he had interviewed Moore, Digger had noticed that the short, somewhat "thick" (not really fat) fellow blinked often, so much so that Digger had begun to think of his own blinking, discovering that he hardly blinked at all!

Looking at the other adjuncts, Digger noticed that a few were missing, as usual, since part-timers seemed to have busy summers, family obligations. He thought of the typical student excuse for absences and missed assignments: "family emergencies!" Still, several part-timers were in attendance, not only Bill, Johna, and Jay, but also John George, a quiet, capable former high school teacher; Patricia Pauley, a slightly eccentric little lady who knitted during office hours (might as well make them productive!) and beamed when talking about her three cats; Dave Jepson and Liz Lawson, whom Digger thought of as a pair since both were furtive but pleasant enough when cornered. At the moment, the two were whispering, and Patricia, left out of any conversation, looked like she regretted leaving her knitting needles at home. She taught just night classes, but Digger had forgotten why—must work during the day.

Elena Bonner was, of course, not present since she had years ago returned to SVCC to take a full-time position. Although Digger never heard from her, the humanities secretary, Gloria Swanson, kept him informed—whether he wanted her to or not! Elena had apparently left poor Will Watkins behind, too, the bespectacled Psychology professor, who had been Elena's boyfriend several years past. After Bonner left Ocean View College, Gloria had suggested repeatedly that Digger should email Elena, but that had been years ago. Even Gloria recognized a dead end.

Facing the now quiet crowd, Digger felt a bit like Jesus at the Last Supper. He said hello and that he hoped they were having fine summers and then he thanked them for coming. "We don't have a whole lot to do this time, so this meeting will be shorter than usual." At this announcement, heads turned and words bubbled out, happy little hoots. Digger continued, "I want to introduce two new faculty members, talk about our Bridges software, and discuss what seems to me to be our students' biggest weakness: reading skills."

"Or a lack of them!" said Lou Knightly, and a tittering swept the room.

"Definitely," said Digger. "A lack of them. But first maybe we could hear from our two newest members. I won't have us all introduce ourselves, because the new people would just forget everybody's name, no doubt, and because we will all meet them sooner or later during the semester." Even as he said this, Digger knew that it wasn't true since part-timers rarely ventured beyond the adjunct faculty office, where full-timers rarely tread. However, he had decided to dispense with what he considered a tedious beginning to these summer meetings—everybody introducing themselves.

"Johna," smiled Digger. "Let's start with you, Johna." He gestured to her, not to stand but to begin.

"My name is Johna, obviously," she started, and Digger noticed her blush (it made him feel more connected to her). "Johna Adams. I'm teaching two sections of English 101, and I've been teaching writing for about ten years, mostly at Sea View Community College, where I will also still have courses. I'm looking forward to teaching here, and to asking you all for help!"

*Good ending*, thought Digger, who knew that humbleness worked with this crowd. Fertilizer for the prestige!

Digger smiled at her, saw a shape entering the room and turned to watch Don Domberg's unsuccessful attempt at being invisible. The shovel-bearded fellow bumped into a desk, said "Sorry," nodded to Digger, nodded to others, moving like a bull in a china shop toward the full-timers, choosing an empty seat outside of the big rectangular table.

"That's Don Domberg, head of Tutorial Services, trying to be inconspicuous," Digger announced to the two new adjuncts, and everyone twittered a bit, especially Domberg, who also bowed, looking even more religious than normal with that prominent dark beard. Digger smiled at Domberg and then turned to the Blinker. "Jay," he said.

"Jay Moore," said the Blinker, and then he blinked twice (one for each word, wondered Digger?). "I'm teaching a night English 101. And I'm going to need your help more than Johna because I have not been teaching for ten years, only for a couple. I used to be a realtor. In fact, I think I recognize a couple of faces here. I probably sold you your mansions." Everybody laughed at that. No OVC professor lived in a mansion, yet the word made Digger think of Tobias, who before his murder eight years back had owned a big house. Jay wasn't done: "I decided when the economy dipped that I wanted a career change, so I went to night school myself, and now I'll be teaching night school. I'd like to pick up another class or two, too, but the new guy has to wait."

Everybody smiled at the new guy, even Diana Pell, whom Digger had labeled the Reluctant Smiler because her grin formed so slowly. Her mouth was wide, like a boxing turtle's, and downturned on the ends, too, so that it took that long line quite a while to transition upward and finally to divide into a gleam (sort of) of teeth—almost like a sunrise on a really cloudy day. Digger saw her teeth appear now. He saw a couple heads nod at the Blinker. Everybody wanted to help the new guy, but Digger knew that few after today would even see him because almost everyone would be gone long before five o'clock or so when Jay Moore would arrive for his six o'clock class (until nine at night—*oh, god!* Digger remembered those!).

Digger switched on the computer, using the keyboard at the top of the long table, and the screen behind him transitioned from gray to blue to the home page of his own Bridges site revealing links to his courses both future and past. He clicked on a link to one of his three previous spring semester ENG 102 courses, and immediately the screen showed a more specific image, one with a calendar, a note about the course, and a full tool bar on the left. The Chair wanted to urge colleagues to use the course software as much as possible, especially to collect and return papers—all digitally—a step that few faculty had taken so far, one that he had embraced years ago. For close to half an hour, he walked the room through his Bridges site's tool bar, focusing especially on the Assignments and Resources tabs, offering tips and suggestions, apologizing to those who already knew Bridges well, occasionally asking for questions, responses, reactions. As always, a few people (not just adjuncts) asked sort of dumb questions, but Digger realized that not everyone was familiar with the course software. Most colleagues, as usual, pretended to be experts, beginning their comments with "I use …" and then going on for a couple minutes (or hours!) about their *use.* This subjectivity was nothing new, happened with every summer meeting, with every meeting of teachers in fact, even in informal gatherings. Everybody wanted to show "I know!" Nobody wanted to reveal any vulnerability, and perhaps, thought Digger yet again, that's a good thing, a required quality for this profession—acting!

After covering his Bridges site and hearing that nobody had any more questions, Digger transitioned to his next topic by clicking on one of his spring semester student's summary assignments, pointing out that the student had not understood the writer's argument, had just repeated the main idea but not broken it down into clear supporting reasons, apparently did not see those reasons in the reading. Digger concluded the presentation with this: "Because the author implied her points, as is always the case with any literary work, the student could not see them, as you can see through his essay. He lacked the required reading skills, and most of them do. Why? More importantly, how can we supply those skills?"

These questions led to a spirited discussion and to multiple "In my class" soliloquies. Nobody took notes, reminding Digger of his own students, who for years had ended his brief lectures or their peers' presentations by extending their phones at the board and snapping photos, rather than choosing and annotating ideas from it. His students all had backpacks for their laptops, but rarely did a written notebook appear. Same thing with this summer meeting—minus the backpacks. After half an hour of "reading" conversation, thousands of words having been driven through his mind, Digger synthesized the proceeding: "In short, we need to focus on reading skills, especially early on in the semester, and especially by stressing annotation, even requiring it in class and for homework, and we can use the Does-and-Says tactic, too, to get students to see how a writer builds an argument. In other words, with 'Says' ideas, some points stated, most points implied, and with 'Does' information, with evidence, with language and rhetorical tactics, ethos, pathos, logos, and for our 102 literature classes with elements of fiction. Those elements are the logical 'Does' ideas for stories and poems, even plays. We need to focus on their understanding of the readings, and our assignments need to reflect that understanding. Our lessons need to stress it, especially early on. Maybe next summer we'll explore those lessons in more detail than today's discussion. Maybe we'll all type up a lesson plan, one focused on reading skills, and share them. How does that sound?"

It sounded good, mainly because it signaled an ending to this summer's meeting, and Digger thought of bobble-heads. Lou Knightly licked his upper lip; Jay Moore blinked twice. Diana Pell frowned, her smile long gone. Maybe the old poet didn't want to go home. Maybe Digger could raise that grin again with his final main announcement, his book.

"Okay," he said, seeing the crowd shifting, ready to rise up and vacate the premises, and hearing it murmur, making Digger think of a field of dry autumn wheat in the wind, the clacking of seed husks. "Just a few things before we go and enjoy the rest of the summer. As always, thank you for coming."

"It's mandatory!" yelled Bill Jacobs, and everyone twittered, the wheat field vibrating.

"Thank you everyone but Bill," smiled Digger. "Okay, for you new people, you can find printed syllabi in the copy room, or just ask Gloria for help. Gloria has all the answers!"

Everyone looked over at Gloria, poised by the door. She had just now showed up, not needed for the meeting but apparently in tune to its conclusion. With her big head of black hair, held in suspension by chemicals more so than genes, Gloria Swanson looked like a 1950's schoolmarm. Seemingly unaffected by the attention, the sociable woman nodded to the field of faces and then slipped out the door—work to accomplish!

Digger continued. "I will be available mainly on Tuesdays and Thursdays in case any problems arise, but to see me you will have to enjoy dogs because my two often come to school on those days." The wheat field glistened and twittered at the mention of Digger's dogs, who were well known at OVC, especially the lion dog, Simba, old now but unaware of it.

Digger continued again: "Of course, you can always email me or call me at home. Gloria has my number if you lose it. I'd like to hear how things go, and I wish you all a successful semester." Wind swept the field, words evaporating: "You, too, you, too …"

"On a personal note," said Digger, "today is my birthday." An image of Bilbo Baggins arose in his mind, along with the words "an unexpected party."

The crowd chanted "happy birthday" but not quite together, the words blurred like an impressionist painting or like a Catholic congregation responding to its priest: "Peace be with you."

Like Bilbo, Digger humorously thought of saying that he knew few of them well and liked even fewer of them less (i.e., "I don't know half of you half as well as …"), but he discarded that silly idea, saying instead, "It's a big one, I'm afraid." Suddenly reluctant to mention his big surprise, his published book, he uttered, "Half a decade old almost." He had not planned on mentioning any numbers, nor on using the wrong word, but when the wheat field erupted in rippling laughter, reminding Digger of fire, of violence, he realized that he had once again confused "decade" with "century" and thus declared himself to be four-years old. "Century," he yelled to douse the flames. "Century, of course. I'm just a little dyslexic with those two words."

"Maybe some dementia," yelled Bill Jacobs.

"That, too," laughed Digger, but the mirth was just a mask. He was thinking of his published book, his murder mystery, based very loosely on his experiences with young Danny Jones, the boy who flew from the Bay Bridge, forever towering over OVC's south campus. Digger felt an odd reluctance, a premonition?

Time and mumbled silence pushed the composition teacher to act. Into the rippling field of faces, Matthew Diggerson said quickly, "I gave myself a book for my birthday, my own book, a murder mystery. I wrote a book, and it's been published." He smiled to hide that he had run out of words.

The wheat field went still, completely silent, a hush having swept past. Digger noticed that many people's mouths were open, little O's, and the image almost made him laugh. Then Lou Knightly clapped, and the hollow sound caught on, others joining in, everyone. Digger bowed and then the applause ended, sort of abruptly, and the standing man thought of the word "synchronization." Was it his imagination, or did this crowd look a little hostile? Digger felt compelled to explain.

"I've tried to write a book, fiction, many times, but always ran out of plot. I never knew where to go, but with a murder mystery, the plot's built in. Solving the murder! My protagonist's a composition teacher, a professor turned sleuth!"

Digger had thought that this fact would amuse and interest his peers, yet they didn't look too entertained.

Was Bill actually scowling? And Diana Pell? The box turtle's mouth was clamped closed.

"None of you are in it," Digger laughed, or tried to, and it's not about Tobias, not about Dan Pinsky, those two murders. It's fictional. Anyway, I'd enjoy telling you about the book, which I will give to our library when I get a few copies, and I thank you for coming and for doing such a good job with our students."

Not exactly an organized conclusion, but Digger stepped to the side toward his seat next to Lou, signaling the meeting's end, but then he remembered one more announcement: "Be sure to let Gloria know your office hours!" But the crowd was on the move. He would have to email everyone this reminder.

Lou's tongue made its passage, and its owner, looking down at Digger, said, "A book, Digger, a murder mystery! Congratulations! That's really something!"

"It's been fun," said Digger, glad of the connection. "And I'm writing a sequel."

"Wow, an explosion of creativity! I wrote half a book one time, non-fiction, though."

"What was it about?"

"I don't remember now, something to do with my home town," said Lou Knightly, and his tongue flashed past. "American life in a small town. Angst. Disappointment."

Digger didn't know what to say to that, but luckily Johna Adams then joined the pair, the line becoming a triangle, and Digger thought of his term "bookending," a tactic he had labeled so that his students could better remember an effective way to begin and end their essays—with related specific content, such as a story or interesting quotation. This summer meeting had begun with two of these people and now seemed to be ending with them. The group just needed Bill now for the bookending to be complete. Jacobs was approaching with the retreating crowd, but with his head down, the long-time adjunct appeared to want no part in any concluding tactic.

"I didn't know that you were a writer," said Johna Adams. Her hair was brown and not as long as Anna's, not nearly as shiny. Anna had always seemed to Digger to be a mythical figure—even more so now.

Digger had been wrong about Bill Jacobs, again, for the always bearded and sometimes angry man broke into the trio with "A writer with such beautiful eyes!" as he passed by, and Digger laughed honestly because it felt good to laugh and because Bill's statement seemed benign. He hadn't stopped to join the group, though.

"We're all writers, right?" said Digger to the standing trio. "Lou here wrote a book, or part of one, and he'll finish one day. Honestly, you just need to find the right genre. And then I took my own advice, something I've been telling students for decades—not centuries!"

"What's that, Digger?" said a passing Don Domberg. "Put your phones away!" Digger and Lou laughed at that, and Don patted Digger on the shoulder as he kept moving along. As usual, Digger pictured the man's manicured beard as an old-fashioned train's cattle guard. *Coming through, move aside!*

"Well," said Digger to the remaining two teachers, "not just that. Don't we always tell them to write about what they know? To use their experiences, limited as they are? That's what I did. I made my main character myself, with some major differences, of course. His name is Billy D Wilder, and he's a bit of a cad, bit of a drunk. He, uh, left his wife."

"Were you using your experiences there?" asked Johna, and Digger admitted that he was but didn't embellish his point, didn't mention the contrast.

"I wrote about something that happened at OVC over a dozen years ago," he said instead.

"Not the old Chair's murder?" said Lou.

"And I remember reading about a janitor, too," added Johna, who explained, "I was just at Sea View Community College then. But it couldn't have been twelve years ago."

"Before Tobias and Dan," said Digger. "That was eight year ago, and this was years before, when I was just barely full-time and still …" He had been about to say "still married," but he transitioned to "still a faculty tutor. At Tutorial Services, I had met a student named Danny Jones and he ended up killing himself."

"That's awful!" said Johna.

"Oh, yeah," said Lou, his tongue following those words, and Digger thought, *I wish that he wouldn't do that!* "I heard something about a student's suicide. He took a dive off the bridge, right? I didn't know that you knew him, Digger."

Took a dive? *How well do we know anyone?* "I didn't really know Danny," Digger admitted, "but I tutored him a few times and talked to him a couple other times. And, of course, I saw him jump."

"What!" declared Johna, and Lou's tongue flashed and slashed.

"Yeah, I saw him up there. I had been driving over it one night, going to get a pizza."

"Mario's!" said Lou.

"Mario's," said Digger, adding "I haven't had one of those in over a, uh, decade."

"You were about to say 'century,'" laughed Lou Knightly.

"I was," said Digger. "I drove past and saw Danny clinging to a pylon. I didn't know it was him until I got out to talk the person down. I failed."

At that, all three humans fell silent, each picturing the failure, the fall.

"I use that bridge all the time," said Johna, "but I don't like driving over it. The wind up there makes the car go side to side. You feel like you're driving through the clouds, and the lanes are so narrow, too. It's scary when you pass a big truck. I can't imagine stopping on it and getting out."

"It was late, not much traffic, none actually," said Digger, adding "For many, many years, I tried to blot out the memories, but then I decided to use them instead, to write about them."

"But I thought you said it was a murder mystery," said Lou, "not a suicide."

"Write about what you know," said Digger, "but make a lot of stuff up, too! I changed just about everything, out of respect for Danny and his mother. I won't tell you the details, just in case you want to read the book!" Digger laughed at that, thinking that of course all his colleagues would do so.

"Definitely!" said Lou.

"I will," said Johna, but then she added, "Not right now, though, because I have too much prep to do."

"Me, too," said Lou.

"Of course," said Digger, but he couldn't help feeling a bit let down. He had pictured many of his colleagues' ordering e-books, at least, that very night. After all, August had barely begun.

Maybe his peers were doing exactly that, rushing to their computers to access Amazon, for the room was now empty, the field of wheat harvested, just the human triangle remaining. Then the three people began moving toward the door, Digger last.

"What did you say was your protagonist's name?" said Lou, turning back to Digger.

"Billy D Wilder," laughed Digger. "My mother's maiden name is Wilder, and my character's full name is

William Daniel Wilder, but everybody calls him Billy D. He's a bit of a swashbuckler, outgoing, confident."

"The man you want to be," smirked Lou, and Digger laughed.

"Seems like the man you are," declared Johna, and Digger laughed at that, too.

"Not so much," he said, adding "But Billy D's far from perfect. Perfect's not really interesting, you know."

"Better to write about all of us leading quiet lives of desperation," agreed Lou.

"What's it called?" asked Johna.

Digger felt a little foolish. He had chosen a melodramatic name, partly to fit the mystery genre, partly to make the accomplishment less serious, mainly to stress his niche, the unique angle that made him feel especially good about reaching this goal.

"It's called *Composition Murder*."

## Chapter 2: To Balance

Students often create run-ons, two statements that lack grammatical connection. A semicolon is a mark that could be used between the two statements in order to balance them correctly, as shown by these lyrics related to a famous song by Leonard Cohen.

If you write two ideas that don't sound smooth,
Well, listen for the connecting groove,
Like a "since," an "and," a "but," or something other.
If there's no connection for your thoughts,
Perhaps some punctuation's sought,
The force of a period or balance of a semicolon.
Hear a run-on? Use a semicolon. Hear a run-on? Semico, oh, oh, o lon.

As August counted down, Digger awoke each morning a little more disgruntled because none of his colleagues emailed him about his book. *Busy preparing*, he told himself, but he didn't really believe that excuse. An obsessive organizer, Digger had been prepared for the fall by June, and at this point in the summer, he was merely tweaking his lesson plans and Bridges course sites. As the Chair, he had just three courses now, not the normal four, but he had to be in the office more often than in the past in order to deal with the myriad problems that blossomed suddenly like spring mushrooms: a student dissatisfied with his or her teacher, a professor concerned with a student, some sudden order from the administration, etc. Still, living just a mile from OVC, during the semester, if he didn't actually bring his pups to school, then Digger often skipped home to say hello and to let his dogs run around out back. In fact, he had just done so (let them out, the fall semester having not yet begun), and standing in his kitchen doorway with his morning cup of coffee and a growing irritation at his

OVC peers, he watched Simba and Snodo move about his little fenced-in yard, the grass baked golden dry by the August sun and the sea's salty breath.

Simba looked golden, too, lighter than ever. The Corgi-shepherd mix's black fringes had long gone gray, white muzzled now where once she had sported black fur, white tufts sprouting from her ears like an ancient man's, her thick lion's mane pale tipped where once it had been jet black, but she still trotted about fairly well, just slower maybe, perhaps less often. Less enthusiasm, for sure, and that was hard to see in a dog who had once absolutely beamed. Digger wondered about her ears, too, because Simba didn't always seem to hear him rattling the food bowls or opening the back door. The veterinarian said that her ears were pretty clean, just a little wax to remove, and she prescribed a bottle of blue ear-cleaner. Simba also slept more often, that deep sleep beneath those soft wrinkles that make a slumbering dog so heart wrenching, failed to jump up on the couch as much, and often licked her paws, both front and back. The vet flexed her limbs, said "No real rough spots," and recommended glucosamine pills. Simba's brown eyes were glazed by a green sheen, too, the breath of Time, but the vet said that cataracts were to "be expected" and that the old dog—about sixteen now—was in great shape for her age. *Beautiful Simba!* As he stood in the doorway, Digger smiled because the lion dog had just made a rare dash and scattered a troop of sparrows, many of whom had nests softened by Simba's double-coated fur, which Digger often brushed out and left scattered across the back yard. Simba looked back at Digger in the doorway, checking in, something that she had once done continually but that now occurred just sporadically.

Waving at Simba and smiling, the composition teacher then turned his attention to Snodo, his "new" dog, a little nut named from the Baggins' clan, at least that's how Digger thought of his Snow Doe. Eight years past, he had found her, a sister for Simba, at the local pound, and every day he wished he had gone sooner since Simba had lived alone for five years. As "tall" as Simba but not nearly as long as the Corgi-shepherd mix, Snodo was a strange sister: an energetic playmate, a soothing companion, and at times a vexing, growling adversary. Especially lately, Digger had noticed that the two dogs played together less, slept further apart, looked mainly to him for…what? Camaraderie? Entertainment? Meaning? Guidance? *Food!*

Younger, more full of life, of "piss and vinegar" (as his mother would say), Snodo was physically the size of a long beagle, mentally as large and alert as any human, and spiritually huge, with a soul that beamed from her light-brown orbs, which always seemed to ask, "What! What! What!" That's how the dog had seized his attention at the pound eight years back. He had been looking for a bigger dog, a black one (Digger had always loved black dogs), so he had just glanced into the little white dog's cage and continued on. However, as he was cooing at a big black-and-brown lab mix three cages down on the aisle's other side, something pulled his mind and head back. It was that little white dog. She had been sitting up against the bars, quite still, and staring at Digger with a look that had to have had telepathy embedded. What else had turned his head backwards, rather than forwards toward all the dogs yet to be seen?

Digger had stared back, the two creatures united by a thickening interest, and then the man had returned to the white dog's cage and looked in again. The dog that would be Snodo had not moved at all, other than a slight head swivel to match Digger's movement, and when the man knelt and said hello, the animal began a tail wagging that continued until this day. When he had reached through the bars to stroke the little white head, Snodo had licked his fingers, and when he brought Simba to the pound later to meet his future sister, the two had reacted very positively, hopping and bouncing about, actually reaching their paws toward each other as Digger and one of the pound's officers sat in the office and watched the new friends. The cop had said that she had *never* witnessed two dogs more compatible.

*Not so much now*, thought Digger, noting the *friends*' separate pursuits in the back yard. Simba was squatting (Digger would deal with that later), and Snodo was stretched out on her back and rubbing against the earth, enthusiastically, making a comma shape to the left and then to the right. Had the door been open, Digger knew that he would have heard her emitting happy little grunts. Short haired, Snodo was as white as a Disney movie horse, and she even had a magical equine mane, not as thick and rounded as Simba's, but long white hair running down her head and ending halfway along her back (the pound cop had decided on a beagle-wire terrier mix). Sometimes, Digger called her "Pony," but the name "Snodo" had come to him almost immediately at the pound since Tolkien's hobbits were never far from Digger's thoughts—their love of nature and simplicity, their loyalty. The happy little dog had immediately reminded Digger of a Shire dweller.

That spirituality existed in this backyard world, where Digger spent most of his happy times. He liked to stand at his kitchen door or the sink and look out the windows, watching the blue waters ripple and sizzle with white lines, to feel the slow passage of floating clouds, to fly and soar and dip with the birds. To hear the nasal sounds of the winds pushing their way through the twisted and stunted maples and pines, which separated many of his neighbors' yards from the short public beach. Then Digger would gather his gaze from afar and focus closer, taking note of his backyard sparrows snatching Simba's fur tufts from the grass or holding heated discussions at the feeding tube—on it, below it, on the fence—and the chickaddees as they darted back and forth into the spindly blue spruce, its arms waving as though to fend them off. And at times he would imagine that if he turned back to the kitchen table he would find *her* there, sipping her coffee, reading the Sunday paper with that look of concern she would get, her brow furrowing and creating a V above her nose, her light eyes narrowing. *Oh, Anna; oh, Anna!* He would close his eyes to the empty table, the sky, the sea, and think, *Time, time, time, time, time*, as though that were the combination to unlock and rewind life. And sometimes he would turn and open his eyes just to make sure that she was in fact *not* there, but usually Matthew Diggerson would not bother. Sixteen years makes a realist out of just about anyone.

On this late August day, he did not turn back. Instead, he pulled the two leashes from their hook behind the back door and joined his friends out back. Snodo charged over and bounced up and down several times, recognizing the leash and what it meant, the next-best thing to dinnertime: a walk! Simba hadn't heard Digger. She was still sniffing around beneath the spruce, the chickadees cocking their heads at her and complaining in little peeps. When Digger approached, the black-and-white birds shifted an eye each toward him and then zipped away. Unaware, Simba was still exploring something invisible near the spruce's base, the tree's trunk as thick as a man's leg now. Digger's eyes on the brown dog, his mind on her hearing troubles, the composition teacher was startled when his neighbor's head popped up over the six-foot wooden fence that separated their properties.

"Digger!" announced Graham, who had lived next door (with his wife, Donna) even back when Digger and Anna had moved in. In the folds of memory, the older couple had presented the younger one with champagne, but the pairs had never really grown close. Digger considered Graham and Donna, whom he saw less often, "good neighbors" because they didn't complain and kept fairly quiet—sort of a sad way to define a relationship, he knew.

"Graham," said Digger. "You startled me. Did you grow during the night?"

"I'm on my step ladder," smiled Graham. "What's with that lion dog?" The two men looked at Simba.

"What do you mean?"

"She doesn't come when I call her anymore."

"Simba's a little deaf. That's what the vet said. Just typical age. She's sixteen now, almost sixteen. You can never be sure how old a pound dog is."

"Wow," said Digger's neighbor, transitioning the dog's sixteen years to himself. "We're all getting old, aren't we? Except that white dog, that little horse. Look at her stomp about, the world's her oyster!" Graham was always like this, always used descriptions instead of names, and Digger wondered if his neighbor did that to people, too, said "that fat guy," "that big-nosed woman," "that sour puss." He imagined Graham's reference to himself—what would it be? That *sad* guy? That *deserted* teacher? Maybe the *wife-less* one. No use going down that path. Some people just didn't refer to pets by name, perhaps considering them not to have names, personalities, souls. His neighbors had no pets, didn't feed the birds, didn't even attract feral cats or the wild animals that ambled about the edge of the sea: skunks, opossums, raccoons. Especially skunks. Because of the wild, Digger never fed his dogs out back, but the bird seed still attracted attention. Before letting his pups out, the composition teacher always checked for critters in the yard.

Are animals attracted to certain people, or do certain people feel attracted to animals? *Probably both, as usual*, thought Digger. Then his neighbor, looking down from above, surprised him again.

"I thought I saw someone in your back yard last night."

"You did?"

"Before bed, I tend to take a look around. Remember those college kids who painted swastikas on your house?" Hard to forget when neighbors resurrect the incident yearly!

"Oh, yeah. I remember, but I try not to think about that." Digger was good at blocking bad thoughts. He sent them to his black river, which slid by just beneath his consciousness, gurgling only occasionally. Digger often thought of the story of Abraham Lincoln and the pigs (he had heard it back in college but couldn't remember the class or the teacher): Beset with anxiety over the splitting union, President Lincoln looked down from a pedestrian bridge to see some pigs wallowing in the mud, and for a moment he wished he were one of the happy hogs, who seemingly had no worries, no responsibilities. Then, of course, Lincoln chose to be a man, to forgo ignorance. Digger always sided with the pigs.

"Maybe it was that weird neighbor kid," continued Graham, and for a moment Digger struggled from his muddy thoughts to regain reality.

"You mean the Hoodies?"

Graham laughed. "Donna and I call them that."

"I know. You told me, and the description fits. Even the mother and father wear hoodies, and that teen does all year round."

"A cut-off shirt with a hoodie attached—is that what young people are wearing these days? Do you see that at the school?"

"Not at OVC," said Digger. "The students are mainly Ken and Barbie there."

Graham laughed again. He laughed easily, as did his wife, and Digger was usually happy to have them as neighbors. They helped to keep life simple.

"I wonder who I saw," said Graham, "or what I saw," and Digger again had to shuffle through his thoughts to find the right card: oh, the tresspasser!

"Probably just your imagination, Graham. My two little security guards would have set off the alarm otherwise. Nothing enters my property without Snodo's, especially, knowing all about it."

"Yeah, I'm glad of that. That little white dog sure has a big bark. You didn't have her back when that wacko attacked you, though, did you?"

Paul Smith! Digger often thought of his old peer, the stork-like ex-professor who had tried to kill him, wondering what Smith was doing at certain times, what he was thinking. Digger knew that Smith was "housed" a few towns to the north—not too far away. Digger pictured him as a tall Renfield pinching flies that buzzed from the sky past the vertical iron bars of his cell window into hell.

"He's up at the Detention Center, a lifer. Two counts of first-degree murder and a failed insanity-plea defense. Paul Smith used too much logic to be considered insane."

"He had that big knife, I remember. I saw a cop bringing it back from the beach."

"That was his family heirloom," said Digger. "I always wondered why he threw it into the sea since it meant so much to him. Maybe he was just scared or it could have been a symbolic act, I suppose. Or maybe he really was crazy in that moment." Then Digger wondered where the knife was now—probably nestled in a box surrounded by a roomful of other evidence bins. He thought of the first "Indiana Jones" movie.

"He can never get out?" asked Graham, and pulled from his fictional image of a cavernous room full of pine boxes, Digger had to think for a minute. *He?*

"Never," he finally remembered and said. "You can't kill two white people and get out." Digger hadn't meant to make a societal judgment; it had just popped out. But it sailed past the other man.

"Maybe you should call the prison and make sure the guy's still in his cell. I saw something last night."

"What time?"

"Right around bedtime, around ten. It was a dark night, though. Maybe I just saw the shadow of something. I made a point to tell you about it, though. That's why I climbed my ladder when I saw you out here."

Picturing the ladder and his neighbor's no doubt green lawn, Digger felt a little embarrassed about his own brown and sandy soil, the skeletal bushes that lined the fence on his side. Anna would have gardened better. Then he thought of his happy dogs and of the birds, chirping and zinging about, pulling the skies down into his little life, and the negative prickles evaporated.

"I'm going to write about Paul Smith next," he said, having already told his neighbors about the first book, *Composition Murder*.

"What are you going to call it?"

Digger said that he didn't know, even though he had thought of a title, *Murderous Mistakes*. He liked campy titles, ones that reflected college writing and his composition-professor protagonist, Billy D Wilder. But he regretted mentioning his book, felt something else prickle at the subject (something rising from his black river), and wanted to leave the subject. Niether Graham nor Donna had read his first book yet (*or ever!*), but how could they? Even Digger had not received a print copy yet. *Well*, they could have ordered a cheap e-book download, right? How long did that take?

"I better get going," said Digger to his neighbor's head, the light-blue sky an appropriate backdrop to his seemingly floating noggin. "Look at Snodo! She knows we're going for a walk on the beach." And at the word 'walk,' the white dog began her high bouncing again, occasionally rebounding right off of Digger's chest.

"I wish I still had that energy," said Graham, looking down.

"I sometimes wish that she didn't," laughed Digger, but he didn't mean that. He loved Snodo's joy of life, that *joi de vivre*. Digger bent down to the happy animal and hooked on her leash. Then he stepped over to Simba, petted her back (the startled lion dog trembled quickly), stroked her head (feeling the velvety ears), and attached her leash, too. In the past, when Digger had scratched behind Simba's ears, his first dog would rub her head against his fingers, petting him back, her tail sweeping the air. *Simba's joy*. Sporadic at best now.

"Off we go," Digger said to his old dog, to his newer one, and to Graham's head, which watched Digger and his dogs as they went through his back gate, slipped past the long, strong sea grass, and moved up the beach, inland, where the sand stretched past several homes' back yards until ending at a concrete jetty.

At the distant jetty, not the one just to the south of Digger's cottage, the beach had a public access point, but few people seemed to know about it, the area residents' keeping their mouths shut, too. Nobody yet, neither neighbors nor invaders, had this morning taken advantage of the pretty oceanside area, so Digger unleashed the hounds, Simba first since Snodo could catch up with her so easily. By the halfway point, Snodo had surged ahead, and when she reached the distant jetty, the little horse reared around, grinning wildly at Digger and waiting for her slow sister. Simba used to act just like this, always looking back to Digger, always judging her place in the world by his proximity, yet now she just stood before the concrete jetty as though wondering what it was, why she had to stop, *or perhaps thinking of nothing at all,* thought Digger, picturing old people with walkers and vacant faces, stuck physically and mentally in front of walls. *No!* Not yet, not Simba!

Snodo was exploring the bay's gently lapping little waves, which could hardly be labeled as waves, being more like breaths, wind-driven heartbeats from the canal's depths. The white dog was careful not to let the water touch her. She hated baths, too, something that Simba had never minded. Simba had not minded much, really, just Digger's going through the back door without her. Digger experienced a little expansion in his chest, a lament for the past, for a time when Simba would already have been back by his side, looking up at him, wondering what wonders were next to come.

Turning, he looked back at his Anna-less cottage, seeing just his roof and no sign of his neighbor, other than the second story of Graham and Donna's house, which was bigger than his, two stories to one, fatter, too. Digger loved his little home, tucked into the bay's bend. From this distance, he could just make out the top of the Bay Bridge, where long ago Danny Jones had climbed the sky and failed to reach it—or perhaps he had. In his book, Digger had used the bridge as a looming presence, but not as a suicidal scene. In fact, in his fictional account, the Danny student (named Yusef, a Saudi-Arabian exchange student) had actually been murdered—by a white supremacist group camoflaged as campus Young Republicans. Three of its members had forced Yusef to a bayside spot known as the Whirlpool, where the bay's currents met and fought, creating dangerous undertows. They had followed the Saudi from the library, having studied his typical schedule, and during an early nor'easter storm, had made Yusef walk the jetty—the plank—until he could walk no more. The waters swallowed him. Had the haters actually meant for their Saudi peer to die? Digger never answered that question, but they certainly tried to cover it up, going so far as to murder another person (this time quite calculated!), a composition teacher (not Billy D, though) who had discovered the crime.

Digger had enjoyed—if you could call it that—writing the Yusef murder scene because he had simply pictured Danny Jones climbed atop that Bay Bridge pylon, the winds, the darkness, the stars, the terrible emptiness and uncaring power of the universe. Into his fictional scene, Digger had poured all of his experiences, just substituting swirling snow for the stars, and the written words had healed him, he who had thought that he was no longer wounded by the memories of the witnessed suicide, the long fall. His fictional words had squeezed the non-fictional pain that had sunk into his bones and platelets, evaporating the hurt. *Write how it actually transpired*, Digger had thought then, and he immediately turned that thought into an acronym, WHAT, knowing that he would use that idea if he ever taught Creative Writing I or perhaps Introduction to Mystery Writing, a course that did not currently exist.

With *Composition Murder*, the writing teacher had followed his own advice, using the Paul Smith experience to pen his book's second murder, and he even employed his teaching into the book, both in chapters that covered in-class lessons (revealing clues) and as chapter titles, such as "Focus Clearly," "Develop Specifically," and "Listen for Awkwardness," all writing-process steps that he preached repeatedly in class. These titles also loosely guided each chapter's content, too, the "Focus" one leading to Billy D Wilder's search for suspects. William Daniel Wilder. Digger had paid homage to his mother's side of the family, the wacky Wilders, which now included just his 81-year-old mother, her deaf brother (John), and her two older sisters (Mary and Carol), widowed and quite happy about it, keeping away the reaper through a continuous enthusiasm for the present.

To these remaining family members, Digger had not dedicated the book (he would for the next one). For his first novel, Digger had said this: "Dedicated to the memory of Daniel Jones, a student, a son, a brother, a friend." Before okaying the final manuscript with his publisher, Digger had sent a copy to Danny's mother, who had given her blessing to the book. In a note returned, she had written that she wanted Danny to be "remembred," spelling the word incorrectly, but who cared? On the book's cover, Digger had asked his publisher to depict the Bay Bridge, but only in the background, suggesting that the Whirlpool and a handful of figures be highlighted, and the design had ended up pleasing him. The image looked a little campy, dark (with streaks of deep blue, cobalt but almost purple), stormy, like a novel from the 1950's perhaps. For his second murder mystery, Digger imagined a crimson cover showing a darkly receding hallway, with the words "Murderous Mistakes" hanging in red above and maybe dripping a bit. He would, of course, begin these chapters with the names of grammatical errors, which he would briefly explain and then use to guide each chapter's happenings, such as "Fragments," "Run-ons," "Dangling Modifiers," etc. Already, he had planned several chapters, taking notes and jotting down thoughts, but he didn't yet know who would die or who would kill. Billy D would find out; he had become Digger's constant companion, a friend, a voice, a second pair of eyes on the world. This second novel would balance well with the first, provide it with a partner, creating an actual series, a world.

In the real one, out on the beach, Snodo snuck up and licked Digger's left foot, bringing the writer back to reality. Billy D Wilder had lived with two dogs but no wife (he had dumped her!), and Digger had been playing with the idea of having one of the dogs pass away in the second book—but which? The older one, probably, but maybe the new killer would take the younger dog. Would readers accept that trauma? In movies, Digger would yell at the TV if a *dog* were killed. *No canine corpses!* For his story, Digger would take a lot more notes and then decide on deaths, on the killer, as he wrote, probably over winter break, which seemed far away from this warm morning. Simba was still rooting around up at the jetty, so Digger said, "Go get Simba!" to Snodo, who cocked her head a couple times, making Digger smile. He had never seen a dog that would look up at passing planes, but Snodo did consistently. At those times, Digger marveled at her consciousness and wondered what she thought of those heavenly objects. Today, just gulls speckled the skies. Digger pointed at the lion dog and motioned with his head, too. "Simba! Go get Simba!" And this time the little pony understood and dashed away, enjoying the game of point and go.

But Simba didn't return with her seeker. To get Simba back, Digger had to walk to the far jetty, redirect his startled friend, hook her to a leash, and through the thick, dry sand, with Snodo capering on his other side, slowly lead the old lion dog home.

## Chapter 3: To Separate

Commas are marks of separation, usually showing where word groups end, and as this melody from the iconic classic rock band Jethro Tull shows, to use commas correctly, you need to listen for a pause. If you hear one, then put the comma down.

In syntactical Madness, put the commas down
So that you can show your readers, how your ideas sound,
Your phrases and subordinate clauses, your transitions, too.
If you want to lead your readers, you know what you have to do.
Put the commas down, put the commas down.

Don't put one after "Although," it's a subordinate clause,
But add a comma before "but" to show your readers the pause.
Right after you add "However" to start another thought,
Right there you slow the reader, so punctuation's sought.
Put the commas down, put the commas down.

You need a comma before an "and" if there's a second thought.
And to set off extra info that's what you've been taught.
So put one before a "which," but not before a "that."
To show your readers where to slow and where to rush right past,
Put the commas down, put the commas down.

At Ocean View College, the fall semester began the Tuesday before Labor Day, which didn't occur this year until September 7, and the day before classes commenced, the last day of August, Digger found a lunchbox-sized package in his mailbox. *His novel!* Now he could begin the new semester as a real author and show the book off to his peers! The cover appeared exactly as it had looked in the attached email, even better since the book was real. He could hold it, flip it around. The object had thickness, weight, substance, life. Digger couldn't take his eyes off it that Monday afternoon and night, propping the novel up in various places, calling his mother to brag a bit (always welcomed by mothers), wishing that Anna could see it (he did have her mailing address!), even showing it to his canine friends. While Simba just panted and walked away, Snodo licked the cover, and if Digger had not hidden the book on higher ground, the strange unicorn dog would probably have consumed it exuberantly, page by page.

Tuesday was Digger's shortest at OVC, a noon-to-five schedule, no classes, but the happy man arrived an hour early, book in hand. First, he showed it to the only person present, Gloria Swanson, who cooed and congratulated him, complimenting his picture on the inside back cover. "Oh, Digger, the female readers will love this!" she said. He didn't believe that.

Then he sat in his office and popped out (*like a spider*, he thought) whenever he heard anyone in the corridor. When Mary hovered by and was accosted, she looked at the book but didn't touch it, saying that she had "never really enjoyed" mysteries. Undeterred, Digger responded, "You'll like this one. It's about a writing teacher." She moved on down the corridor, unconvinced. When Jolie's neat, sharp footsteps echoed down the hall, Digger called out, saying "Here's my book, Jolie. Just came in the mail." The short-haired woman glanced at the cover, nodded, and then said, "I'm writing a book, too."

"About what?"

"It's literature, about being gay in academia, about prejudice and overcoming obstacles. You know, real stuff."

"Mine's about a writing teacher."

"Who solves murders?"

"Well, yeah," said Digger, feeling a little defensive. "That's the genre."

"That's the genre," Jolie had repeated, adding that she wrote songs, too, and then showing Digger the back of her sawed-off haircut. He had lost some of his shine at that point, starting to feel the sharp edges of separation, of ragged, gray resentment.

Then Eliot had appeared *in* his doorway—not just disappeared into his own office—and Digger as usual felt a wisp of concern for the heavily-breathing older man, who had predated even Digger at Ocean View College. *Eliot Gladstone*. When Digger had told Anna his name, she had called him "Professor Happyrock," and Digger had loved her for that, for the way she could slip seamlessly into play, just like a dog. How easily she still emerged in his thoughts—his Anna—and Digger realized that she appeared because he wanted her to, that other men would have blocked out a divorced spouse, a source of pain, but that his time with Anna acted like a magnet, a glow.

"I hear…you have…your book," said the Breather. Digger's pilot light blazed. Gloria must have been doing some promoting.

He showed the older man the cover, and Eliot reached out for the novel. He shook it up and down, as though weighing it. "It's definitely a book," he said. "A little short, but a book." *Happy Rock*, a juxtaposition, an oxymoron, for how could a "stone" be "glad"?

"I discovered online that anything over fifty thousand words is considered a book, and mine's about fifty-five." Digger felt that prickle of defensiveness again, pictured the "stone" side of the old man's name—the "rock." Eliot flipped the book over, read the synopsis on back, then read it out loud, as though Digger didn't already know it: "When murder occurs at Oceanside College, composition instructor Billy D Wilder turns from professor to sleuth to solve the crime. Is the killer a student, a fellow teacher, an administrator, or just a madman? Billy D teaches as he investigates."

"What does *that* mean? Teaches *what*?" added the Breather, creating spaces between each word, putting an extra puff on "that" and on "what."

"Look," answered Digger, turning to the first chapter (nobody had yet opened the book, except for Gloria to see his photo) and pointing to its title: Hook the Reader. "I begin each chapter with some writing advice, which loosely guides the chapter's content. This opening chapter's about this one Saudi student, Yusef, whom I want readers to like. I want to hook them with Yusef."

"Then you *kill* him." Same spacing, this time a hard breath on "kill."

"Well, I don't want to give it away! I'm going to give our library a print copy, and the book's available on Amazon, too—really inexpensive e-book version."

"I don't read e-books," announced Eliot Gladstone, deflating Digger again. His "friends" were putting up walls, and a flash of irritation rippled through the new author. *This old guy says everything in four-word statements!*

"This is still a teaching college, is it not?" continued Eliot, who handed the book back to Digger and added, "I spend my time preparing to teach." Digger nodded, and the Breather turned and progressed on his way, back up the corridor, no doubt to wrestle with his current lesson plan. *Gladstone*—a name that went full circle, both the yin and the yang, darkness and light. The beginnings of an anecdote flashed through Digger's mind, something about Eliot and a famous writer, some past pain, but Digger's brain was too rooted in his own ego to see other people's viewpoints or concerns.

The new author slunk back into his office and flopped into his chair. *Only noon now.* Five hours to go! He pictured Anna's talking about Eliot. "How's Professor Happyrock?" she had often asked even though Digger could not remember her ever having met the man. She had just liked his name. Anna, *light Anna*. Like Eliot's ancestral name, her memories brought not only the dark pain that Digger was alive, but also the light certainty that he had lived, really lived.

*Composition Murder* was like that now, a shining yet shadowed thing. All afternoon, alone in his office, Digger kept trying to connect through his book, but none of his colleagues mirrored his enthusiasm:

From Jeff: "Quite an accomplishment. I remember my first book."

From Todd: "Impressive. I will read it when I have time." (The word "impressive" sounded humorous when riding a mid-western drawl.)

From Catherine: "I don't read mysteries, Digger."

From Bill Jacobs: "Making any money?"

From Patricia Pauley, another part-timer, the night teacher: "Does it include any cats?"

"No cats," he had told Patricia, thinking of his long-ago feral felines, Shyla and Skittles. "But the next one will." She had said that she would read the *next* one.

From John George, the stately adjunct who actually requested eight o'clock classes, having gotten used to that schedule after a life of teaching high school: "This is a teaching college, yes? We don't have to publish, right?"

"No," Digger had said, wondering if this adjunct had been conversing with the full-timer Eliot, "but *Composition Murder*'s not exactly a publish-or-perish piece. It's not peer reviewed, not scholarly. It's more or less entertainment." Digger couldn't help showing a little irritation, putting emphasis on his 'p' words.

"If I had to publish," concluded the somewhat stiff fellow, "I would definitely perish." Then he laughed. The man seemed to think that he had made a joke, so Digger gave the retired secondary-school teacher a smile.

By five, Digger felt run-over, all his joy squashed right out of him, but by looking at *Composition Murder* again, rifling through the pages, focusing on his name (in white) against the darkly threatening cobalt cover, checking the chapter titles, feeling their connection to his own teaching, he re-energized. At least enough to still strut a bit as he walked the long sidewalk to his car, a black Toyota Yaris (he had traded his pick-up for this little car so that his two dogs could ride along inside with ease, space, and safety).

At home that night, the writing instructor was subdued, his mood reflected in a clouded twilight—beautiful really, but sad, too. The day had not gone as expected. How could a man live for fifty years and still be blindsided by humanity? "By being stubborn," Digger concluded.

Wednesday offered not only three of his own classes, but also a different round of teachers (a Monday/Wednesday/Friday schedule), yet Digger tempered his eagerness. No hallway pop-outs today. Feeling almost as alone as he had sixteen years earlier, after Anna had left him, he sat in his office—between his three classes—and waited for visitors. This tactic paid off, if not in dollars, at least in change.

Prior to his first class (11 a.m.), the Reluctant Smiler emerged from her office opposite Digger's, the creative writing teacher, Professor Diana Pell, the former State Poet. She stood in his doorway, and after Digger greeted her and showed her the book, *it* began—the snail-like process of her smile, fascinating to watch. It commenced as a frown (her usual countenance but not necessarily her attitude) that slowly rose, wrinkles that had been tethered to gravity now becoming like a puppet's strings, pulling the corners of that long mouth up, like a sunrise almost, the brightness held off by the dark but rising and then suddenly breaking through. *Beautiful!* A light usually hidden, a slumbering eyelid opening into crystal blue depths (her own orbs softly streaked with red lightning). Diana Pell's smile took a decade of hard living off her face.

"It's quite something, isn't it?" she said, and Digger understood the 'it' to mean "publishing a book," not necessarily this one.

"*It* feels good," agreed Digger, and he stood up, approached her, and held his text out. The old woman took it and shook it, just as Eliot the Breather had, and Digger hoped and prayed that she wouldn't judge his tomb skimpy, unsubstantial. She didn't. Diana Pell didn't say a thing, just leafed through the book as though its creator were not standing before her. She skipped to the end, looked at his smiling photo, read his short biography, and handed the book back.

"Very nice indeed," the old woman concluded. Digger could live with those words.

"I'm giving the library a copy, Diana, if you have a chance to read it."

"I read only poetry these days, Digger, but my son would enjoy this. He reads everything." *Okay, a strike and a single.*

"I thought I remembered that your son lived far away—in Europe, right?"

"He used to live in Switzerland, but now he lives with me."

"That's nice," said Digger, but he wasn't sure if it were. What would make a middle-aged man return to his mother's house? "I'd like to hear what he thinks," Digger added.

"Oh, Michael's not shy with his opinions," said the woman, but her long mouth remained clamped down. And as she moved away down the corridor, Digger thought of her reluctant smile and wrinkles and slow treading through life as a wise old box turtle. Not that she was heavy or leathery or even unattractive, just that Diana Pell knew it all, had seen it all, had turned the chaos of living and shuffling emotions into verse, the little triumphs and the long sadness and sorrows, and that made him think of Jefferson Starship's great song "Ride the Tiger," which contained a poignant cultural comparison: "a tear in the hands of a western man, he'll tell you about salt, carbon, and water, but a tear to an oriental man, he'll tell you about sadness and sorrow and the love of a man for a woman." Something like that, anyway. Diana understood the *tear*; she was oriental at heart, and that's why her smiles rose so methodically, when they ventured forth at all, and why they bloomed so sweetly.

After his two afternoon classes, Digger scored again, this time in the form of Lou Knightly, Lip-Licker Lou. He too appeared suddenly in Digger's doorway, his rectangular head nearly touching the frame, but this skinny peer strolled right in and took a seat.

"C'mon in, Lou," smiled Digger.

"Professor Diggerson," said Lou in mock seriousness. "Or should I say Supreme Author Diggerson?"

"That would be fine," laughed Digger, reaching for the recently ever-present copy of his achievement. He handed it to the sociable man.

"Nice!" said Lou Knightly, and Digger thought, *Why does everyone weigh a book like it's a gaggle of grapes?* Like Pell, this teacher began to root through the text, adding commentary, though, such as "I like these chapter beginnings," "Always good advice this," and "Whose this good-looking guy at the end?" *Lou!* Digger enjoyed his visit, and after he had gone, the Chair relaxed for the first time in days. Looking out his narrow office window at the quad, Matthew Diggerson noticed that shadows were reaching out from the two-towered library building on this late, sunny September day. A seagull sailed silently past. Digger was happy. Soon he would return home to his two dogs.

*Soon* came, and as he swept up the Humanities hallway to begin his short journey home, he greeted two adjuncts conversing in the adjunct faculty office, the two OVC newbies, Johna and Jay, both of whom had Wednesday night classes.

"Your first night classes," he said, looking from one to the other. "Are you looking forward to three hours of teaching?"

"Can't wait!" said Johna, smiling. Jay seemed to think that her response covered them both. He blinked three times.

"Any problems with Bridges?"

"No," said Johna, continuing to smile. "Worked just like you said it would in my noon class. Really helpful. Sea View has nothing like that, no software course sites."

"Too expensive for a community college," responded Digger, adding "What about you, Jay? Any troubles or questions?"

"All set," said Jay, continuing not to smile. Although the one-time realtor had been somewhat verbose and humble during the summer meeting, Digger now had the feeling that the other man wanted him to leave. A condensed body language. Then Jay opened up a bit: "Johna and I will trade experiences before classes, but I don't foresee any problems." *Stop blinking!*

"Who does?" responded Digger, and Johna laughed at this.

"What are you going to do later this long weekend?" she added. "No papers yet. Are you going to write more of your next mystery?"

Digger felt his soul swell a bit. *Yeah, his next book.*

"I think so," he said. "My next one mirrors a couple murders that occurred right here, one right where I'm standing!"

"The janitor," said Jay Moore flatly, his face inscrutable, his tone the same, and at that, Digger deflated, ashamed suddenly of his own cavalier attitude, now reflected in this relative stranger. How could he have turned two people's deaths, two people he had known, no less, into superficial conversation, into entertainment?

"Who's that?" said Johna, saving him.

"I don't mean to sound flippant. I miss those two. Our former Chair, Tobias Mann, and Dan Pinsky, who cleaned the building. A guy who used to share this room murdered them eight or so years ago. Then he tried to kill me, but instead he sort of woke me up. Paul Smith."

"I know that name," said Johna. "Everybody at SVCC talked all about those murders, but your name didn't arise, Digger. Maybe Johnny said it once." *Johnny Lambmann.* Digger's old SVCC boss, and mentor of sorts. A lost friend. Why did Digger always seem to fail with connections?

"How's Johnny?"

"He's still the Chair. Nobody wants him to leave, and nobody wants all that administrative paperwork. He's the Vladimir Putin of writing department heads. Without the sanctioned executions of course! You can't help but love Johnny. He told me to apply here, told me that you were Chair now, that you would be great to work for."

Digger wondered how he knew. Digger didn't seem to know anything about anyone.

"I need to contact him," Digger said, as much to himself as to Johna. "Maybe I'll send him an email this weekend. Is it just jlambmann at svcc dot edu?"

"Yes indeed," said Johna, smiling. Jay Moore had turned away.

"Okay," said Digger. "And thanks. I'll let you two get back to your conversation. Probably talking about me!"

"Don't be so egotistical, Digger!" laughed Johna Adams, but the other man just looked up and blinked.

That night, Digger felt strong, connected, and he celebrated with a Bud Light, then another. But he stopped at two; he no longer had trouble stopping. For several years, he had felt more controlled about his life, and for that strength he thanked Paul Smith, who in trying to take his life, eight years past, had actually reignited Digger's will to exist. Simba and Snodo lay on the couch with their human, who watched a cop show on TV, enjoying it. Simba had needed a little help up, a boost, for when she had tried to reach for the soft heights, the Corgi-mix had made it just halfway, her back legs turtling, her front a little too weak to support her long body. As the night progressed, both dogs kept their eyes on their human, Simba's dark brown orbs covered with that green sheen (the vet having said that she could still see "fine" and just wanted to keep an eye on them—"No pun intended!"), Snodo's lighter ones, offering more depth, perhaps even seeing more. Digger always imagined that the dogs wanted to read his mind to determine when their next walk would occur. *No walks tonight!* Too cozy on the couch. "The son!" said Digger to the TV screen, for he had determined the fictional killer. Snodo cocked her head, trying to decipher that word, but Simba just stared greenly, panting repeatedly, as though in slight distress, confused and lost.

A couple miles away, in the seedier part of Ocean View (for every town has one of those), a cop show began in reality. Johna Adams was beat, physically and mentally exhausted. *Three classes all in one!* Driving home to her cheap apartment, she had been thinking that night classes might not be for her anymore, that they were just too long, that they required constant in-class monitoring and re-planning, that perhaps she lacked the flexibility to succeed with those continuing-education students, many of whom were older and more judgmental of teachers and their choices. Like Digger the day before, Johna Adams was feeling a little blue. And perhaps that was why she failed to notice the lights that followed her obediently all the way to her apartment building's lot, stretched out in a double row before the complex that looked more like a motel than a home. At least she had gotten an end apartment so that she could look out her side window and see trees (at least she had a side window!). For the past month, she had actually enjoyed the place, the simplicity of the half kitchen, the inviting front room, where she spent all of her time.

Johna had been married once, had known the feel of an actual house besides her childhood one, but that union and that home were long gone. Fred had wanted kids, and although that disagreement had been their main problem, plenty more had arisen, too. Johna was basically happy now, and Digger was an interesting man. The secretary had told her all about him, about his *bitch* of a wife (Johna's word, not Gloria Swanson's), his loyalty to her memory, his love of dogs. Johna had never really enjoyed animals, but she could learn to, no doubt. Dogs weren't really kids, after all. Dogs could be locked up and left at home.

When she stepped out of her old sedan, Johna recognized autumn's whisper. Getting cold already. *Another summer gone!* Johna had begun to think of Time that way, as something past, something just a little bit squandered. On the way to her door, she searched in her big handbag for the door key, which she didn't keep connected to her car one, mainly because she had heard that heavy keys could turn a car off at dangerous times, such as while careening down a highway. Johna was a practical human being.

But she had forgotten to leave her outside light on again, or maybe the damn thing had burnt out. This really was a *cheap place*. After she got a few OVC checks, maybe she would find "more attractive digs." That was Johna Adam's last thought before the pain and the darkness.

He snuck right up on the stupid woman, knocked her unconscious with his handy little club, and as he clamped both hands around her neck, he thought, *Why am I doing this? Why don't I just jump off that damn bridge? Isn't that what broken bastards like me do? Why don't I?* But he didn't. He just kept squeezing, realizing that he enjoyed the sensation, the control, the vice-like feel, the rag doll in his hands, the small sounds of leaking air, ruptured cells. He imagined the blood vessels popping in Johna Adams' eyes, could even hear them pop. He squeezed and dug with his fingers and said nothing at all. Like life, the experience lasted forever—until it was over. It actually hadn't taken too long, maybe a few minutes. Nobody intervened. The world had given him its okay.

Laying the body in the shadows beneath the apartment's big front window, he thought, *No love to be found here. No joy. No connection. No victory for you, Matthew Diggerson!*

## Chapter 4: To Highlight

Two marks seem to scare students, who somewhat rarely use parentheses and almost never try dashes, two marks with one fairly simple function—to highlight. The stressed information must be "extra" though—i.e., unnecessary to the sentence (so that if the set-off words were to be deleted, the sentence would not be affected grammatically). To hear how both marks work, imagine Simon and Garfunkel's long, sad, famous ballad, perhaps as they play to a sea of humanity in New York's Central Park.

Parentheses, you have succeeded
To set off info that's not needed
To add a detail or clarification
Some non-essential information.
But when I add you to a quote, you change your shape
To a bracket
To show the reader, my addition.

To use a dash, a daring mark,
Two little hyphens must embark,
To stress unnecessary information,
Perhaps with "i.e.," an abbreviation.
Or to end a statement with a dramatic little thought,
I have been taught,
Type two hyphens, but no spaces.

Until Friday of that first week, nobody at OVC knew that Johna Adams had taught her last course. On Thursday, watching the evening news, Digger had learned that a forty-two-year-old woman had been murdered on the edges of Ocean View, a surprising fact but not necessarily a shocking one.

Yet Digger, no stranger to death, did feel a tingle when Gloria Swanson appeared in his office doorway that Friday afternoon and said, "Johna missed her noon class. Some of her students came to see me. They had waited the fifteen required minutes, they said, even though it was just twelve-twelve. I checked my watch. Did she contact you about missing class?"

"No," said Digger, who had just checked his email and who had no flashing lights on his office landline phone (he still didn't own a cell phone—*never would!*). "I haven't heard anything."

"Did you hear about that murdered woman? Forty-two. You don't think ...?"

"Oh, god, Gloria! We don't need that again! A murdered woman doesn't mean that it was Johna. How old was Johna?"

"My guess would be about forty-two," said Gloria with none of her usual zeal.

"That old? I guess you're right. Do you have her application? No, wait. I have it here somewhere." And Gloria said not a word as Digger checked his bottom desk drawer for the handful of applications dealt with over the past two plus years. He found hers, and both people leaned down into it.

"Doesn't say her age," said Digger.

"But look at her college dates, her graduations."

Digger counted in his head, back from twenty-one or two from her undergraduate graduation date and then up to the present.

"I count forty-two," said Gloria.

"Yeah," answered Digger. "Forty-one or two or three. Around there, anyway. But, Gloria, that doesn't mean much. That doesn't mean anything!"

"It could mean much." Gloria rarely talked in single statements. Her terse words made him even more nervous.

"I'll call this number," he said, reading off of the application as he dialed. The phone, far away it seemed to him, rang and rang and rang, but Digger hung up before the fourth ring, which would, of course, lead to an answering machine.

"Nobody's home," said Digger, and Gloria's eyes got even bigger. Digger could almost see white showing all around the dark-brown circles, black pupils like bullets. It made the secretary look freaky, the face of a person who had died of fright.

"Why didn't you leave a message?" she asked.

"Uh," said Digger, wondering why himself, deciding on fear as the motive. *Fear?* "I just didn't want to leave a message, but I'll try again later. After class. I can't call the police now, Gloria! What would I say? I have a missing adjunct and would like to know if she's last night's victim. They would send me to a psychiatrist. I'd end up on Will Watkins' couch!" William Watkins was the longest-tenured OVC psyche professor, a famous man, actually, but not one loved by either Digger or Gloria Swanson, who used to work in the Psychology Department before transferring to Humanities.

"It's not possible," agreed the black-haired woman, but she didn't say what "it" meant. Digger took it as Johna's being the victim. Then Gloria continued, "But Johna doesn't strike me as being irresponsible, does she?" Digger shook his head—*no*. "She would have called me, Digger, or called you. Where does she live?"

Digger looked at the application again, noted the address, didn't recognize the street. "Do you recognize this street?" he said.

"Barksville Avenue? No, but it might be on the line with Middleburg. It might be that sort of downtrodden spot." Middleburg was the next town north, an overdeveloped, underfunded little city. Digger wrote down Johna's street address.

"Says 'Barksville Lane Apartments.' I could go and take a look on my way home tonight. I could call you after that, around dinner time."

"I would appreciate that, Digger. I'm very worried, and this is going to be a long weekend anyway, with the holiday."

*Labor Day*, Digger thought, brushed coolly by a premonition, yet he told his secretary that he definitely was not worried and asked for her number so that he had it handy. He wrote it under Johna's address.

Barksville Lane Apartments appeared suddenly, just past a leaning line of large but malnourished fir trees (Arborvitaes gone wild? Every fourth one was brown and seemingly dead), and as he turned quickly into the short driveway, Digger immediately saw the OVPD SUV and then the crime tape wrapped around the porch posts and enclosing the end apartment. *Johna!* Right then, he knew. The tape was bright yellow and took Digger's mind back eight years to the Humanities corridor in the Faculty Offices Building, the Hallway to Hell as some had referred to it back then when Paul Smith had killed two people there. Now Johna Adams was dead, too. That's all Digger could see, and his mind said, "No, no, no, no, no, no," until he saw the female cop watching him drive up. Illogically, the cop—for despite wearing no uniform, she had to be police due to her steady eyes, her cold attitude, her firm stance—had immediately reminded him of Anna. Pulling into a close spot facing the road, Digger got out and looked again at the cop, who just stood and waited, probably used to the public's intrusions into her detective work. That's what she was, Digger knew, just like the little detective (Doyle!) whom Digger had grown close to eight years past and then had never seen again, never even contacted again, except for once to enquire about Paul Smith's whereabouts. Doyle hadn't known—good bye!

This detective looked like she could be Anna's sister gone Goth, dark where Anna was light, closed where

Anna was open, shadowy where Anna shined. Digger felt nerves ripple, and then he caught himself. Johna was dead, and here he was thinking of his long-ago ex-wife and her in-person, un-personable doppelganger. Behind the cop, Digger saw a chalk outline, but he looked immediately away from it. Dark Anna noticed, of course.

"I'm Professor Matthew Diggerson," he said to the silent, dark policewoman, shorter than he, thinner, but somehow taking up more space. His introduction apparently failed to impress her. "I teach at OVC. I'm the Chair of the Humanities Department." *Who cares!* "I heard that a forty-two year old woman had been murdered, and one of my teachers didn't show up for class today." *My teachers?* "Her name's Johna Adams, or was. My secretary and I checked her application and saw that she was forty-two, the same age as the woman killed on the news." Murdered *on* the news? "Anyway, we tried calling her, and I wrote down her address. This one. When I saw your SUV and the tape, I knew that Johna was gone, that she was the victim I heard about last night on the news."

The woman had said nary a word, but now she cocked her head a bit, reminding Digger of Snodo. He had to repress a smile, just in time focusing back on Johna, on the crime tape, on the cold concrete's chalk outline. Was that a small blood stain?

"You should be a detective," said the cop at last, and Digger had two thoughts, one stumbling over the other, the first being that her voice was nice—deeper than Anna's, but pleasant—the second that Detective Doyle had expressed the same thought upon meeting Digger almost a decade past.

"I've had some experience," he smiled and then frowned. "I worked with, or talked often to, Detective Doyle back when we had some troubles at OVC, the murders, Professor Tobias Mann and our janitor, Dan

Pinsky, eight years ago." He was stammering, and just like Doyle, this cop just let him stumble. "I assume that I'm there again. Another murder, I mean. Was it Johna, Johna Adams?"

The cop had not introduced herself, just stared at Digger with her head tilted a bit, dark and mysterious. Digger had trouble focusing on Johna Adams, on anything.

"We just released the victim's name to the press, after contacting family. Your assumptions are correct. Johna Adams, age forty-two, murdered." Then the woman stopped, her head tilting back, vertical to the earth now. "What can you tell me about the victim?" she added.

Digger saw a nametag and tried to focus on it. She wore a dark green buttoned-up shirt, reminding him of a cow girl, and that made Digger think of Billy D Wilder, his protagonist, who would have impressed this cold cop by now, probably bedded her later, and that thought made Digger happy and then sad. What did her tag say? Little white letters—J. Zorn? Then Digger saw that Officer Zorn saw that he was looking at her chest.

"Officer Zorn," he said in acknowledgment, "I hardly knew Johna Adams, who was new at our school this semester. I hired her this summer to teach two composition classes, one at noon on a Monday, Wednesday, Friday schedule, the other a night class, Wednesday night." Because Zorn was typing into her phone, Digger paused, waiting for her to catch up, but she already had.

"You type fast," he said, smiling again and feeling immediately inappropriate and stupid and even guilty. "I hired Johna in early August, saw her at our August meeting, talked to her this past Wednesday, two days ago, and that's it. She was friendly, sociable, had a good record as a teacher, ten years at SVCC, Sea View Community College." He didn't know what else to say.

"Last Wednesday, two days ago," repeated the dark Officer Zorn, her eyes the color of her attitude, "you talked with Johna Adams. Where? What about? When exactly?"

Digger saw behind these questions. Johna must have been killed after class that night. His eyes were drawn back to the chalk outline, which showed one outstretched arm, as though Johna had been trying to get someone's attention, like a student wanting to be called on or a traveler hailing a taxi. Snodo sometimes slept like that, her head resting on one extended arm.

"Was Johna killed after her Wednesday night class?"

"The victim's body was discovered in the ten o'clock hour on Wednesday night, September second. That information has now been released."

"Her class would have ended around nine, but maybe she had stayed late to talk with a student or two. Do you think that a student could have followed her?"

"No conclusions have yet been drawn, Professor Diggerson. Please continue about your dialogue with the victim." *The victim*. Cops and their cold tones!

"I saw her at OVC when I was leaving, about five o'clock. She was in the adjunct faculty office in the Faculty Offices Building. She was with another adjunct, a part-time instructor, Jay Moore. I recently hired him, too. They were waiting for their six o'clock classes."

"Did the victim seem upset in any way?" The question bothered Digger for some reason, and then he realized why.

"Listen, I wish that you would not refer to her as 'the victim.' I know that this is your job, but that's a little cold for me. Could you call her by her name, Johna Adams?"

"Did Johna Adams seem upset in any way?"

This woman knew how to focus, just like Doyle, and Digger realized that all cops, all detectives, must be single-minded in their pursuits, had to be. He thought of the word 'purpose' and the way he would urge students to stick to their reason for writing, to not deviate from their assignment's mission. Cops and writing teachers.

"No, she was not upset at all. She said…said that her first class, at noon on Wednesday, the second day of the semester, had gone well…I think she said that, anyway. She wasn't worried looking, just her normal self, as normal as I can tell you, anyway. She asked about my weekend, about my book." With the latter word, Digger felt both big and small, then just small after realizing that he was calling Johna "she," almost as bad as "the victim." He said, "Johna seemed happy with the beginning of her semester, but I hadn't had a real talk with her yet. The fall semester just started this week."

"This other teacher, Mr. Jay Moore, Professor Moore, how would you describe him last Wednesday?"

Digger thought about that, decided not to blurt out, "He blinked a lot" or "Did you hear me say 'my book'?" Instead, he paused and concluded, "He seemed fine, too. He's not as friendly or talkative as Johna, but all kinds can teach. He and Johna seemed to be having a productive conversation. They definitely weren't arguing."

"Moore was there after you left?"

"Yes, as I said, they were both waiting for their night classes, an hour away. Both classes were in the Classroom Building, down in South Campus, just up from the Faculty Offices Building." Digger didn't know if these directions were at all helpful. Officer Zorn kept typing away. Waiting, Digger had an image of the Blinker and realized that Jay Moore could probably take over Johna's M/W/F noon class. He couldn't teach two night classes at once. *Too bad.* Then he glanced at the chalk outline and felt far worse.

As he waited for Zorn to respond, though, Matthew Diggerson's empathy shifted to himself again, a normal transition. There went the *holiday* weekend—no book, no emailing Johnny Lambmann. Just emergency staffing, and Digger realized that he would have to take Johna's Wednesday noon class. That would mean teaching for four straight hours—four classes in a row almost—since he taught at eleven, one, and two. He wouldn't be able to zip home between classes to let his pups out. Digger groaned and then noticed that Officer Zorn had stopped writing. He should stay focused on Johna, but the past and future kept flapping about, as usual. *Ghosts and specters!* Black Annas.

She was fiddling with her shirt pocket, the one with her pinned nametag, and then Digger noticed the little white rectangle for what it was: a business card. He was about to be dismissed. He didn't want to go yet.

"I know, I know," he said as Officer Zorn handed him the card. "If I remember anything pertinent, I will contact you." *But what if it's just that you remind me of Anna?*

"You seem to have had a lot of criminal experience, Professor Diggerson." He wanted her to call him Matt, but he didn't think that she would.

"Just like you, though, just on the right side of the law." *Did she smile?*

No, she just wanted him to leave.

"I'm curious," Digger added. "Why are you here? Does this place still hold some unseen evidence?"

"Crime scenes always do, Professor Diggerson." His name again, his formal title. Dark Anna wanted him to leave. He was used to that.

"Did you release the way Johna was killed, the method …of murder?"

"Johna Adams died due to strangulation."

Before turning to leave, Digger glanced again at the chalk outline, expecting what? To see pale strangulation marks? But the macabre sketch held nothing at all, just a little plum-sized and colored stain near the top, down from the outstretched arm. Walking to his car, Digger pictured the Statue of Liberty, then thought of its image at the end of the first *Planet of the Apes* movie. Then he thought of holes, always more holes. Johna's outline had looked like a hole, but blurry, as though a child had drawn around her fallen shape, which had then fallen in.

On both Saturday and Sunday, and even on the holiday Monday, with his restless pups mulling about, wanting his attention, willing him for a walk, Digger's mind was bombarded with thoughts. OVC would be Killer Kollege again, Murder U., and Time shrank until Tobias' and Pinsky's deaths happened just last week. But why would that be? Johna was killed far from campus, had hardly even worked at OVC, but what did that matter? The journalists would see Ocean View College as her workplace and leap to the Killer Kollege connection, licking it up. The TV reporters might even rehash events, and they did—just a bit, just one line about the school's "having suffered murder before." *Suffered.* Digger admired the rhetoric.

As early as Friday night, a couple hours after leaving the crime scene (and Officer Zorn), Digger had emailed Jay Moore about taking over Johna's Monday, Wednesday, Friday noon class, hoping that he wasn't already teaching somewhere else at or around that time. On Saturday, he received good news: Moore would be happy to take that class. He didn't write anything about Johna, and Moore had not asked. On Sunday, he found a taker for the Wednesday night class, the Cat Woman: furtive Patricia Pauley. Replying that she had heard the "terrible news," Pauley had gladly accepted the extra course. What's more, neither Moore nor Pauley needed Johna's syllabus since all English 101 teachers had a common guiding document, and since the semester had just begun, Digger decided not to use Johna's first essay assignment, but instead to let the two new teachers go with their own. All three papers had a summary purpose, anyway, Digger was glad to discover. Just different readings. Digger was also relieved that Jay Moore could take over immediately, Wednesday at noon, so Digger didn't even have to take that one class. Still, he emailed both teachers that he would introduce them to their first classes (both on Wednesday due to Labor Day Monday) and talk a bit about Johna. They both replied favorably.

He had forgotten to call Gloria Swanson that Friday night, but remembered on Saturday. She had been very upset, and Digger had stood uncomfortably listening to crying sounds bubble from his landline phone near his back door. Out back, Saturday's sky had been as blue as a robin's egg, as calm as a sleeping puppy. *Sleeping and sobbing*. Digger had thought of yin and yang, how darkness in a picture illuminated its beauty. Then he had broken into Gloria's sobbing to request that on Tuesday she find out where the services would be held and to send flowers at the bequest of the Humanities Department. He hadn't known what else to say, so he had told Gloria that he would see her on Tuesday and said good bye.

Over the long weekend, Digger thought about writing a letter to Johna's family. Although she had never mentioned family, he assumed the existence of a mother and father since she herself was only forty-two. She had looked even younger, too. She had been attractive, and Digger wondered what would have happened had she lived. Would he have dated her? A colleague? Don't "poop" where you eat, that's what he always heard, yet it had been so long since Digger had eaten. *So long!* Officer Zorn passed through his thoughts repeatedly, dark and cold, two themes to his life, really. Digger wondered what the "J" stood for. Probably "Jennifer," maybe "Janice" or "Janet." Nobody was named *Janet* anymore, but Zorn didn't look too young, probably about as old as Johna. In his range, anyway. Nobody would say that Digger was robbing the cradle. *Silly thoughts!*

What could Digger tell her parents, anyway? That their daughter had been friendly, that she had fit in well at OVC, for one day and one meeting, anyway, that she had admired his blue or green eyes, had actually asked him about his book—more so than people who had known him for twenty years!—maybe that he had imagined asking her out? *All stupid thoughts!* He tossed the letter idea away, but it floated back occasionally, smaller and flimsier each time, until darkness took it completely. Digger had too many other concerns.

That Wednesday after his own first class at eleven, Digger moved up the Classroom Building stairs to where Johna's class would have been waiting for her. Peeking inside the room, he noticed that Jay Moore was nowhere to be seen, and Digger felt something whisper—annoyance or maybe fear. For close to five minutes, he stood waiting outside the room, wanting to enter it with the new instructor. Time passed, slowly, quickly. He would have to start without the Blinker. When Digger moved into the classroom alone, he found about fifteen students already seated and quiet. Most were staring into their laps—their cell phones! As always, that image annoyed Digger. Why couldn't he just let it go? Why couldn't he let anything go? Where the hell was Jay Moore!

"Hello," he said. Nobody said it back, but at least they all looked up at him.

"You probably don't know why I'm here," continued Digger. "I'm Matthew Diggerson, Chair of the Humanities Department, and …"

"Our teacher was murdered" came a voice from one of those fifteen faces.

"Uh," said Digger, and then the voice came again, and the composition instructor was able to wind it back to a face, a young-looking fellow (they all looked that way to Digger, but especially some freshmen).

"We read about it online," said the boy-man, and he held his iPhone up as though offering proof.

"She was strangled," said a girl from the front, and did Digger imagine that both students looked flushed, excited almost, or did he just see killers everywhere now? Or maybe the red tinge was simply embarrassment, the effect of speaking up in class. The word "strangled" seemed to unlock something because all the students started jabbering and exclaiming (and smiling?), giving Digger the overwhelming urge to scream "SILENCE!" Instead, he allowed Johna Adams' students to let it all out, and before long, the words stumbled back and disintegrated into empty space.

"I didn't know Johna, your teacher, well," continued Digger, "but I liked her. She was friendly, open, smart but willing to listen. She had a lot of experience teaching writing. I expect that you will miss her, as both a person and a professor." Some of the heads nodded a bit, some were bent back into their laps. Digger wondered if they were reading more info about Johna. "You've had just one class with Professor Adams, so you have not gotten far into your first project. Your new teacher will have his own first project, but it will be similar to Johna's, Professor Adams'." At this point, Digger looked toward the door, expecting a grand entrance from Jay Moore—nope, not yet. Although Digger was not happy with Moore, the Humanities Chairperson did not want these students to see that, didn't want to give them an excuse to disregard their unreliable new instructor. Digger decided on the spot not to waste this class, which apparently was relying on him for today.

"Okay, your new instructor probably cannot make it in today on this short notice, but he will be here Friday. Did Professor Adams begin your first project last week?" A couple students nodded, including both speakers so far. Some just looked at him with blank faces, as though they couldn't remember last week. Some looked down into their laps, beckoned by the siren call of their addictions.

"I'm assuming that your purpose was to summarize a reading," said Digger.

"'Letter from a Birmingham Jail,'" said the girl in front, "and a rough draft's due next class." *Next class*!—that was pretty quick. This female student had a halo of black curly hair, reminding Digger of a young Gloria Swanson because of not only the hair, but also her enthusiasm and social forwardness. He realized that Jay Moore was lucky to have this enthusiastic student in class.

"That's a good reading," said Digger, trying to remember it, but retrieving instead the famous "I have a dream" speech. "Birmingham" was a very long letter, if he pictured the piece correctly. "That's a long letter, right?" he asked, and the head-nodders went up and down. "Did Johna put the reading on Bridges?" Up and down again—*good!* "Let's go to your Bridges site then," said a smiling Digger, who had just decided what to do. He looked over a male student's shoulder at his laptop screen, which showed the course site, then links under a Resources tab, and then Martin Luther King's long letter.

"How many pages?" he asked the boy, who scrolled through the text.

"Nine or ten."

"Thanks," he said to the boy, and to the whole class he gave a little lecture, using the board in spots (all white boards now, the old chalk ones having slipped into history). He first wrote "Says" and "Does" on the board, adding "main point" and "supporting reasons" under the former and "evidence types: factual, authoritative, descriptive, comparative" under the latter. He turned back to the class: "Okay, did Professor Adams give you this does-and-says reading tactic?" Side-to-side head shaking ensued. *No problem.* "She was probably planning to do so today, and I wish with all my heart that she'd had that opportunity. Okay, when you read, to be an active learner, you must annotate as you read. In other words, take notes, such as labeling main points, asking questions, noting comparisons, et cetera. A great annotation tactic is to determine what a writer 'says,' is his or her main point, and what a writer 'does,' mainly meaning giving evidence to support that point, in each paragraph. The writer's points are often just implied, too, making them harder to see, so sometimes you can determine the 'does' idea first. In other words, what type or types of evidence is being used. Is it factual, like statistics or maybe examples? Is it authoritative, meaning quotes from others, from experts hopefully, not from the writer him or herself? That would just be the writer's own opinion, not evidence. Or maybe the evidence involves descriptions, maybe definitions, or maybe comparisons, even creative ones. When you can label the evidence, you can often determine what that evidence is proving, in short, the writer's point, the 'says' idea. That's what we're going to do now for King and his letter. I'm going to put you in pairs, assign you a few paragraphs each, have you do a does-and-says analysis of those paragraphs, and present your ideas to the class. You would be wise to take a lot of notes today because you will be helping each other to generate plenty of ideas for your summary essay."

With this latter suggestion, past students would pull notebooks out of backpacks and conjure up pens or pencils, but nowadays the young people had no paper or pens, just laptops and cell phones. Digger sometimes missed paper, which had made prior students seem a little more engaged. These days, he would often have to implore students to take notes on their laptops. All they wanted was to use their phones to take pictures of notes on the board. To Digger, that seemed very passive, a bad way to learn.

"Okay," he added. "Pair up. I'll come around and give you some paragraphs."

The exercise worked well with most of the students although a couple of the pairs seemed to communicate only through "telepathy," as he described non-talking students. These people's presentations were unorganized, too, but overall Digger felt satisfied—except for the fact that Jay Moore never came through the door. Digger had decided not to give the absent Jay a choice of topics for Project One; the substitute professor would have to use Johna's choice, "Letter from a Birmingham Jail." When the class' hour was up, at about twelve-forty-eight, Digger said, "Your new teacher will be here Friday, and I'll let him know that you're writing about King's letter since we did all this work today—good work, too! Just go with your present schedule, having a draft ready next class, as your previous teacher requested. I'm very sorry about Johna Adams, as I'm sure that you are, but your class will proceed smoothly. Come see me at the Faculty Offices Building if you have any problems." Some nodded, some smiled a bit, and they all left. Digger didn't expect to see any of these faces again, but in that assumption, he was incorrect.

## Chapter 5: To Guide

Note: Punctuating correctly is important because each mark guides readers through your sentences, and since the marks follow fairly simple rules, you can learn to punctuate well. Let Bob Dylan help (or you might remember Guns N' Roses' version better)—can you hear the slow melody?

Put a comma if you see, extra word groups that appear.
A comma, you simply will not need, if a pause you do not hear.
Set, set, setting off some phrases
Pace, pace, pacing through the mazes
Guide, guide, guiding all your readers
That's how commas act like leaders.
Put a semicolon down, when you make related thoughts.
You can listen to the sound, when one idea stops and another starts.
Bal, bal, balancing at strong pauses
Sep, sep, separating two main clauses
Div, div, dividing a pause that's not small
That's where a semicolon does fall.
Put a colon on the page, when you introduce some information.
Those two dots will set the stage, for lists and quotes and explanations.
Show, show, showing what comes next
Lead, lead, leading to more text
Point, point, pointing to the rest
That's where a colon does work best.

That Wednesday, after leaving Johna's students, Digger taught his own two English Comp 101 classes, so he didn't hear about Jay Moore's excuse until he returned to the Faculty Offices Building and saw his secretary, Gloria. She was holding up a note and shaking her head. While her eyes still looked a little red, job duties seemed to be focusing Gloria Swanson.

"I don't know, Digger," she said, and he knew what she meant: she didn't know about this new guy, Moore. "Not much of an excuse," she added, handing Digger the note, which read "Previous engagement—had forgotten about it, couldn't break it. Tried to call you, left a message."

Digger thought of his landline phone, which would now be blinking, eager to give him Jay Moore's mysterious message. A flash fire of guilt swept him, for if he had given in and bought a cell phone, then he would have received this message, wouldn't have waited and wondered during Johna's class. But he didn't want a cell phone, didn't want to be reached anywhere. *Damn it!*

"Previous engagement!" smiled Gloria, and Digger knew that this note would ride the office grapevine, probably already had. Everyone would think that the Blinker was on thin ice. Wondering if the man's "engagement" were an eye-doctor visit, Digger said that Jay "would be fine," thanked Gloria for the note, and headed down the hall to his office. Although the door to the adjunct office was wide open, the room yawned emptily, making Digger think of Johna's absence, her murder. All throughout the extended weekend, he had wondered who had killed her, but not with the obsession that he had once tackled his own Department Head's murder, Tobias Mann. For one thing, Johna's death obviously had nothing to do with OVC, whereas Tobias' had actually occurred *on* the campus—in the very room that Digger now occupied, in fact! Digger had hardly known Johna Adams, too, while he had had a dozen or more years of shared experiences with Mann. Then there was Officer J. Zorn, too. *The Dark Anna!* What did the "J" stand for? Certainly not "Juanita." She was dark but not Spanish dark. Looked more like Eastern European dark—sort of pale and dark at the same time. And his published book often intruded on Digger's mind these days, not to mention the one still to be written. *Light and shadow*, the two sides of life. None could exist without the other.

None of his colleagues was home, so to speak. All the doors were closed, like a long corridor in a nightmare. Was this emptiness typical at three o'clock on a Wednesday? Or were quiet professors keeping their doors closed so that they wouldn't have to see Digger, wouldn't have to talk about his book? The green-eyed monster—jealousy—was that keeping the doors closed? Not even old Eliot appeared, and he never kept his door shut. Digger closed his eyes, tried to hear Eliot's breathing, but all he sensed was his own pounding blood.

"Hello!" yelled Digger, and he heard Gloria Swanson way down the hall echo that word. "Just testing," he yelled back and then heard her laugh. All of the gray metal doors held their breaths.

Entering his unlocked office, he thought of Tobias Mann, of how his killer had snuck up on him, stabbed him. Paul Smith, what was he doing right now up in that concrete penitentiary? Digger often wondered that, pondered Smith's new life, his wife-less life. Did Paul read a lot, write? Did he *like* his days? Did he sleep peacefully? Dream of that saw-toothed knife? Since the sick man had actually helped Digger to restart his own life, Digger hoped that Smith was relatively happy. Not suicidal, anyway. Paul had even had a hand in Digger's office décor, for the desk was no longer faced away from the door. Turning just a bit to his right, Digger could always see who was coming. Right now, no one. Last week, no one. Just about no one, anyway! Digger had expected a little more conversation about *Composition Murder*. After all, they were all writing teachers, right? Indifference. Jealousy. Sad words. Dark and gray and sickly green.

*Jealous. Green.* Digger suddenly pictured Eliot Gladstone, for he had remembered the old teacher's sad story from his younger days, a tale told a dozen years back, when Digger had been a fairly young teacher at

Ocean View College and right after he had published his first scholarly article. Eliot the Breather had seemed old even then, but he must have been just a decade ahead of Digger himself. How else could the odd fellow still be gulping at OVC air today, otherwise? Digger could still picture how Eliot had looked that day, repeatedly opening his mouth to snatch the next breath of air, as though he saw bubbles, opportunities, missed by everyone else. Like a fish out of water, Digger had thought, but he had been too excited about the article to worry much about an asthmatic peer. His newly published piece dealt with a class activity involving a model essay, multiple-choice questions, and minutes of freedom earned. *Earn and Learn*, Digger had called both the article and the activity, using it still, now putting the questions in PowerPoints. To develop his article, he had studied "student motivation," playing around with various key-word searches and using the database sources' evidence to support his contention that actively focused students learned more in less time—less since they had the chance to earn their way out of class sooner. Upon the article's publication, Digger had told Tobias Mann, the current Chair (back then), expecting him to inform all the Humanities teachers and perhaps to email them all the link to the article or the pdf file of the piece itself. Instead, Mann had responded that OVC was not a "research institution," that it was a "teaching school," meaning that Digger had not had to publish any article. Mann had said little else, and because Digger hadn't wanted to beg his Chair to share the news of his accomplishment, he had given up, acquiesced.

Upon leaving Mann's office that day, in Time's grip for a dozen years, Digger had noticed Eliot's open door and knocked, after which the conversation had gone something like this (with a series of pauses within the Breather's dialogue):

Digger: "Eliot, can I tell you something?"

Eliot: "Anything, Digger, although I am not a priest."

Digger: "Nothing like that. It's just that I've published a peer-reviewed article."

Eliot: "Congratulations. There's not enough of that around here. *Teaching* school, you know."

Digger: "That's what Tobias just said, and I knew it already, was informed of it by Gwena when I became full-time. But I didn't write the article so that I wouldn't 'perish.' I wrote it because I'm a writer."

Eliot: "I used to write, too."

Digger: "You don't write anymore."

Eliot: "I am content with my career, Digger. I have accepted that I probably will not write the great American novel. Teaching is its own reward."

Digger: "That's true, but I'd still like everyone to read my article. Tobias wasn't interested in emailing it out, though."

Eliot: "A short article? I would like to read it, Digger." Then Eliot had gulped a couple of minnow breaths and continued, "You have to understand your audience, you know that. Do you have time for a story, an illustrative tale, Digger? It will tell you all about envy and egoism. It will surprise you."

Digger: "Yes, Eliot. I'd like to hear it."

Eliot: "You know that I went to graduate school at the University of New Mexico, right? Late eighties. Albuquerque. Oh, those desert skies at night, Digger. All the stars anyone could ever dream of! Anyway, one of my fellow TA's was a star already, had already published a book, which I heard about from a friend. Plus, someone had made copies of the cover and taped them up in the hallways. *A Step Behind.* That was the name of the book. I will never forget that title. The author's name was David, and I hated him for various reasons, mainly because of his success, for at heart all of us writing teachers want to write a book, want to be published. This David had two last names, and I knew that because I read them on the photographed book cover and because I had shared a class with the, uh, jerk. The professor of that class had been a sarcastic bastard, too, Digger, had told us all on the very first day of class that he would 'with the greatest pleasure fail' us if we did not do the work."

Digger had remembered Eliot's face when he had mimicked the teacher's words, the way he had spit out "pleasure" and then swallowed air.

"That class is also why I remember that my nemesis David had two last names. Because that professor had used them every time he addressed my peer, who always sat behind me, behind everyone, more like he was observing the class than taking it. And, oh, Digger, David Two Last Names asked the strangest and most detailed of questions, far beyond any ideas that we other grad students could have imagined, and those questions were always just a bit off track of what the professor was lecturing, so that I would steam and think about the money I was paying for the class and the time that David Two Last Names was wasting just so that he could stroke his ego and send us all on tangents. Those two, the sarcastic professor and my successful-author-already peer, turned each class into an intellectual ping-pong match, one with just two players, two equal combatants, the rest of us students just an audience, just witnesses to their intellect. I hated that class, Digger, and I hated myself for staying quiet, for not joining in and smashing a few ping-pong balls!

"You see, Digger, I could always write, had always written, had received an endless string of A's on all my college papers, graduate and undergraduate. Writing was my main way of defining myself, and because of another student, I now found myself lacking.

"For years, Digger, for years! For after graduation, I kept hearing about a writer making great waves in the literary world, a David with two last names, but I never pursued these snippets of information, did not want to know if the achiever were my old nemesis from New Mexico. With each passing year, I would hear more news, more accolades for a David Blank. Books, chairmanships in creative writing departments, guest appearances on major talk shows! Jay Leno if I remember correctly. But I shut out all this information, Digger. The Green-eyed Monster, you know?"

Besides nodding and smiling, Digger had not interrupted Eliot's sad story, but at this point, he had offered, "The only David writer with two last names that I know is David Reed Winslow, but you couldn't have gone to school with *him*! He's a giant in the literary world. What are the odds that any of us could have crossed paths with an immortal?"

Eliot had lowered his head then, breathed deeply three or four times, concerning Digger, but then looking up and smiling, said:

"I don't know about odds, Digger. Nor immortals. But you have guessed my antagonist, and I should have known that you would. You're young but you're sharp. I saw that in you years ago, when you were still an adjunct."

Digger had broken in again to thank the tale teller and to announce again that "It could *not* have been Reed Winslow!"

"But it was, Digger. David Reed Winslow! 'Mr. Reed Winslow,' how many times did I hear that? How many times did I see it on that Xeroxed book cover? *A Step Behind.* I also heard that name one more time on the news, just a year or so ago, Digger, when I heard that David Reed Winslow, the literary giant, had hanged himself."

That old-but-new news had shocked Digger, too, for he had not heard about the author's death, having been more or less dead himself at that time, twelve years ago, Anna-less in body but not mind or spirit, clutching at a buoy labeled "love" in the stormy sea of life. He still held tight to this image, but Digger had long since accepted his main character flaw. And Eliot's twelve-year-old tale had been one of acceptance; that had been its moral. And for that reason, the older man had unburdened it onto his younger colleague.

"Jealousy, Digger," Eliot had continued. "It will hide and whisper to you, tear you apart from the inside. When I heard about Reed Winslow's suicide, I sought out more information. I used Wikipedia. For the first and last time, Digger. I typed in his name and then scrolled down to his publications. All I needed to see was that first book, and there it was, *A Step Behind*, a novel that I never bothered to read, that I never allowed myself to know even existed! Then I scrolled further and saw that he had, in fact, graduated from the University of New Mexico, in 1983, same as me. And I read about his suicide, read a quotation from his father about 'David's having battled depression for twenty years.' Twenty years, Digger! That would take us back to New Mexico, and that fit my memories of him, the way that he would separate himself from others, sitting in the back of the room, conversing just with the professor.

"Digger, I never bothered to talk with David Reed Winslow, never tried to get to know him, basically just shut him out because I was jealous. Petty, small minded, jealous! And even at an institution of higher education devoted to teaching, not to 'publish or perish,' we all feel pain and envy when somebody else *does* what we just *teach*. Do you follow me, Digger?"

Sitting in his office all those years later, hearing nothing from the hallway, from all those closed doors, absolutely nothing, no breathing, no tearing jealousy, Digger had understood (at least, he thought that he had), and he still remembered Eliot's story's summation: "I had set myself up beside a giant, been jealous of a literary god."

A giant or even a god so unhappy with his heights that he had cut himself down. Even today, Digger found Eliot's tale almost unbelievable. What a life lesson! Why had Eliot hidden it for so long? Not only to brush up against greatness, but to have maintained his wall of ignorance for two decades. Both facts were amazing. *The bliss of ignorance!* Like Eliot, Digger had blocked out the jealousy tale because his life back then (still?) had been full of blinders, denials, Anna-less days. Alone in his office, Matthew Diggerson thought of his ex-wife, *Anna*, and of the ideal love he had imagined them to possess. Definitely not bliss; more like a wall of ignorance. Yes, good fences make good neighbors, and maybe that's what was happening now. Maybe his colleagues were putting up Robert Frost fences. Emotional walls of silence, physical walls of closed doors. Digger thought of Reed Winslow, pictured finding him hanging, and then transitioned to the suicide he himself had witnessed on the Bay Bridge. *Poor Danny Jones*. Digger wondered which suicide affected which man more. Jones' had led Digger to creation, to a voice, a legacy in print. What had Reed Winslow's self-destruction done to Digger's old colleague? Had it sparked Eliot to write, too, to seek something more than the rewards of teaching? Digger had never asked Eliot, had never mentioned Reed Winslow again, but he had heard nothing of any publications—not from any of his colleagues, actually. Jealousy. Ignorance. Bliss. A green-eyed monster. For an instant, Digger thought of the poem "The Second Coming," of the "rough beast" emerging from the desert. What beast had *Composition Murder* unleashed?

Thinking about jealousy, about the shadows stretching from the main library's towers, and about Simba and Snodo, about their need to use the back yard, Digger actually flinched noticeably when the phone rang. It was Jay Moore.

"Professor Diggerson, I'm so sorry. I had every intention of meeting you before today's class. I had forgotten about a prior engagement." His voice came in little spurts, making Digger think of the far older Eliot.

"It's okay, Jay," said Digger (even though he didn't really believe that). "I taught the class myself. We covered the does-and-says tactic. Johna had them reading King's 'Letter from a Birmingham Jail,' and I had them pair off and analyze a few paragraphs each and then present their does-and-says summaries to the whole class."

"That sounds like a good lesson," said the other man. "I do a similar one."

"I'm afraid that you will now have to use King's piece for your first essay, Jay, because Johna's students have now spent a couple classes on it, and Johna actually scheduled the paper to be due the next class. Will that King topic be a problem?"

"No, no problem. I know that letter, and I'll find it online."

"I have access to Johna's Bridges page, so I can send you the file. I'll do that right after we're done talking."

"Thanks, that would be convenient."

A long pause ensued, and Digger pictured the other man blinking. He wanted to ask him about the "prior engagement," but wasn't sure of his words. People were entitled to their privacy.

"I have one problem, though," continued Jay Moore, adding quickly, "I can't make it to Friday's noon class again. I'm sorry, Professor Diggerson. I wasn't expecting this responsibility."

Silence again, and Digger wondered whether "this responsibility" meant Johna's class or his Friday excuse. Then he thought again of an eye doctor, an ophthalmologist, right?

"Okay," he said at last, just a little reluctantly. "I can take that class again. I'd rather not just cancel the class for Friday. Those students need some continuity. Did you have a plan for the class?"

"Well, my Wednesday night students have a paper due, tonight actually, and you said that Johna's students had one due Friday, too, so I was going to do an exercise on comma use. None of them know how to use commas, so I like to get to that grammar early in the semester."

"That makes sense," responded Digger, although he actually thought that "getting at grammar" so soon didn't make a whole lot of sense. "I can do a comma exercise with that class," he said instead. "That way, you can keep going with your usual schedule after that. You aren't going to have any more, uh, engagements, right?" He laughed at his own question, partly to make the other man feel better, partly to open up the topic.

Jay laughed, too, said "No, no," but he kept the topic closed. No disclosure.

"You'll be coming in soon?" said Digger, elevating the "soon" to form a question.

"I will," said Jay Moore, but offered no accompanying words.

After the two men hung up, Digger accessed Johna's course site, downloaded her "Birmingham" file to his own desktop, and then emailed the attached file to Jay Moore. Then he thought about that Friday class on commas. Maybe he should have some fun with Johna's students. Maybe they could use some laughs. He certainly could.

Johna's students, or as he should think of them, Jay's, didn't look surprised to see him. "Hello again," he said to the same fifteen or sixteen faces, and although Digger saw some heads nod and lips move, he failed to hear a thing. Maybe he needed a hearing test. "Your new instructor, Professor Moore, will meet you on Monday, but he could not start today. But he told me that he wanted to work on commas today, and since your prior teacher (*the murdered one*, he thought but did not say) had requested your first draft of your Birmingham summaries today, a little comma use could help. In fact, you need to remember that the writing process goes in loops, that you're probably not even done generating ideas for this paper, that you most likely will need to go back to King's letter and add more proof to your papers. You see, nobody gets a paper 'perfect' the first time, or even the last time. 'Perfect' is a subjective idea, but you *do* want clear and specific content, and you can edit as you go along, not just at the end. However, I do want to suggest that you don't think about grammar as you write, or you might block ideas and create a skimpy paper." Digger stopped. *Okay,* he thought, *that more or less covers why this early grammar review's acceptable—at least, it would persuade the students, anyway.* He fiddled with the room's computer, clicked "On" the overhead projector, and accessed a document titled "Stuck Inside My Sentence with the Comma Blues Again."

"We're going to have some fun with commas, can you believe that?" The students didn't seem to believe it. "I have an exercise I call Grammar Jam, which involves making up helpful lyrics to well-known songs. My latest comma song may not be so well known. Do you know Bob Dylan?" Bobble, bobble, smile, smile. They were getting interested, and before long they would be laughing and focusing, Digger knew, because he had used Grammar Jam for over a decade. In fact, he sometimes brought his acoustic guitar to class to spruce up the presentation. After the Paul Smith Affair, Digger had bought the guitar and taught himself to play. He especially liked the E-minor chord because it was a little sad but still defiant, too, and he thought of himself as that chord. He really wanted to be a straight E, the chord that symbolized his protagonist, Billy D Wilder, but that power rang out of reach. The E chord was played in his song today, Dylan's "Stuck Inside of Mobile with the Memphis Blues Again," but he had decided not to bring the guitar, because he didn't want to lug it from one class to the next, not unless he were also playing it in his own classes, which were still focused on paragraphing issues, not grammatical ones.

"Dylan's going to help us to understand the most complex yet important punctuation mark, the comma, the mark that guides readers through your sentences. Do you know his song 'Stuck Inside of Mobile with the Memphis Blues Again'?" More bobbles, more than Digger had expected, yet that knowledge was common because classic rock transcended time. College freshmen all knew the Beatles, the Rolling Stones, David Bowie, Led Zeppelin, etc., having heard their parents (and grandparents!) play the hits all throughout their kids' childhoods. "You know how it goes," Digger continued, and then he imitated the famous chorus. Although he wasn't sure that he had gotten all the words quite right, nobody corrected him, but some of the bobble-heads laughed—*good!*

"Good," said Digger, "so now you can help me to sing," and he turned to the screen, scrolled down on his computer, and showed the students the four stanzas. Then he scrolled back to the top. "Ready?" he asked, and then he sang and scrolled, revealing these lines as the song progressed:

Oh, a comma, it appears, every now and then.
I don't know where to take one out
Or where to put one in.
But I hear that there are guides to use, to help me with my plight.
Three rules of separation, will set my commas right.
Oh, comma, I hear the period at the end,
But I'm stuck inside my sentence with the comma blues again.

The first rule, it seems to me, is an easy one to use.
If I start my sentence with a word that flows,
Then I add a comma, too.
So if a sentence starts with an "If," or maybe with a "When,"
I'll listen till that word group ends, and add a comma then.
Oh, comma, you help me with my thought.
I add you when I hear a pause, subtract you when there's not.

The second rule for commas, involves words like "but" and "so."
If they lead me to a second thought, a comma before them goes.
Those words, they coordinate and link, connecting where they drop,
So if an "and" leads to a subject-verb, a comma shows the slight stop.
Oh, comma, you help me with my thought.
I add you when I hear a pause, subtract you when there's not.

The third rule I need to know, to add commas that work right

Involves extra information, to show shifts that are just slight.
A "which" within my sentence, a "meaning" near the end,
To separate unnecessary phrasing, a comma I must send.
Oh, comma, you help me with my thought.
I add you when I hear a pause, subtract you when there's not.

In his own classes, students usually joined in, at least after the first stanza or two, but Johna's students didn't help much, some mouthing the chorus, a sort of mumbling in the crowd, but Digger saw lights in their eyes and smiles on their faces. Who didn't love music? What students didn't love seeing their teacher make a fool of himself? Johna's students applauded his efforts, and Digger gave a mock bow. Then he wrote this sentence on the white board, using a green gel pen:

When a sentence begins with a flowing word a comma will be needed fairly soon and a writer needs that mark again to show two connected statements guiding the readers through the sentence.

"Okay," he said, "now we can use those lyrics to determine where this sentence needs commas. The first sentence begins with a flowing 'When' word, as mentioned in the second stanza, so where does its word group stop in my example?"

Young Gloria (in Digger's mind) from the front row raised her hand. "After the word 'word,'" she said, and a handful of other heads bobbled.

"Exactly," said the composition instructor. "Anytime a sentence begins with a word that flows, not with a noun like 'The writer' or a pronoun like 'She' or 'He,' then find where the flow ends and add a comma. Now what about the third stanza, the second comma rule, the one involving coordination, in other words, words that connect equal ideas? In my sentence here, do you see the coordinating word? Yes, the 'and.' Does it lead to another subject-verb, to another statement? If so, you need a comma before that connecting word."

"It does," said 'Gloria' (Digger didn't actually know any of their names; he had not even taken attendance), and Digger agreed.

"Everyone messes up that comma, too," he added, "but it's not *that* hard to get right. If the 'and' leads to a second statement, pause the reader. If the 'and' leads to just a word or phrase, then don't add the comma. Except, of course, for items in a series. I like adding the comma before the 'and' and last item so that the last two items in the series look more separate."

The boy in back, the same one who had spoken on Wednesday, introducing the topic of Johna's murder, said, "My high school English teacher said that you never use a comma before the 'and' in a list."

"Some teachers do say that," said Digger, thinking about how he should put this, "but as a writing teacher, I can rarely use the word 'never' for any grammar rule, and all I can say is that the comma in that spot could help the reader. Grammar's all about helping your audience to navigate your sentences and understand them with no distractions, such as wordiness or errors."

The boy's question made Digger forget about applying his song's last stanza (the third and final comma rule) to the sentence. Instead, he explained what he wanted students to now do: "Now it's your turn to create a song, actually just one good stanza, a song on comma use, and one that could contain some of my lines from my Dylan song. Working with one or two or maybe even three other people, choose a song melody and then build your stanza. Use my lyrics to do so. Make sure that your song offers specific advice on comma use so that when you sing it to yourself it will help you to edit your papers. You can make groups yourself. And for added motivation, you can leave after you sing your songs!"

The young people looked apprehensive about that possibility (i.e., singing aloud), but most of them quickly formed trios, an effective number since three brains led to different views but not to too many of them. Digger mulled about, checked songs, inquired about the bands (which he often did not know), and advised that students use info from his songs and offer specific words related to commas, too. Some groups accessed YouTube and played their songs, using the melodies to construct lines, others practiced a cappella style, and one trio even Googled "comma use" to get ideas. All the students laughed and connected in their groups, and Digger smiled. If teaching could be fun, why not?

Ten minutes before the end of the fifty-minute class, one group (the only quartet) said that they were ready to present. The three females sang the lines while the one male chimed in on the repetitive words, creating an entertaining presentation. One girl announced that their song was Taylor Swift's "Shake It Off," and it went like this:

I don't use a comma, got no rules in my brain.

My teacher says rules, mmm hmm, always says rules, mmm hmm.

I need one before "but," but not always before "and"

And after words that flow, mmm mmm, where the phrase does go.

Cause the commas gonna show, show, show, show, show

Where the pauses gonna go, go, go, go, go
Like items in a list, list, list, list, list
Where the sentence shows a shift, shift, shift, shift, shift
I use a pause, I use a pause.

Clapping broke out, caught hold, and then died off, Digger's applause lasting longer than anyone's. That was a nice song, maybe not the most helpful in terms of specific tips and words, but still useful and definitely enjoyable. Since no other group was ready to sing, the quartet happily got up, gathered their ubiquitous backpacks, and exited looking pleased with themselves.

Then another group, a trio, was ready, and after Digger nodded, one of the three boys said, "Our song's to, well, you'll know it," and then the trio sang, the voices blending fairly pleasantly:

Comma, comma, little mark, before an "and" you will embark.
If I add a second thought, that is where a pause is sought.
Professor Diggerson sang his song,
Now that Professor Adams' gone.

This "Twinkle, Twinkle, Little Star" ending didn't elicit quite the applause as the first song had, and suddenly Digger heard just one hand clapping, his own. He stopped. *Not again!* he thought because the lyrical twist had reminded him of the macabre contributions of a former student, George North, whom Digger had once considered a possible murderer, Tobias Mann's. Could history be repeating itself? It often did. To an ignorant humanity's demise!

## Chapter 6: To Compare

Note: Besides functioning to balance, a semicolon also can be pictured as a comparison, one statement equally related to another, side by side. As the following melody from Radiohead's most famous rock song suggests, think of a semicolon as a soft period. That comparison will help you with this oft misused mark.

When you choose a semicolon, to balance two main thoughts
It works just like a period, that's just a little soft.
It implies there's some relation, between one idea and the other.
You can often add transitions, like "therefore" or "however."
Cause a simple semicolon, often is misused.
Side by side it compares, like a pair of shoes.

Jay Moore had no more issues, and the fall semester settled in and became *normal*, for lack of a better word. To Digger, each semester had a similar rhythm and progression—the September enthusiasm of a fresh beginning, the October tiredness of no end in sight, the November promise of completion, and the December euphoria of a job finished, of the promise of *space in time*, as he and Anna had called it when responsibilities were completed and Time became a friend, rather than an adversary. *Friends and adversaries*. Those two opposites had become hazy and merged in Digger's mind, for his colleagues basically ignored his book, which now sat waiting in the library's shelves. Alone and forgotten, like an old tombstone leaning forgotten in the corner of a cemetery, Digger imagined. Had these people ever been his friends? Just work colleagues, not friends. Digger had *no real friends*, other than Simba and Snodo. The composition teacher allowed himself to feel slighted, to dip his toes into the black river that flowed just below his consciousness but that bubbled up occasionally, such as this moment, in his empty cottage, with his dogs asleep in the living room and the sun mocking him in its brightness and omnipotence. Sulfur bubbles, stench!

*Oh, get over yourself!* Whose fault is this lonely life, anyway? How many people had Digger invited to his home over the years. Nobody! And he liked it that way, didn't want a roomful of people holding cocktails and talking about their complex, meaningful lives. He chose *this* existence—well, sort of. Anna had chosen, too. Digger thought of Anna, of the Christmas card and note that would appear in his mailbox. *Long off now*. Only mid-September, but already Digger felt the burden of the semester, the weight of all those classes and papers and problems that would arise and need capping. His usual enthusiasm had been squashed out of him by Johna Adams' murder, by the extra work that opening had created (Jay Moore!), and especially by the department's lack of reaction to his book. That was the main drain, he realized, feeling guilty that his own ego hurt him more than Johna's death, but Digger was almost always honest with himself.

This day, for instance, this sunny, mild September day—the glory and wonder of a New England early autumn—had brought with it the desire to skip school, and since Digger had no Thursday classes, he had given into that weakness. That morning, he had called Gloria Swanson and said that he was staying home today, that he had work to do, and that she should use her discretion about giving out his home number if anyone came looking for him. "Don't give it to any students," he had added.

"Matthew Diggerson," the Humanities secretary of almost eight years had chided him. "Do you think that I would give your number to a student? Now maybe if she were a continuing education student having come back to college after raising a child and then getting a divorce, and if she were quite attractive and didn't seem too crazy, well, then, Professor, she might get your number." Digger was glad that Gloria had recovered her humor after the *Johna Affair*, as he had labeled his short stretch of knowing the woman.

"Not even her!" Digger laughed about this fictional older student, and the two disconnected. Gloria Swanson—always the matchmaker! Digger was glad that she had not mentioned Elena Bonner, or whatever her last name might be now. If he wanted to stay in frozen loyalty to a run-away wife and live amongst the canines, well, that choice should be accepted. It was even honorable. On the national news awhile back, right at the end when the station would offer an uplifting story, a human-interest piece, Digger had enjoyed the tale of a World War II soldier, one of the few remaining from that Greatest Generation. Although Digger could not remember the gist of the story—maybe it was just due to the former airman's age—he recalled always that the old fellow's wife had died a couple decades earlier and that the journalist had asked him why he had never remarried. "I'm still married," the wrinkled, shrunken wonder had retorted. "I'm not alone, not without a woman, she's just not here right now." *That's it!* Digger had thought and actually said aloud, both his dogs having swiveled their heads up from a dream at his exclamation. That *was* it. Digger *was* not alone; Anna just was no longer present. Why couldn't Gloria understand? Even his own mother, Jean of the eighty-one years, continually asked him if he were seeing anyone. Sometimes he would joke and say, "Besides Simba and Snodo?" while at other moments he would lower his head and offer a soft "No." Mothers always seemed to hold the power of guilt.

Digger heard the sea breeze push against his kitchen windows. If he got up from the table and looked outside, he would see sparrows camped out beneath the bird tube, maybe a dive-bombing blue jay or two (always in small squadrons), perhaps the crimson blur of a male cardinal, his greenish lady love more hidden in the fir tree. In the distance, the gulls would be dipping and screaming prehistorically, and perhaps Digger would see a flying V of geese, practicing for their southern journey or maybe even starting it. But Digger did not get up. On the table waited his notebook—the print kind, paper, which his students no longer seemed to need. On the open page, Digger had made two columns, the left side's titled "Tobias," the other "Johna." He had started to compare the two murders. Under "Tobias," he had written "knife," "on campus," and "full-time," while under "Johna," he had correspondingly added "hands," "off campus," and "part-time." Under both, he had jotted down "OVC employee" and "known by me," and one more notation lengthened the "Tobias" column: "known by the killer." Across from this, beneath "Johna," Digger had made a question mark.

What else was there to say? Under "Tobias," Digger added "hated by Killer," "hurt by killer," and then "killer suffered a loss." Turning his eyes to the other column, he applied each idea to Johna Adams. Who hated her? How could Digger know that? He jotted down "ex-husband," and turned to the next idea. Whom could Johna have injured, besides that ex-husband? She had not been at OVC long enough to hurt anyone, had she? And what loss had she caused? Her transitioning from Sea View Community College had to be considered a move up the ladder—more money, more prestige at a four-year school, more opportunities. Could that move have "hurt" any of her SVCC colleagues? Digger thought of his old community-college friend, Johnny Lambmann, the Dean of Humanities there. Maybe Johnny would know.

*JayLamgmannatsvccdotedu*. An easy email to remember. Maybe Digger would reach out at last. *Later*.

He turned back to his notebook and flipped the page to a blank sheet, filling it in by listing names without really thinking: Eliot, Jeff, Jolie, Diana, Mary, Lou…all the full-time OVC faculty and then all the part-timers, too. Across from the names, he jotted down how each had reacted to his book. Eliot had mentioned his own book, so had Jeff and even Lou, although the Lip Licker was definitely the most enthusiastic about *Composition Murder*. One or two people, Catherine, Jolie, had dismissed the genre, and Bill had asked about money. Others had been cold, talked of Time (as though it stalked only them!), or didn't talk at all—closed doors. Diana had been open, though, a bit distant, sure, but at least she had touched his book, opened it. Most had acted like vampires when offered a crucifix! What did this page two list have to do with his page one Tobias and Johna columns? Nothing that Digger could connect. However, the creation of page two's content felt oddly satisfying, painful but productive, and Digger thought of those sad teenagers who cut themselves with pocket knives or nail files. Were they punishing themselves, brain washed, or did the bleeding and throbbing prove that they were actually alive?

Digger chose not to pursue these thoughts.

Flipping the notebook to page three, he wrote the word "Emma." His big sister had been gone for a couple decades almost, a good sixteen years, anyway, Digger realized, and his father for even longer. Both killed in single-car accidents, both ruled accidents. A very strange coincidence. And then Danny's death, then Tobias', Dan Pinsky's, now Johna Adams'. All these people who died so young. Then Digger thought of his mother, his uncle (John), and his aunts (Mary and Carol). The elder Wilder clan members were really getting up there in years, but they were still alive while all the others had been swept from the earth. Digger's eyes fell on his sister's name: Emma!

For weeks after the news of her death, Digger had simply been unable to believe that she was gone, especially since he had lost so much that spring—Anna, Shyla (the feral cat that kissed him with her eyes), and then his only sibling. Throughout that summer, Digger had counted each passing week after Emma's crash: one week past, two weeks gone, three, one month since she lived, five weeks into death, six. But at seven weeks, he had no longer felt any surprise, realizing (and accepting perhaps) that Emma had floated off into Time, a colorful leaf in a stream full of brown ones, old and wrinkled leaves, all drifting away. The image was both beautiful and terrible, bright and cold, for Digger had known that that brook was irresolute in its motion, a force that would stop for no one, that would collect everyone, sooner or later, a fact known by the mind yet unaccepted by the heart—at least for six weeks.

He had been fairly close to his sister, at least at one time, connected in the way that blood united people, an unstated knowledge of acceptance and assistance, even when two members were quite different. Emma had been five years his senior, a lifetime when Digger had been a boy and then a teen and then a young man, and Emma's life never seemed related to his: she read novels while he poured through comic books; she obsessed over music, musicians, and clothes while he wrapped his head around dinosaurs and plastic airplanes, snakes and turtles; she drove off to meet friends while he simply rang doorbells for his. But Emma had always been his big sister, and he carried fond memories of her. For instance, when he was just a boy, a pre-teen, they used to play the Animal Game involving the family dog, a scruffy Scottish Terrier mix named Little Bear. Each sibling would look at the dog and connect his appearance to another animal, such as a "wart hog," an "elephant," a "baboon," and even an "ant eater." They played this game for years, coming up with new connections that both fit and didn't, but the game fizzled out when Emma got her driver's license and drove away all the time. Then she moved away. Then Little Bear died. His father drove off with a lethargic dog—the sick Scotty looked like a sloth, Digger would have told Emma, had she been there—and returned with empty hands, just a sad series of statements: that Bear had had a bad disease (Digger later learned that it had been stomach cancer), that the vet had suggested he be put down, that he had not been in pain, that he had been left at the veterinarian's office. "Why?" the little Digger had asked his father, who had misinterpreted the question and begun to talk about Little Bear's illness again, trying to make the boy understand. But Digger had not wondered about that, but rather about why the body had been left at the vet's, why Little Bear's earthly remains (he had not thought of it in those terms, of course) had been left in a cold building, why they were not going to bury their dog out back, at home.

*Our Scotty really had looked like a little bear*, Digger thought, and he turned his head and mind to the living room. At this motion, Snodo's white, fluffy noggin popped up, her light brown eyes searching his own, her floppy ears straightening and pivoting. But finding no promise of a walk, she lowered her head with a soft sigh and closed those wondrous orbs. Simba was laid out on the couch, too, but she did not stir. The ears that used to triangle about, searching for him, were still. When inside, Simba spent nearly all her time on the couch now, or more often just below it on the floor, and just earlier, Digger had had to boost her up beside him again. The lion dog had tried to hop up but only half succeeded, her lower body dangling and then succumbing to gravity.

"Up you go," Digger had said, hoisting her short legs and double-coated bottom up to the soft couch, old and lumpy. Maybe Digger should get a new one. He wouldn't.

Beneath Emma's name, Digger added no words, instead turning the notebook over to page two again and thinking of Paul Smith, Mr. Morbid, the stork-like composition professor who had tried to kill him eight years in the past. Could there be another monster among the faculty, Digger's peers, his "friends"? *What friends!* He ran his finger down the list of names. Could teaching composition drive a human to madness? Digger wondered if he could Google an answer. He had once heard or read that certain vocations—Air Traffic Controller, for instance, and even Veterinarian—led more often than others to despair, but he never thought of Writing Instructor as one of them. One too many notes to "listen for a pause," to "state your point clearly," to "show, don't just tell." Digger sometimes felt as though he were throwing information at walls, blackboards (whiteboards these days), and hoping that some advice would stick. Jackson Pollack teaching! However, he rarely felt angry about his job, rarely wished that he had taken another track, especially now that he had finally created a book, a life goal. Still, any job could drive a man mad, couldn't it? The repetition, the only sporadic success, the loneliness, the endlessness—at least on Mondays, right?

*Silly!* Johna's murderer had not been caught on this page. It was probably her ex-husband, it was always ex-husbands. But wasn't *he* himself an ex-husband, too! *No, don't go there*. Was it really silly to disregard his peers in Johna's murder? Probably not, and this time, anyway, he was not involved. The little detective, Doyle, he was not even involved, and then Digger thought of J. Zorn. Were girls named Jay? Maybe Jerry, but wasn't the actual name Geraldine with a "G"? *Dark Anna.* Why had Zorn reminded Digger of Anna? The shape of her eyes, just a little almond-ish, the hint of something exotic, or maybe the shape of her hair, soft looking, and the way it flowed naturally off her head, as though caressed and held by a breeze. Digger's thoughts were getting him nowhere, as if a place to get to actually existed! He probably should have just gone to school today.

OVC, Killer College, Murder U. At least no journalists had contacted him this time. None seemed to have made the connection. Could another killer walk its halls, maybe at night? *Night classes*. Johna had been followed and strangled after a night class, or had she been followed? Maybe the killer had just been waiting, but Digger didn't think so. Could any student have done it? He thought of the bobble-heads in her noon class, the way that one group had referenced her murder in their Grammar Jam song. *Innocent play*—unless! It would have to be a Psych student, he concluded, and he flipped over the notebook again (back to the beginning two columns) and wrote "Psychology" under Johna's name. Since OVC had a nationally renowned Psych Department, attracting mind-probing teenagers from around the globe, those students tended to see their pursuits as more worthy than their peers' interests from other majors. Beneath "Psychology," Digger added "arrogant" and then "confident," and beneath those dual sides of ethos (*darkness and light*, thought the writing teacher), he listed some generalized comments about OVC's most famous students. "Don't take advice," he wrote, followed by "the only students to sleep in class" (underlining the word "sleep"), "don't smile," "don't work well with others," "don't care about anything but case files," and then "don't sleep, stay up all night reading." The white space under the "Johna" column gradually disappeared. While realizing that he was not being fair, that in fact he had had some great psych students throughout the years, Digger also knew that most generalizations had a toehold on the truth—certainly this one, for psych students were usually frustrating, beyond reach, uncoachable. A teacher could lead a horse to water, but he couldn't make him (or her—*gender didn't matter with psychos*) drink it.

Digger let himself get a little righteous for a spell, for OVC psych students didn't care about writing, about him, about his tips, his models, his logical and practical suggestions typed into their papers, the transferability of all those skills. They spent all free time reviewing cases, apparently, delving into the abstractions of personality and abnormality, both nature and nurture, as though the two weren't part and parcel, thought Digger, shifting his harangue to an image of his shiny wife, then to himself. He could connect just about any topic to Anna, even after sixteen years, but what was that small amount of time really? Years passed like pages in a book. Slowly, methodically, but suddenly the book is done. Hadn't he heard a quotation like that somewhere? *Life is long until it isn't*, something like that.

Then the phone blared, and Digger actually heard a flutter, like a book's pages being swept back (that image again!). He jumped up and snatched the phone from its wall cradle just as it began to shout again. He was about to be quite surprised.

"Digger?" came an old woman's voice—his mother? *No*. "Matthew Diggerson?" The voice sounded a little irritated now. *Could it actually be!*

"Gwena?" said Digger into the phone, and then from it he heard the retired OVC humanities professor laugh, a pleasant-sounding release that bubbled on and on before stopping abruptly.

"The Grammar Nazi!" she said then, and Digger laughed, too, honest but short, as Matthew Diggerson's joy always seemed to be.

"I've heard that you're an author now," his old colleague and friend said, making Digger's stomach glow and rise slowly. "You're a murder mystery writer, eh? I hope that you're making some money, too."

"Not much of that yet, Gwena," Digger admitted, but he didn't feel any accompanying guilt at the financial reference, which he had heard before. Gwena's mind held less dark rooms than the brain of Bill Jacobs, the part-timer Digger had known the longest.

"Who cares about that!" added the old woman (*she must be eighty now*, thought Digger, his mother's age almost). "Ocean View will make you rich," she added sarcastically, "so you can just write for yourself. A writing teacher who writes—who would have thought of it! How are your peers treating your newfound success? Has Don Don Don Don Domberg read it yet? And what about the great poet Diana? She probably just reads verse. How about Mary? She probably just reads poetry, too!"

Digger enjoyed her words, his one-time peer's conclusions. "The reaction has been a little underwhelming," he admitted, and the complaining felt good. He had lamented the same message to his dogs, of course, and while Simba had just closed her eyes, Snodo had cocked her head a couple of times, trying to understand. That sweet, funny image actually helped the one-time author.

"What can you expect?" said Gwena Schmidt, and that question ignited a torch within the present Humanities Chair, creating the following track:

Digger: "I used to think that life was like a story, that people you know cared about your own story, that they were interested, loyal, like Tolkien's hobbits. I used to think that life could be the Shire."

Gwena: "Life isn't a story, Digger."

Digger: "You mean that life tells no tales?"

Gwena: "Just as Chekov said."

Digger: "Chekov was wrong. Remember in *Three Sisters* when a cow sticks its head in the window, remember how funny that was? That's a story right there. It's just that it's a little story, nothing big, but still great."

Gwena: "But all the cow said, Digger, was 'moo.'"

Digger: "What did you expect it to say, Gwena? If the cow had said 'Hello' or 'I'm hungry' then I'd agree with Chekov. No story there. Reality is the story."

Gwena: "But reality means no hobbits!"

Digger: "Yeah, no hobbits, no Shire. Maybe."

Gwena: "You didn't really think there was, Digger, did you?"

Digger: "I did, I used to, yeah. I thought there *was* peace and beauty and loyalty. Magic. That's the Shire, Gwena. But you're right, I suppose. Nobody much cares about anybody's story but their own."

Gwena: "Why should it be any different?"

Digger: "Because there should be party trees and dry hobbit holes, and loyalty. That's why. There should be loyalty."

Gwena: "Loyalty? You're a romantic!"

Digger: "When I hear the name 'Baggins,' I feel a light, the shine of loyalty."

Gwena: "You're definitely a romantic, Digger, an incurable condition."

Digger: "Why would anyone want the cure?"

That ended the conversational transgression, one that made Digger feel just a little bit embarrassed, the anxiety of opening a soul for public viewing.

"I'm sorry about all that, Gwena," he said. "I've been feeling a little down about my book's reception and about some other things. Thanks for listening. I really miss you. I don't know why I never stayed in contact."

"You weren't the only one," broke in Gwena, "but I'm contacting you now because I heard about your book. I'll get a copy from Amazon. Richard and I get everything there. We hardly go out at all!"

"You can get the book for free at our library, you know."

"No, no, no! I don't go back to OVC *ever*. I would end up talking to so many people that I would never get home to Richard. Either that, or more likely I wouldn't recognize anyone anymore. No, no. I want to *buy* the book. I want you to get some *money*."

"Thanks, Gwena. But I don't really care about the money. It's your support that means a lot to me. Do you like murder mysteries?"

"Oh, yes. I read them all the time. In fact, I was obsessed with Agatha Christie as a young person, and I've been reading them again. They're quite engaging. I read all the time now. Poetry and plays, literature, it all seems too heavy now."

"Have you tried Tony Hillerman?"

"Tony Hillerman? Does he write about that private detective from New Orleans?"

Digger laughed. "Go West, young woman!" he said. "Hillerman writes about a Navaho cop, cops actually, from the four corners region."

"No, then. I don't know Hillerman. But let's not start talking authors, or I'll forget why I called!"

"Okay, okay, Gwena, but just let me ask about Richard. How is he?" In his mind, Digger still pictured Gwena's husband as the tall, stiff man whom he had last seen well over a dozen years ago. The white king on the chess board. Digger had been glad to hear Gwena's speaking of him in present tense!

Gwena didn't respond right away, but then she said, "That question's not an easy one to answer. Richard has Alzheimer's, you know? He has good days and bad, good moments and bad. We get along, Digger. We're fine."

"I'm sorry," said Digger. "It's too easy to think about and talk about just your own problems, isn't it?"

"Sometimes it is actually harder to focus on them, Digger, so I'm going to order your book as soon as we hang up, and I'll call again when I'm done reading it. Maybe you could come over some night. That is an ancillary reason for my call. I still cook a bit, you know."

"I'd love that," said Digger, meaning the words. The two said good bye, and after Digger hung up the phone, he thought of his notes but instead glanced out the back door's window and saw a female cardinal halfway up his spindly blue spruce, now a fine and healthy accent tree, about fifteen feet high. The bird cocked her dark green head, her orange beak opening periodically, calling to her mate, no doubt. "Cheep … cheep," Digger heard in his mind and then laughed because he had thought of a wife's calling her husband "cheap." In his sunny back yard, though, the blood-red husband failed to appear.

## Chapter 7: To Obstruct

If you misuse punctuation, you send readers in the wrong direction, making both your writing and yourself look less believable. Thus, use this Green Day melody about loneliness to remind yourself how *not* to punctuate.

I used a comma wrong, I put it where there was no pause at all.
My subject was too long, so I put one down before the verb, but I was wrong.
Hear no pause, no comma belongs, hear no pause, no comma belongs.
My semicolon is not right, it divides a simple sentence type.
So I must see the sight of two balanced statements, then it's right.
Like a soft period, a semicolon's right, like a soft period, a semicolon's right.
To use a colon make a statement,
Then add your list, quote, or explanation.
Don't use a colon after "says," "such as," or "including"
Unless you add "the following."

October brought its usual bipolar weather, not only Indian summer for one three-day stretch, but also northern winds that required winter coats and caps. Halfway through the month, Digger had not heard from Gwena yet, nor Officer Zorn, nor a whole lot of other people, for that matter. On this late Tuesday afternoon, the Humanities hallway was empty. Another office hour in the process of being scorned by students! The effects of technology, email. Having expected the solitude, Digger had brought his dogs to work, a choice that he had made less often after getting Snodo, who could now offer Simba a companion on those long afternoons with Digger gone. Now *he* needed the company. Four-thirty on a Tuesday afternoon. *Not much to write home about!* But Patricia Pauley would be arriving pretty soon since she had a night class that evening. Digger wanted to inquire about the Wednesday night class inherited from Johna, especially about its students—any troublemakers? *Any killers?* Although he didn't believe this thought, it wouldn't quite leave his mind either. Then he noticed Simba strolling out the door.

"Simba!" he called, but his old Corgi-mix friend didn't seem to hear. She took a right and disappeared—head, long body, then tail. Snodo looked up at Digger, her eyes probing, her head clicking to the left.

"Go ahead!" said Digger, and the little white unicorn took off, disappearing after Simba in a flash. Digger felt a puff of happiness and then a silver lining of sorrow. *Simba.* The lion dog seemed especially disconnected these days, more and more lost, and Digger recognized those feelings and wanted to soothe them. He got up from his chair and looked down the hallway. Snodo was nosing Simba's furry ears, bone white now, but the latter paid no attention and just continued to stroll away. She had that singular, straight-forward focus almost all the time now, Digger realized, as though if left to her own choices she would just amble off into the horizon, maybe the sea, maybe the sun. He trotted down the hall and guided Simba back with her brown leather harness. She came without complaint, but looking back, Digger saw no white dog anywhere.

"C'mon, Snodo!" he called, and a white face appeared low down around the corner and then a white bullet sped toward him, stopping right before the man and smiling, smiling, smiling. "Good, pup!" said Digger, stroking the animal's thick white mane, the mantle that made her look like a tiny horse, sort of, or sometimes like a hyena. He and Emma would have had a fine time with animal names for this dog!

Then he saw a figure down by the secretaries' desks, a young man looking his way. *Was that Twitch?* On the first day of classes, Digger always did a group exercise involving student interviews and presentations; in short, he had them present each other to class. One of the questions involved how the person wanted to be addressed, and Twitch's peer had announced him as "Twitch." Digger had later asked the boy about that name, obviously carried along from high school or even earlier, because it didn't seem exactly positive. But the lad had assured Digger that he did, in fact, want to be called "Twitch," that he liked the name even though it stemmed from a nervous habit, a tic that fairly often resulted in a little hitching movement to his shoulders.

"Twitch?" Digger called down the hallway.

"Professor Diggerson!" called the boy. "I think there's some kind of animal loose in the building, like a skunk or an opossum." The last word came out "posum."

"That's just my dog Snodo," laughed Digger, motioning his student to come down the hall. At her name, the white dog had poked her head out the door, and now she took off toward Twitch, who said, "Wo-uh," and put his arms up, as though he were being arrested.

"Don't worry about Snodo," laughed Digger. "She'll just lick your toes. She won't bite."

The skinny, lanky boy still had his arms up, surrendering. "Okay," he said reluctantly. Twitch was all arms and legs, and as he approached, Digger thought of a spider, a Disney one, though, nothing like Shelob from Tolkien. Twitch was sort of a goofy spider, good natured, harmless.

"You don't like dogs?" asked Digger, for the boy had frozen up again, as though the small white dog were an actual threat. "Look, Twitch, put your hand down, let her sniff it, and then give her a little head pat, but show your hands first. That's how you greet a dog. Show her that you have nothing to hide."

"Okay," said Twitch, bending down and cupping his hands, as though offering Snodo a drink of water. The squatting young man made Digger think of Gollum, but the little horse lapped up the empty palms, making Twitch laugh. “She tickles!” he exclaimed.

“She does,” said Digger, adding “Come on in and meet my other dog.”

“Another dog!” said Twitch. But when the boy entered the small office, Simba failed to acknowledge him, just slept on, half beneath Digger’s desk. Twitch didn’t seem to mind the non-greeting from this canine. The student crumpled his appendages into Digger’s visitor’s chair. For the next few minutes, Snodo spent the whole time studying the strange, gangly human, her ears twitching in unison when the boy’s shoulders lurched in spasm every minute or so.

“I have a question about my paper, my Project Two.” Twitch leaned forward and pulled a folded copy from his back pocket, and Digger’s mind traveled back to when he used to collect hard copies. A long time ago. Twitch spread the paper out on the corner of Digger’s desk and tried to flatten it.

“We could check the online version,” said Digger.

“No thanks,” said the lad. “I like to work on paper.”

“Actually, I do, too. I like to write it out first and then type it into the computer.”

“Me, too.” Snodo tilted her head at the boy.

“Right here, you say that I’m off purpose here, but I don’t know what you mean. I don’t see that I’m ‘off purpose’ because I’m just explaining the writer’s point.”

“You are, Twitch. In your mind. But what the reader sees is this sentence that relates not just to the writer’s quotation, but to life itself. See how you aren’t mentioning the writer’s name in your sentence?” The boy’s shoulders did their twitch. Digger wasn’t sure if he had just acknowledged his teacher’s question or given a spasm of disagreement.

"See what I mean?" he repeated. "You need to get the author, 'Selzer,' into that sentence, or else you will seem to be talking about slaughterhouses in general, not about the writer's view of them."

"Oh," said Twitch. "Now I see what you mean. That sounds like my own argument against slaughterhouses." Then the student abruptly shifted topics, going off purpose in reality. "Have the cops figured out who killed your friend?"

*What? Who?* Digger was momentarily thrown back into the Tobias Mann episode, which he was currently taking notes about for his second book. Fact and fiction swirled around the composition teacher. "Do you mean Professor Adams?" he said.

"The lady who was strangled. I saw you with her this summer, during orientation. I recognized you because I saw your picture on our Bridges site. I knew that you were my writing teacher."

"But how did you recognize Johna, Professor Adams?"

"Yeah, that surprised me because I'm usually not good with faces," said Twitch. "But I saw her picture in the news and recognized her right away. She had been smiling at you and talking. You two were walking down near the Psyche Building."

Digger thought back to Johna's interview. They had walked together past the Psychology Building. All the way to the faculty parking lot.

"I could tell that she liked you a lot," said the boy, "and I just remembered her face for a change. Usually faces just merge into a blur in my mind. I'm sorry that somebody killed her."

"Me, too," said Digger, adding "You should major in Criminal Justice, Twitch. With your facial-recognition skills, you could be a great detective."

"Oh, I don't have any skills like that," said the boy. "I could hardly tell you what my roommate looks like. I'm going into psychology. I'd like to figure myself out, other people, too." Then his student's shoulders lurched and fell, and Digger realized that the young man did indeed fit that major, sort of. The composition teacher couldn't actually remember a psych student ever coming to his office hours for help. Then Digger felt a tingle of forethought, a premonition that Twitch's future would involve law enforcement in some way, on either side of the thin blue line.

"I looked you up, too," said Digger's student, further dividing Digger's thought about the lad's future.

"Looked me up?"

"Online, on 'Rate Your Professor.' I looked up all of mine, and you had the best reviews."

"I did?"

"Yeah, your reviews were almost all positive, unlike some of my professors. Professor Watkins had terrible reviews."

"Wait, Twitch! I don't want to hear about any names! I don't want to see these people and think about what you said."

"Okay," said Twitch, "but yours were really good, and they were right, too. They reflected what we do in class, how you're always having us work together and teach each other. I like that. That's how I learn best. I'm learning about learning in Professor Watkins' class, and he's not as bad as his reviews sounded."

"I'm glad to hear that!" Digger had never Googled his own name, had no intentions of ever doing so, either. He believed that any student who took the time to critique his teacher online must have some agenda, some emotional guiding force, such as a bad grade on a paper or test. Otherwise, why would anyone bother to click and type? Digger could hardly get students to check their paragraphs for dropped quotations (i.e., those with no introductory phrasing, such as "According to the narrator,"), so why would a regular student, one not in the grips of resentment, make the effort to create actual sentences about the past?

Suddenly, Simba raised her head, turned it toward Twitch, stared for two full seconds, emitted a little sound, sort of a falling "Hoooooooh ..." and then slumped her noggin back down.

"Your dog just hooted at me," said Twitch.

"Yeah, it did sound like a hoot. Simba's never hooted before."

"What does a hoot mean?"

Digger didn't know, but it worried him a little. That attenuated *hoot* had been rimmed with emotion. Confusion? Pain? It had almost sounded like a soft cry for help. The composition instructor bent down and stroked the slumbering dog's furry head and neck, but Simba had drifted even further back into silence, into an untouchable level. Beneath her thick fur, Simba seemed to be shrinking.

"Did they find the killer?" Twitch had shifted again.

"No," admitted Digger. "Not yet. From the news, the cops don't even have a suspect, but I haven't spoken with any law officers for over a month, and none have called me." He thought of J. Zorn, of her dark presence, so dark that it glistened a bit. Was that why the cold woman had reminded him of his warm Anna? Not *his*!

Twitch launched himself out of the chair, startling his writing instructor, causing Digger to picture a Jack-in-the-box, one from a horror movie, frowning, snarling, holding a big knife. Towering over the seated man, the thin fellow then announced, "I have to go, Professor Diggerson," and then he did, seeming to do everything abruptly, in a tangle of appendages. Snodo accompanied the lad down the hall, and Digger got up and watched as

Twitch repeatedly bent down and touched the strange white dog with the bottomless eyes. The boy even talked to her, but Digger couldn't hear the conversation. "Bye, Twitch," Digger called, and when the pair disappeared around the corner, he felt a stab of concern. *Snodo?* "C'mon, Snodo!" he called, and immediately the white pony came trotting back around the corner alone and then pranced down the fairly long hallway toward him—past all those closed doors. *Empty rooms?*

Where was Patricia Pauley? Could she be in the adjunct faculty office, perhaps doing some prep for tonight's class? Digger walked up the corridor, greeted Snodo after just a couple of steps, and then knocked on the adjuncts' door. When nobody answered, he turned the handle and looked in. *Empty*. The silence of the room and then the corridor enveloped Digger as he returned to his office, saddened him a bit, but Snodo made little breathing sounds, happy ones, not like Eliot Happy Rock's laboring ones. *Look, Eliot, you too have two last names, Happy and Rock!* the lonely professor thought, but then he glanced down at his beagle-sized white dog, perked up immediately, and said, "We'll go home soon, yes!" Snodo seemed to understand, at least the word "home," for she flopped down near Simba's back, brushing up against the sleeping lion.

Digger thought of Twitch, sort of a sad fellow, sort of alienated. Why? He was a little strange, true, and those shoulder twitches! They made his arms seem even longer and thinner. Digger pictured an orangutan. He had occasionally seen other students smiling and gesturing at Twitch's repeated spasms (not too often, thankfully), and the boy himself was perhaps too enthusiastic, pushy at times. But Digger liked the student's attitude, talked to him often after class, for the teacher would choose enthusiasm over apathy every time. Then he thought of what Twitch had said about those online grade-your-professor sites, which he had heard of before, usually back in his pre-chair days when a student wanted to enroll in a class. Invariably, the boy or girl would say that she had read about his classes online and heard "great things" and therefore wanted in on all that greatness. *Rhetoric!* The art of persuasion. Although most students didn't much enjoy writing about an author's use of rhetorical tactics, some of them sure could use those techniques, such as appeals to emotion, themselves! Then he thought again of Twitch.

When his phone jangled, Snodo leaped up, but Simba didn't seem to hear the noise. Digger answered before the second ring, saying "Hello."

"Matthew?" It was his mother, Jean Diggerson, eighty-one years old. Her son wondered how long it would take until she brought up that number.

"I called you at home, but you weren't there."

"I was here."

"I know that now, Matthew." His mother often sounded just a little exasperated. "You're working late," she added.

"Just sitting around with my dogs actually."

"They let you bring your animals to school, do they?"

"This school's full of animals," laughed Digger, "and I don't bring them too often anymore, but since I don't teach on Tuesdays, I thought they'd be good company. Simba's mostly slept, though."

"She's getting old," said Jean Diggerson, and Digger thought, "Here it comes—eighty one!"

"I am eight-one years old now, Matthew, you know that?"

"You are? Eighty-one! Now how could that have happened?"

"Don't be facetious," said the eighty-one-year-old woman. "I'm calling to tell you that John has fallen and broken his hip. He can't hear and now he can't walk!"

"That's too bad, mom," said Digger, "but men recover better from broken hips than women, that's what I've heard."

"Where did you hear that?"

"I'm not sure," said Digger, who suddenly wondered if he had heard the exact opposite, that men go downhill fast after breaking their hips. He decided to stay positive. "Uncle John will be up walking about saying 'What?' before you know it."

"Hmpfh!" said his mother, a sound that Digger had never heard her make. He thought of Simba's little "hoot."

He decided to change the topic. "Mom, you once told me that blood is thick, so the roots are strong and deep."

"I did? I don't know about 'blood,' Matthew, but roots are deep. Family is all connected. Death does not part us."

"Blood nourishes the roots, right? But family can be extended, even to work colleagues, right?"

"I wouldn't know about that, Matthew, but why do you ask?"

"Oh, it's just that my colleagues around here are not as interested in my book as I thought they'd be." It felt good to admit this again—cathartic.

"And what do you want your colleagues to do, gather around you like little kids around a storyteller? Matthew, you're old enough to know that people do not act like that. Your problem is that you're a romantic. You still pine for your wife, for Anna, don't you? You need to find another woman. Then whatever your colleagues do wouldn't bother you."

Digger ignored this soliloquy, which he had heard before. "Blood and roots. That's what I had with Anna, Mom, and that's why I held onto her so long. Still do. I can't kill those roots, they're too deep. They're nourished in my dreams."

"Now you're getting a bit imaginative, Matthew. Most things can be gotten over. It just takes some resolve. Look at me with your father, with Emma."

"Resolve and acceptance."

"And acceptance."

"You know, Mom, that's really the key to a good life, istn't it? Acceptance! Without it, this wild world will tear you apart."

"You're getting creative again, Matthew. You should write that down and save it for your books, for that Willy Wilder fellow."

"Oh, sure, so that everyone around here can read about him," said Digger sarcastically, but then he corrected his mother. "Billy D Wilder. Aka William Daniel Wilder."

"I like that, Matthew. Billy D. I told John about that name, but he didn't hear me, the big dope!"

"I'll send him a card, Mom, and even a copy of the book, but I can't visit yet. October's the longest month in the fall semester. No real breaks. November brings Thanksgiving, and then December comes fast. It will be Christmas before long."

"And I won't see you until then!"

"Probably not, but I'll write to John, and Christmas will come fast. Do you still want me to get you a dog?"

"Matthew, I do *not* want a dog! What could I do with a dog? I'm eighty-one years old now!"

"You are?" said Digger, whereupon his mother made that strange non-word noise again, and then the two said good bye.

Snodo had joined Simba in snoozeland. Digger looked out his tall, narrow office window and watched the library towers' shadows reach for him. They would miss his corner office, of course, always did, the dark yet pale arms passing to the south-east, out to sea. Where were all the seagulls? He hadn't heard a pterodactyl bellow for hours. Right on cue, a shadow arced across the quiet quad, and then, from the open door, came the sound of another door creaking open from down the hallway. The Cat Woman, at last!

As Digger rose from his chair, he saw Snodo's butt already disappearing around the doorway. Dogs and cats. Neither species should be too curious! Then he heard a loud "Oh!" followed by a series of softer ones and a "Where did you come from?" Digger got up to talk with one of his more recent adjuncts, Patricia Pauley, who requested only night classes, two per semester (Tuesdays and Thursdays this semester), but who had agreed to take on Johna Adams' Wednesday night one, too. He heard Patricia's cooing at Snodo and then found the two in the adjunct faculty office.

"Yours, Digger, I assume!"

"Oh, yeah. One of my two kids."

"One of your fur babies!" Patricia was letting Snodo lick her chin, the little ham!

"You have some of those, too, of the feline variety. Three if I remember correctly, Patricia."

"Up to four now. They just wander into our yard and never leave." Digger smiled at that, but he thought that the opposite took place at his home: everything wandered out of the yard and never came back. But Simba had stayed, Snodo, too. Eight years already past for his prancing pony, and so much longer for the lion dog. Patricia was talking again: "My husband says that half our cats come from the neighbors, that they like our food better. But I know what they like better. How they're treated. Even Bob loves the cats. He just pretends to be tough!"

Bob Pauley. Digger had never met the man, but a rumor had cast him in a negative light: that he was abusive. Digger smiled at Patricia again, wondering if one eye didn't look just a bit darkened. *No*. He was looking for monsters and thus finding them.

"Patricia, I've been wondering about Johna's night class. You haven't emailed me about any problems, so I just assumed that there weren't any, but I should have checked with you earlier. Time has gotten away from me this semester. Already half way through October."

"We'll be shoveling snow soon, but the extra night class has been fine. At first, when you take over for another teacher, the students seem to resent you, as though you were responsible for them losing their teacher. But now we all get along like peas in a pod. No problems."

Digger was thinking about Johna's being followed home after her first class. "None of the male students seem …" he started to say, changing to "none have said anything odd to you or done anything strange?"

"Like what?" Pauley's face looked confused, curious.

Digger laughed. "Oh, I don't know! I'm a little crazy. I talked with a cop, a policewoman, soon after Johna's death, and she—well, mainly I—thought that Johna might have been followed home after her night class."

Patricia's eyes widened, her mouth opening, forming an almost comical "O."

"No, no, no!" said Digger. "I don't mean to worry you! I was being a little paranoid. Remember that I got all mixed up in Tobias' murder—before your time here. Have you heard about that?"

"Everybody's heard about that, Digger."

"Well, Johna's death, her murder, has started my mind working like back then, even though this time everything's different. It can't be a fellow teacher this time, right? How many of us can go crazy like that!

Anyway, Johna's class doesn't seem to have any crazies in it, does it?"

"Just me now, Digger!" Patricia Pauley said, but then she laughed. "Actually, Bob's already gotten me paranoid about that class. 'Taking over for a dead woman' is how he put it. He just wants me around at night more."

"How is Bob?" Digger thought about those rumors.

"He's fine, thank you."

"And I've forgotten what he does, what his job is—did you tell me?"

The Cat Woman laughed. "If I had, you would have remembered. Nobody forgets Bob's line of work. He's a private investigator!"

"No kidding?" said Digger, getting a sudden image of Humphrey Bogart wearing a hat and smoking a cigarette, holding a gun, too. He thought of asking Patricia if her husband wore a hat. Then he thought of asking her if she had read his book, if she had any interest in his accomplishment at all. After all, it was about a writing teacher, for God's sake! Then Matthew Diggerson chastised himself for being as abrupt as Twitch and made a small joke: "Maybe Bob should take me on as an apprentice."

"Maybe he would—as long as you'd work for nothing!"

"Well, I do that around here," said Digger, but he didn't really feel that way. And as he bid Patricia good bye and good luck with all three of her night classes, calling to Snodo as he left the adjunct faculty office, he regretted the financial comment because part-timers often did feel grossly underpaid. Many were, too, especially at the community colleges and technical institutions. Back when he had been an adjunct, before coming to OVC, Digger had taught classes for a variety of schools and experienced a range of financial compensation. He was grateful that those days were over—except, of course, that some of those days had included Anna. Digger would go back to those rich poor days in an instant.

Whenever he brought his "fur babies" to school, Digger would take the elevator, at all other times walking the two flights of steps to the third floor Humanities corridor—for exercise. On this late Tuesday afternoon, the composition instructor met nobody on either end of the elevator, saw not a soul as he strolled up the path past one of the smoking gazebos, enjoyed the soft pull of Snodo's lead. She was a dog who wanted to get to where she was going—right now, thank you! Simba, though, sauntered along without looking back or investigating to the side, seemingly just mirroring the white dog's forward movement. Digger felt sad about her changes, her aging. A dog never seemed old until it was.

His mind shifted back to Patricia Pauley, who had not mentioned Digger's book, and then to her husband, who could probably kill with his hands alone. Were people really private investigators? Could you make a living doing that? And what exactly did you do? In Ocean View, no less! Then a disquieting thought took roost: Private detectives followed people. And what did abusive private detectives do? Or put another way, what wouldn't they do?

Pondering Bob Pauley, Digger almost ran headlong into Professor William Watkins, who barged right out of the Psych Building, a leather briefcase ever attached to his right arm, and into Digger's little pack. Simba hooted again, and Snodo actually growled, a sound that Digger had rarely heard the happy little fluff-head make.

"Diggerson!" said the bearded, bespectacled professor, and then "Dogs! Diggerson and dogs! You never know what you will discover on this campus."

That seemed to be a joke, so Digger laughed, which calmed Snodo down immediately. Simba just stood silently, gazing off up the path or maybe off within her own mind. Digger had begun to wonder if dogs could get Alzheimer's. Why not?

"Bill," said Digger, bending down to pat Snodo and to stroke Simba. "I haven't seen you in, what, years?"

"Even though your building is right there and mine is right here. That just about explains the human race!"

Was that another joke or just a sardonic outlook on life? Digger decided not to judge this odd man, but instead to take this opportunity to get some psychological—in other words, professional—advice.

"Bill," he said again, wondering for a second if anybody else used the informal form of *William* when addressing this pedagogue. "Did you hear that I published a book, a murder mystery?"

"Sadly, Diggerson, that news has not passed from your building to mine, but congratulations on your success. A murder mystery? I assume that you used your Tobias Mann experience?"

"Actually, I used an experience from before then, one involving a student who jumped off the Bay Bridge. Do you remember Danny Jones?"

"Sadly, no, but I would have thought that Tobias Mann's murder would make for some fine fiction."

"It will," said Digger, adding quickly, "I mean, sort of. I'm planning a second book in the series, which stars a composition teacher turned sleuth and takes place, well, basically here."

"Ah, very interesting, very interesting." William Watkins was even stroking down on his beard as he repeated that conclusion, looking like the stereotypical mad scientist.

To keep from laughing, smirking, Digger got to his point: "I have a favor to ask, some information needed, some explanation."

"Go on, Diggerson. I am fascinated."

*What a dick*, thought Digger, but he went on nonetheless: "I told my writing colleagues about my book during the summer meeting and showed many of them a copy early in the semester, over a month ago now, six weeks, and nobody has yet read the book. In fact, nobody ever mentions it to me, never …" Digger wasn't sure what he meant to add here.

"And you want to know why, eh? Well, that is certainly a complicated scenario."

"They seem to be actively avoiding me, but that might just be a little paranoia on my part. I've always gotten along well with my colleagues, both full and part-time, but I must admit to feeling a little isolated over this past month or so."

"And what about that dead one?" broke in the psychology professor.

"The dead one?" replied Digger, who then made the connection to Johna Adams. "Oh, yes. Johna. But that's not related. But it hasn't helped the semester, either. Is that what you meant?"

"But of course! Did you think I meant that one of your colleagues had gone crazy over your literary success and decided to start killing other colleagues!"

Digger laughed at this, although he was beginning to wonder when this odd man was being serious and when sarcastic. For this very reason, this confusion, Digger had often reminded his writing students *never* to be sarcastic in their papers.

"I hoped you could maybe suggest why my peers are being so indifferent toward my book, why they won't read it. Some human nature angle that I haven't considered."

Watkins looked down at Snodo, who had been staring up at him the entire time, and the professor did a quick double take, as many people did when they recognized the intensity in the little dog's eyes, the depth.

"That is an interesting dog," said Willy Watkins, who remained rigidly upright, and Digger wondered unkindly if the nutter was thinking of experimenting on his littlest girl, attaching wires to her brain.

"If you call her by her name, she'll jump about a yard straight up."

"No, I don't think so. Dogs and children should stay earthbound. And I think we should return to your problem. Your colleagues are jealous, Diggerson. What did someone say, that success involves standing on the shoulders of others. Well, you seem to be stomping on their heads with your book, especially if you have been waving it in their faces. It makes them feel small, so they experience anger, then humility, then perhaps denial, which then transitions into indifference. Simple really."

Digger didn't really believe the psychologist, even though William Watkins was world renowned, at least that's what Digger had heard. He looked the part. Digger almost expected the man to whip a tophat from behind his back, clomp it onto his head, and then float off amidst a crescendo of string music. Snodo made an "urping" sound. She was beginning to tire of the William Watkins experience, and Digger could not blame her.

"Well, thank you, Bill. You've given me a lot to think about. Maybe I should stop mentioning the book, or the fact that I'm now writing another one. Basically,

I've stopped already, but what you've said supports that choice."

"Excellent," said Professor William Watkins, who apparently was headed toward the library on one of the quad's diagonal walkways. The man strode off, but then turned back after several seconds and called out to Digger. "Of course, Diggerson, there is one more possible reason for your colleagues' behavior." Digger braced himself. Despite Watkins' face displaying not a flicker of humor or warmth—none of those raised lips or eye line scrunches—Digger suspected a joke cocked into the chamber.

"What's that?" he finally said, somewhat slowly.

"Maybe they just don't like you."

And if that were a joke, then William Watkins didn't seem to enjoy it much himself.

## Chapter 8: To Listen

To use marks effectively, you need to read your sentences (aloud even) in order to listen for a slight pause, a stronger one, or a stop. After getting help from the following classic rock song, you can "thank" Led Zeppelin for the advice.

If you see a comma "this," or a comma then "however,"
A common error will persist, making readers read it over.
Comma splice, you sound so wrong. Comma splice, you look too long.
Unconnected thoughts, get your readers lost. Your reputation hangs upon a thread.
Read your prose aloud, you can hear the sound
Of where one sentence ends and one begins, so listen in.
Run-on sentence, you interrupt. Comma splice, you must be stopped.

When asked about their favorite month, a New Englander will never say "November," but Digger liked the starkness of the landscape, the barren trees, the unfriendly breezes even, because this was the month that whispered "The End! An end's coming, just around the bend!" Not that he didn't enjoy his job, but the winter break meant weeks without classes, without daily responsibilities, without papers! November was a quick month, too, ending with a five-day Thanksgiving vacation and then a mere two weeks of December classes after that. And within those weeks would come Anna's annual Christmas card, which Digger looked forward to like a junkie, thinking about it around the beginning of November, on any cold day really. Maybe she would ask him to meet her this year, to get together, to reminisce, to rekindle, to … *Oh, God! Stop, stop, stop!* Despite the fact that November symbolized the word "end" and thus "freedom," Anna's word, her justification for leaving him so long ago, Digger still loved the month.

And that Thanksgiving break was just a week away, almost, after another long Monday, another day without mention of *Composition Murder*, without collegial connection. Frowning as he prepared Simba's and Snodo's dinner, Digger craned his head to the left to look out his kitchen window at the sun's bloody dip into the horizon. Clouds lay stripped like long soiled bandages across the sky, creating layers of non-colors—smudgy white, blotchy gray, pale mauve—but as the sun fell, the clouds all turned black and blotted out the stars. Even the seagulls had gone off somewhere, and when Digger opened the back door to let the dogs do as needed (he would pick up as needed, too, the next day), cold air barged right in, uninvited. Within thirty seconds, Snodo was back at the door, barking in her quietly persistent way, bouncing repeatedly, yet Digger had to go out—with a flashlight!—to remind Simba to return.

The lion dog had been staring through the back wire fence into the sea grass that separated Digger's yard from the strip of public beach and then the top throat of the bay, the water's rolling in or out, depending on the tide, the attenuated systole and diastole of the earth. Digger listened to the emptiness of twilight. What was Simba listening to? When he bent and stroked her crown, Simba's head swiveled up, and when their eyes locked, her tail moved back and forth, but only once. The sliver of a connection, yet Digger had felt it. Simba had, too. "C'mon, girl," Digger said to his beloved, disappearing dog. "C'mon, Simba." Snodo had come back out of the kitchen to lead them all back in.

Digger turned on the local news and received a bit of a shock: the story dealt with Johna Adams, seemingly forgotten by both reporters and police for the past month or so. The anchorwoman was reporting evidence released by the OVPD, a long list of nothing: no signs of struggle, no blood under the deceased's fingernails, no bruising other than one cranial abrasion and the ring of death around her neck, no sexual assault, no robbery, no signs of breaking in to either apartment or car, no known motive, no suspects. The latter "no" ended the story, other than that the OVPD was requesting leads from the public, and when the next fragmented tale shifted into a local house fire, Digger muted the sound.

*Listen for the unstated facts*, he thought, for the messages between the lines, for the unconnected thoughts. If Johna's body showed that she had *not* fought for her life, then she must have been murdered by a very strong person, a man, or perhaps by a very cunning one, someone who had snuck up on her and rendered her unconscious. *Or by someone she knew*. Digger did not want to believe that, not again, so he dropped the possibility from his mind. That damage to Johna's head. *Could be a woman.* No fingerprints or fiber forensics were mentioned, and Digger thought suddenly of cat hairs. Patricia Pauley? Her private-eye husband, the gun-toting abuser? *Silly thoughts!* But why had Johna been murdered? No financial reason, no robbery or break in, so it must be personal. Her ex-husband, what had Johna said about him? They had split because he had wanted children, she a career—something like that. Made more sense than Digger's own broken union. And Johna had been coming home (not to *his* home, the ex's) from that career.

Of course, the cops, J. Zorn and company, would have vetted the ex-husband, who would automatically have been the number-one suspect, besides Digger himself. *A silly thought, too!* What had Detective Doyle said about *family*, something to do with strangers robbing you, but family members killing you? Where was the little detective now? Where was Zorn, dark Anna? And what did the "J" stand for? Probably just "Jessica" or "Jennifer," but Zorn was an odd last name, maybe eastern European, Serbs and Slavs. Did they name their girls Jessica or Jennifer? Snodo sat and watched Digger think. Simba slept.

Out back, with the heavens rolling darkly by above, the clouds as big as boxcars, the sky train as long as those mournful metal ones that flowed like rivers through the western desert, the intruder breathed deeply and tried not to cough. The beach sand had been a bit of a struggle, still harder to walk on, even in these colder months, than he had expected, but the path had been easy to follow, as usual. The public access, a dozen or so house lots, all ending at this concrete jetty after Diggerson's little house. A nice, quiet place, almost a seaside cottage. *Diggerson!* He had seen that *bastard* through the window, a kitchen window, it appeared, and the back door was glass, too, and he had seen Diggerson disappear around the corner of the little place, probably into a living room. The dark room had recently cast lightning flashes, which he recognized as the television coming to life and changing screens, light to dark, the eternal cycle.

*Just like me*, he thought. Just like all of us little humans and all our lives of quiet desperation. He could hear the water lapping, the tide apparently coming in, the sea exhaling. Breezes made themselves known, hissing their unintelligible language. Cold and uncaring in November. *Pretty damn uncomfortable!* Why was he standing out here? *Stalking Diggerson!* Why didn't he just walk off Virginia Wolf-like into the bay, into those icy deep waters, into oblivion? Why cling to this November life? Was his own despair really someone else's fault? Perhaps if his corpse washed up on Diggerson's beach, then two birds could be killed with one stone—a release from it all and trouble for the other man. Not joy, not accolades—*trouble!*

The house breathed silence, the sky whispered silence, the sea slept. Where were the great author's dogs? Sleeping on the job.

Light from the kitchen window stretched a path out to the back gate and died just beyond it, just to his left as he stood to the right of that gate. Would that rickety door make a noise, squeak, call the neighbors, summon the authorities? Maybe, but that fear was a bit intoxicating, wasn't that the point? *Johna Adams' neck!* How would Diggerson's feel? The solitary man actually licked his lip in anticipation because the dark side, after all, *was* a side. It *was* a life. He thought of the Emperor in those dumb *Star Wars* movies. "Come to the Dark Side!" *Johna Adams' rag-doll body.* The Emperor was one creepy dude, but strong, too, driven. And with those thoughts, the breeze blew hair about his head and made his eyes blink, once, twice, three times. How could Diggerson live in this windy wasteland? The stalker stood like a pole in the shadows and twitched his shoulders for comfort, once, twice, three times. In his pocket, the gun seemed to pulsate. Like a little heart, it was. Heart shaped, heart weighted. It had almost failed to fit into his pocket, but it felt snug in there now. What would happen if he walked up to Diggerson's back door, found his target, and blasted away? All Hell would break loose, that's for sure. And would that be satisfying? Running off. Would he get away even? Maybe he should run off into the sea. *Coming, Virginia!* Maybe. But not yet.

With that thought, the bipolar man suddenly felt a presence, and he looked down to the left and saw the shadow. It suddenly merged into a shape. It was a cat, for God's sake, a big black tomcat! It sat like a big bowling pin in the pale, attenuating light from Diggerson's kitchen, and it was watching the cottage, too, not even paying any attention to the other human, to him. "Who the Hell are you?" he whispered, wondering if he were hallucinating. He wasn't. The cat swiveled its big black head, *like a damn owl*, up at him, and its eyes flashed in the dead kitchen light, and then he knew, he knew, that this cat was not for him, that there was some damn dark mojo going on here.

"Are you here for Diggerson or for me?" he hissed to the little watcher, who casually turned her attention back to the kitchen light.

The man's mind shifted to the little club in his right hand, the handle narrower and so smooth, so beautifully smooth, the shaft widening and weighted. The cat couldn't see it! How easy it would be to swing the club down and reverse the mojo, *how sweet!* The breathing, lip licking, blinking, twitching man focused on the silent animal again, its eyes no longer blazing but once again locked onto his own, glowing golden. When had it turned back to him? *Don't look at me!* In all this darkness, those two amber orbs unnerved the killer, cracked his confidence. Perhaps this wasn't the time for the author's star to go black. *No, perhaps not.* On another night, perhaps a more moonlit one, he would return. *Yes*, the moon would be a far better companion than this odd cat.

A breeze snaked up from the water and caused a hunch in his shoulders, but the black cat didn't seem to notice the elements. The man blinked down hard at it twice. *Still there*. He could feel his own breath traveling down, pausing, and escaping from his open mouth. The cat had resumed its vigil over Diggerson's cottage. Didn't felines guard Egyptian graves? Or was that the mouth of Hell? *No*, that was a dog, *a three-headed dog, for God's sake*. But cats guarded something.

Turning and picking slowly through the sea grass, the heavy sand, the intruder glanced back repeatedly until he could no longer see the creature at Diggerson's gate. The skies hissed and sent their sinuous breaths to prowl the earth while the dark waters exhaled their mysterious depth and icy siren's song. Only personification, paranoid personification! Yet even the dead sand sucked at his feet, which began to pick up the pace so that the intruder was almost running before he reached the public access path that led to his vehicle and to safety. The world was a strange and dangerous place.

## Chapter 9: To Set Off

Think of parentheses as an aside, such as when a character on the stage breaks from the scene to address the audience directly with information set off from the story. Now listen to this famous Beatles' song to hear how this mark goes.

If you want to set off extra info, put it in parentheses,
Then read the thought without it, edit and see.
If the sentence works without that content, you have punctuated correctly.
Parentheses adds information you do not need.
Parentheses, you will see, offer extra info opportunities,
Put a highlighted detail in parentheses.

The fall semester's classes ended on a Wednesday, which began for Digger the same way that every other December day did: with a check of the mail box. On this day, he had been rewarded. Anna's annual card! For the past few years, she had chosen dog covers, no doubt in response to his own missives. Although she had never met Simba or Snodo, Digger sent a photo of them in his own Christmas cards to her, and most of what he wrote inside dealt with his pups, an enjoyable subject, one that kept him from begging her to return, too. Anna's notes tended to talk of work, her career shift from special education to art, as well as projects, such as a series of watercolors dealing with sunsets, for instance. Digger looked forward to her card with most of his soul, but her words always left him disappointed, mal-nourished. White-bread words. This year, Anna chose to tell him mainly about one of her students, a girl who showed real promise, who really had the gift. *The gift!* Digger had had that once. Bitterness bubbled within, evaporating from his black river below, until he focused on that weak thread and plucked it out.

He had two gifts now, right? They sat and watched him, or at least one did. And he had his book, too, with another on the way. Maybe nobody read his book, yet that didn't mean that the story, the fictional world created, did not exist. It did, and Billy D would live on long after his creator had floated off. That was a gift, too. Existence was full of gifts. *Don't forget that!*

He shut Anna's card and looked again at this year's dogs on the cover. Two golden retrievers wearing Santa hats. Nice artwork, though, not cartoon-like. *Pretty.* Why had he and Anna never adopted a dog in their time together? Would a pet have made a difference? *Definitely, but maybe not.* Maybe a dog would have meant even less *freedom*—for Anna.

As always, he put Anna's card in his briefcase, which also held notes about his lesson plans, gel pens for the board (since they tended to disappear from the classrooms), and copies of the handouts that Digger had added to his online course site. In the past, his briefcase had also held student papers, either incoming or outgoing ones, but he no longer lugged around that burden. All papers were submitted online and returned that way, too. Today, tonight, he would be collecting three batches of them, yet their weight through the computer was far less than it had been when years ago he had crammed stapled essays into this very same briefcase. He really didn't need the case anymore, in fact, except for a place to hold those board markers. And he needed a spot for the pictures of Simba and Snodo, too, of course, and the one behind the dogs, the one showing Anna in their back yard, the light of the sky all drawn to her hair and face, a light that Time could not darken.

Seated, slumped, in his office after his last eleven o'clock class of the fall semester, Digger heard people out in the corridor, happy voices (last day of classes!), doors opened, closed, but he did not get up. He had quit getting up. If his colleagues wanted to connect, they could do the work, not him, anymore. Bitterness boiled, and Matthew Diggerson left the heat on, enjoyed the warmth even. Then he heard a knock, turned, and saw a student, a girl whom he did not recognize.

"Are you the head of the Writing Department?" said the girl. She looked like she was in a hurry for some reason. Maybe it was her body language, angled away from him, or maybe it was the way her chin tilted up. Digger braced himself for a complaint.

"More or less," he said. "I'm Professor Diggerson. How can I help you?"

"My writing teacher doesn't like me," the black-haired student said, and she flicked that hair out of her eyes, challenging Digger to disagree, it seemed.

"What makes you think that?" he responded, hoping that he could get the student to avoid naming the teacher, as well as to dissuade her from this childish yet not too rare view, one that he had heard a dozen times, at least, in his role as Chairperson.

"He disrespects me," the girl said, making Digger think of his oft-repeated advice to students: Show; don't just tell.

"In what way?" he responded, adding, "Would you like to take a seat?"

"No," said the girl, gathering her thoughts, her ammunition. "He won't call on me in class, even when I have my hand up, and he dismisses my opinion when he does call on me. And he gives me lower grades than my papers deserve!"

*Ah*, there it was—the kernel of the problem. *Always grades*.

"You know," started Digger, then adding, "What's your name, please?" She gave it, *Jennifer*, and Digger thought of Officer Zorn. "Jennifer," he continued, "students always complain about us writing teachers' grades because we have to critique everything. Not only what you say, but how you organize it and how you deliver your content, too. Writing teachers grade everything, so even though those grades tend to seem harsh, they actually help you by pointing out the areas that you need to strengthen, like introducing quotations correctly, for instance, or using commas to guide readers through your sentences. Other teachers, in other fields, won't have the time to help you with all those areas, do you see what I mean?"

"I understand all that, but he still grades way too hard. He hates me! He looks at me with anger. Two of my friends say the same thing. I think he hates women!"

*And he licks his lip weirdly or breathes oddly or blinks like an owl*, thought Digger, who realized that this complaint called for action, that he could not avoid naming names here, so he said, "Who's your writing teacher? I'll have a talk with him, if you'd like, and then I'll email you, okay? Or you could come back and see me during my four o'clock office hour."

"You could email me," said the girl, mollified at least a bit. She wrote her email down on the paper Digger provided. As she thanked him (abruptly) and turned to leave (abruptly), Digger started to ask the name of the professor, but she beat him to it, turning quickly and declaring, "And his name is Professor Knightly!" She had accented the "Knight" and then disappeared around the corner. At the name, Digger was a little surprised since most often students complained about adjuncts, no doubt knowing that their teachers were part-time and perhaps less secure in their jobs, more vulnerable to coercion. He had expected to hear "Jacobs," not a full-time faculty member, but at least Lou would be easier to talk to about this complaint than Bill, who tended to get defensive.

The Chair looked through the now empty doorway and thought about how bare the wall looked. *We should put some picture there on the wall,* he thought, and then his mind slipped to the closed door opposite his. Diana Pell's door. She hardly ever seemed to use it anymore. Her office must be like a stuffy museum. Then Digger checked his watch: still half an hour before his one o'clock class, then his last one at two, then the office hour, then home—the end of the fall semester, except for all those final papers, of course. He thought of Lou Knightly's schedule. The Lip Licker should be in his office now. Reluctantly, Digger rose up and went a couple doors down the hallway. Lou's door was open just a crack, suggesting that he was *home* but that he didn't want to be disturbed. Had his student, Jennifer, peeked in at the tall, thin man? Had she scurried by the door? Wasted thoughts! Digger peeked into the crack and then knocked, waited for Lou's "come in," and pushed the door wide.

"Digger!" said Lou, as though happy to see him. *One of the few!* As though reclining on a chaise longue, the tall, thin man was slouched in one of three available chairs, which cluttered up the office. *Why three chairs?* Digger hardly needed even two! Lou's extended legs took up at least half of the room's space.

"Lou," said Digger, getting right to the point. "I have to talk to you about a student who just came to see me."

"I grade too hard, right?" laughed Knightly, and his tongue came out and did its circuit. Did Digger hear a slurp? Like his student Twitch, Lou seemed to be all appendages, topped by a grinning head, dark and square.

"Yeah," said the Chair, "as usual, but this student also seems to think that you don't like her, that you have it in for females."

"For females?" said Lou, smiling. "I love females!" Then the human spider pulled his long legs in, making his knees rise almost above his box top.

"Well, I can't really tell her that, right? She thinks that you don't call on her and that when you do, you don't respect what she says. These are her words, of course, her point of view."

"Who is she?" said Lou, not smiling now. The full-timer had shifted forward a bit, too, his head now higher than his big, boney knees.

Digger was taken aback by this request, not having expected it. Suddenly, he didn't want to tell Knightly the name. To cover this mental deception, he laughed. "You know, I didn't ask her." That was no lie. He hadn't asked; he had just requested her email, which of course revealed her name—last name, anyway.

"Then what does she expect you to do, just to lecture me to change my evil, women-hating ways?" Digger was glad to see that Lou was smiling again. *Stop with the lips, though!*

"She just wanted to vent," Digger decided to say. "And I explained how we English teachers seem like hard graders because we grade everything. And I told her that I'd talk with you, so that's all done. I'm obviously not going to put her complaint in your file or anything. No worries!"

"No worries!" Still, Lou Knightly's body seemed wound tight now, appendages flexed, ready.

Digger thought that he should say something else, something to loosen the thin man again, so he added, "Looking forward to the break?"

"Most definitely. I'll have time to reflect on my meanness [he leered] and to write, too, of course [he stopped leering]. I imagine that that's what you're planning to do, Digger, to write some more, to create a few more fictional murders!"

Digger laughed, too, expelled a couple ha's anyway. "Maybe just a couple," he concluded.

"What's your motive, I mean, the killer's motive?"

"For my second book? I was playing around with the green-eyed monster."

"Ah, jealousy, a formidable nemesis. And will the killer be one of us, you know, a writing teacher?"

"I'm not sure yet, Lou, but if it is, he won't be based on you, probably!" Maybe the lip licking.

"You know," said Knightly, "I once had a musician friend, not a very successful one, he played in a band that did some small gigs, around our home town, you know, high schools, local dances at the Town Hall. Well, this guy would never go to concerts, big shows, because he was jealous of other musicians' success. Isn't that something!"

"Hard to believe," said Digger, and he meant it, and he felt good talking about jealousy, wanted to talk to all of his colleagues about it, to yell a bit. "It's very limiting," he added quietly. Then he checked his watch. The other nemesis, Time, kept pushing on. "Gotta go, Lou. Good luck with your writing. I'd like to hear about it."

"When there's something to tell, I'll tell you," said Lou Knightly, and out came the snake, along with those long legs as Lou Knightly leaned back again. In fact, while the full-timer professor looked like a big spider, Digger was the one who sort of scurried away.

Back in his office, Digger checked his watch again—only fifteen minutes or so, and it would take him a handful to walk to class, but he still had time to fire an email off to Lou's complaining student, Jennifer. He wanted to get that communication out of the way, didn't want to forget it after class. He sent the abrupt girl a short but supportive note, inviting her to return to his office if she still had concerns. She wouldn't, though. That episode was over. With one more look at his watch, Digger grabbed his briefcase and headed off for the first of his last two fall-semester classes.

In the second-floor hallway of the Classroom Building, where most of Digger's classes were scheduled, the composition instructor spotted the administrator Omar Johns, his head rounder than ever, as though gravity were squashing the melon into a state of imminent bursting.

Johns had seen Diggerson, too, and as he strode back to the Administration Building and his own wood-paneled sanctuary, the long-time administrator thought about the long-time writing teacher, the one who had been involved in the suicide and the murders. *Sometimes another man's troubles could lift your own a bit.* Omar had been feeling blue. Safe in the luxury of his office, the administrator stared into the circular wall mirror that had seen his facade a thousand times (Oh, Mirror, Mirror, on the wall, who has the roundest head of all!) and thought, *I'm old. Old and frosted and fat!* Unfulfilled, that's how Omar Johns felt. *Un-appreciated*, he mused. His peers never mentioned the elder administrator's accomplishments—and they weren't just a few!—and the faculty avoided him. He saw that, noticed how faculty members would scurry off in other directions when they spotted him down a hallway, dashing into their offices, their holes. Johns pictured prairie dogs but could not come up with that name. "Weasels!" he decided instead, and in the mirror he saw how his cheeks had drooped almost lower than his chin. "My head looks like a basketball," he admitted and then dismissed, going back to his image of furry rodent faculty scampering for cover at his approach. At the coming of the old lion, he decided, liking that self-title. *Scampering faculty!* Isn't that what Diggerson had just done?

Not really. But perception was reality for most. Digger had barely seen Johns and had forgotten him almost as quickly as he'd noticed the salesman-like administrator. The composition teacher had other topics in mind, such as his last two classes. His eleven o'clock class had gone well. Several of the students had actually thanked him on the way out, wished him a Merry Christmas. That was nice. Maybe just a little fake since he still had to grade those last papers, *but nice anyway*. For this last class, Digger had decided to teach his students how to tutor each other, something that he should have done years ago. *Self-sufficiency*. Wasn't that really what teachers were all after?

In his next-to-last class, the students behaved basically like the ones in the earlier class, paired off and working well on editing for their final paper, which they would submit through their Bridges site within forty-eight hours. This group gave Digger an even cheerier send off, which reminded the writing teacher that one of the elements he loved best about college teaching was the continual starting and ending, the sense of finishing something with each ending semester. Digger didn't think that he could sit in an office for twenty years, didn't know how people could do it, one long process that didn't end until retirement. But maybe these people too had beginnings and endings, projects, for instance. Must have, otherwise how could that tidal wave of future sameness not lead the workers to jump from their impressive office buildings. *Danny Jones' path*.

Digger's mind played with these people's fictional lives and deaths as he waited for his final class, which was in the same room as the previous one (Digger appreciated the Registrar for details like that). At a couple minutes before the hour, only five students were present. "Where is everyone?" he said, but nobody knew. "Well, I guess we still have a few minutes." Twitch was there, and Digger noticed his shoulders roll quickly. "Twitch, how's your paper? Any questions?" A few more students arrived and took their seats. Digger smiled at them.

"No, Professor Diggerson," Twitch finally announced. "It's all set. It's an 'A,' you'll see!" Digger had never liked the word "it," his least favorite one after the to-be verb "is." Weak and confusing words.

"I hope so, but what about that comma splice problem? Did you get to Tutorial Services?"

"More than once. I practically live there."

"Smart," said Digger. "Take advantage of every free thing the school gives you! But if you missed any run-ons, we'll catch them today. Today, you become the tutor."

"I don't know about that, Professor."

Then several students entered at the same time, as though the train had finally reached the station. "The shuttle was late!" said one girl, Susan, a name Digger had not seen on a class roster before this one in probably a decade. Half the females these days had names beginning with a "K" sound.

"Just on time, actually," responded Digger, seeing that the clock showed two exactly. All but two students were present, fourteen faces, and Digger wondered about the missing two. How could you skip the very last class?

"Okay," he started. "On this last day, I thought I'd teach you how to tutor each other. That way, next semester, if you don't have time to go to Tutorial Services, you can work with your own roommate perhaps. When you tutor, you help yourself, too, because you start to see, and hear, problems that you otherwise might have missed. And it's not that hard, really. It's actually just asking questions, sharing the paper and asking questions."

Pointing to the big screen that pulled down behind the front desk, to a series of steps from a file called "How to Tutor," Digger explained what he wanted the fourteen students to do. "First, get your final paper on your laptop or phone, the version that was due today, and then pair off. We have just the right number for pairs."

Then he waited for students to get ready with their papers and peers. "Here's what I'd like you to do," and he read the following from the screen:

1. Share the paper—i.e., put the person's paper (hard copy or laptop) between you both, not just in front of you. Remember that you're working on the paper together.

2. Do not fix problems—i.e., do not be an editor; be a tutor by helping your peer to fix the problems. Remember this proverb: "If you give a man a fish, you feed him for a day; if you teach a man to fish, you feed him for a lifetime."

3. Read each sentence aloud (one of you) and stop at each period to determine if the sentence contains a grammatical need—wordy? Awkward? Error? Punctuation need? etc.

4. Ask questions to lead your peer to edit him- or herself. For instance, you might point to a spot in a sentence and say, "Correct preposition?" or "Sound right here?" or "Is this the right mark?" or "Do you need (or not need) a word here?"

Students were great nodders, and Digger saw several faces bobbing, which made him think of Snodo's head cocking when she was thinking. Simba had once done the same thing. "Let's give this tutoring a try. Any questions? You will first decide whose paper to check first, and then maybe review just one paragraph. Then go to the other person's paper and do one. One of you needs to read, but it doesn't matter which. The key is not to rush, though, not to go too fast after periods. In fact, after you read a sentence, look at your peer to see if the sentence sounded okay. If so, go to the next sentence. Okay, give it a shot."

Twitch was paired off with Cam, a quiet but polite fellow who always sat next to his gangly peer. Although the two often worked together in class, Digger didn't think that Twitch and Cam were friends outside this room. Outside class, Digger had never seen Twitch with any other student. Most humans strayed away from anyone who was just a little off. *Too bad.* Life was all about comfort zones, and Digger imagined, with just a touch of guilt, his empty cottage and back yard.

The writing instructor listened to the babble of voices. "Don't go too fast," he advised again, and then Digger went from pair to pair, listening, offering advice, asking questions. The second time around, he heard Twitch mentioning Johna, calling her "Professor Adams" and telling Cam that she "liked" Professor Diggerson.

"It doesn't sound like you two are reading aloud," Digger said to the pair of upturned faces.

"We were talking about the murder," said Twitch unabashedly. "They still don't know who did it, but at least nobody else has gotten strangled, right?"

That question sounded a little upbeat to Digger, but Twitch was right. At least nobody else had gotten strangled, and then Digger thought of Lou Knightly. Lip Licker. Women Hater. *Lou?* Digger was about to suggest that Twitch and Cam get back to their papers when Twitch announced, "Professor Diggerson has a hooting dog!"

At that, Digger had to laugh, and he told Cam that, yes, it was true, he did have a hooting dog, a poor, old hooter. Twitch summed it up by adding, "I guess we're all going to hoot when we get really old, right, Professor?" And just as his professor was agreeing with this somewhat sad, somewhat amusing life summary, his strange student twitched his shoulders and added, "Unless, of course, we get strangled first."

*Only a Psych student,* thought Digger, who urged the pair to resume their tutoring and then continued to mull around the room, dipping into conversations but hearing no more words about murder. *Thank God!*

After that last class, with his mind still on odd students, Digger waited out his fall semester's last office hour as the December night slowly grew, highlighting the heavens. He seemed to be the only person left in the building, in the world, perhaps, and the new Chair thought of the old one, eight years ago, all alone and then snuck up on and stabbed by Paul Smith. What was Paul doing right now? Maybe sitting on his thin mattress? Eating a baloney sandwich and some Fritos? Suddenly, Digger heard whistling, a sound that he hadn't experienced since the days of Dan the Man Pinsky and his religious hymns, which the former janitor had set loose on the corridor in an aggressive way. Who was whistling now, *Lou? Eliot?* Maybe Jay Moore, whom Digger had hardly seen since September. *Patricia Pauley?* Jay or Patricia waiting for their last night class? *No*, sounded like a male, though, one with no real musical skills, for that matter! And what was that song? Four falling notes in clusters of three, repeated, mournful, almost a dirge. *Ah, yes,* "Bittersweet Symphony." *Pretty*. Digger loved that song, and he almost made the effort to rise from the chair, to investigate, to join in. Instead, he thought of the lyrics, the day-to-day struggles just for finances, the work of survival. *So true*, especially when your colleagues don't care one iota for your life's goal, a book of fiction, even when the tale takes place at their own place of work and in their own vocation. *Bittersweet*, indeed.

Professor Matthew Diggerson sat still and silent, waiting out his last fall office hour alone, listening to those four falling note clusters repeat and then fade, silently singing the words, again and again. Bitterness could taste sweet.

By five o'clock, the day was completely done already, so the department chair exited the Faculty Offices Building without seeing a soul and began to walk the long path to the faculty parking lot through a shadow land punctuated by the cones of path lights along the trail, as well as by the Bay Bridge, towering in the background, decorated as always by its lace of lights. *December in New England!* Beautiful and stark. As he strolled past the Psych Building, the air felt cold, but in a good way, refreshing, not yet probing through sleeves and folds to freeze the soul, not yet January and February nights. The Psychology Building looked dark and deserted already, all the inmates having flown the coop. Digger thought of William Watkins and his point about Digger's peers perhaps not liking him. *Son-of-a-bitch had a point!* Digger kept walking.

Next up, the Administration Building, where long ago a group of wannabe Nazis had spray painted a message to Omar Johns on the back door, not to mention on the side of Digger's own cottage. Danny Jone's memorial. Omar and his round head waxing poetic about the fallen boy, a student he had never even met. *Long ago*. Then Digger remembered having seen a flash of Johns earlier, and he felt a pang of guilt that he had not talked to the man. When had he last spoken with Omar Johns? *Some meeting, probably*. Thinking in this manner, musing about nothing, really, just drifting through Time, Digger glanced into the darkened Admin Building and saw a ghost. A specter with a mop. *A mop?* Digger shook out the sillies. It was just a janitor, a maintenance engineer, rather, but *man-oh-man that one looked just like George North.* At that moment, with Digger's having stopped, gawking, the inside man looked out the window at him, smiled, and waved. *It couldn't be!*

It had to be George North, the one-time student of both Digger and Tobias Mann, the one-time murder suspect (for Digger, anyway). Digger waved back, but the man was walking with purpose toward the building's side exit, apparently to come outside and actually converse. Digger moved toward that side door, too, and suddenly he was face to face with the past.

"George?" he said.

"You remember my name," said the young man, who must now be, what, twenty-six or seven? "I must have been a memorable student."

"That was a memorable time," said Digger, smiling and shaking George's hand. George was a gripper. "That was right after Tobias Mann was killed."

"Murdered by one of you," laughed George North, making Digger remember even more about the young fellow, especially about his cavalier attitude toward death. "You probably thought that I did it back then!"

"No, George, of course not. I never …"

But George North cut him off: "And now there's been another killing, right? Another writing teacher, too. What is it with you professors in the Writing Department?"

*Dan Pinsky revisited!* George seemed to have taken lessons with Paul Smith's second victim because this new janitor was as adept as the old one at steering a conversation. Digger decided not to take the bait, if that's what it was.

"Too many papers," he laughed. "They never end, and they always have the same exact problems."

"Like mine did, I'm sure," responded George, and that journey back seemed to make him pause. "I remember that you didn't like the word 'is.'"

"That's right! *You* have a good memory! Why did you leave school back then, George? Why didn't you graduate?"

"Oh, I graduated, just not here. I have an official degree from Sea View Community College, for what that's worth." Bitter words. *Ah*, there was the George that Digger remembered.

"Why didn't you transfer back here for your last two years?"

"Why else, money! My old man kicked me out. Said my grades weren't up to the *North standard.* Said he wasn't paying a private school's tuition for community college grades. You gave me some of those grades, didn't you?"

George North looked older, even in the semi-darkness of the Admin Building's leaking light. His dark hair had receded, and Digger could already see parentheses forming alongside his nose and mouth. Digger decided to ignore the implied statement about his hard grading.

"Did you get a four-year degree from another school? You could still come back here."

"If I were a four-year graduate, would I be holding this mop!" *Good point.*

"Why did you decide to work here if you don't like our school too much?"

"A lot of reasons. Isn't that what you tried to teach us, to see all the reasons? One was to make steady money, and I'm no longer on my parents' insurance. This job gives me benefits. And I didn't want to keep working in my father's stores, ringing up groceries and stocking groceries and cleaning up spilled groceries. My father refused to make me a manger, said that I had to work my way up. Like *him*. So I said 'No thanks' and here I am. A mop in my hand but free." *Free!* That bipolar word, as exhilarating as a gull in flight, as harsh as its beaky cry, its villainous descent.

"And I don't dislike Ocean View, Professor Diggerson," continued the *free* son. "I had great times here. I actually enjoyed your classes, the way we got to work in groups and write stuff on the board and earn minutes out. And I can take night classes now and pay less for them. This job has lots of perks. I get to work alone. When I'm done, I just mope about, *mop* about, and then clock out. I take nothing home with me, you know?"

Digger knew. He knew all about taking nothing home, or rather finding nothing. *Simba and Snodo*. He thought of them now, waiting by his back door, but then he realized that Simba wouldn't be waiting for him anymore, not really. The Lion Dog would be lost in her dreams in the living room.

"Speaking of home, George, I'd better get going. I'm glad to have seen you, and I wish you luck. If I can be of any help to you, maybe with papers from those night classes, you know where to find me. I'm in my office until five o'clock just about every day."

"I appreciate it, Professor, and I'll remember the invitation. I hear that you're a bigwig now. The chair. A published author. The other writing teachers must really bow down to you now." George smiled darkly.

"George, you would be surprised at how little others care about your own accomplishments, and that's a life lesson, a simple, sad fact."

George North laughed at that, but at what—the lack of caring, the lesson, the fact, all three? Then, just as Digger was beginning to break away from the meeting, George said, "I don't need any writing help, anyway, Professor Diggerson. I took my two-hundred-level writing class at SVCC. I earned an 'A.' And guess who my teacher was?"

The question surprised Matthew Diggerson. How could he possibly know who had guided George North to an "A" grade, a path that seemed unlikely to his older instructor. But before Digger could voice any opinion, George, his hairline receding, already whispering that the young man had forgotten to seek his path, laughed out the answer. "The dead woman! Professor Adams. Can you believe that?"

"What?"

"Sure! I remembered her name, just like I remembered that you didn't like the word 'is,' or broad ideas, for that matter. You were always telling us to be specific. Professor Adams didn't have as many points as you, but you're older, right, wiser? But she really liked my writing, a lot more than you did."

"Well, George, you were a little older, too, right, so you probably had more to say. I'm sure that you wrote some nice essays for Johna, for Professor Adams."

"Johna? I never knew her first name. It just said 'J. Adams' in our schedule, and she told us to call her 'Professor Adams.' Hard to believe that she's already snuffed out."

Digger was thinking of death, of George's at the moment, but then of death in general, all the losses in his immediate life. It didn't seem natural. "George," Digger started to say, but then he lost his train of thought. "You take care," he concluded.

George North was standing just within the side door exit's cone of light, so his features were half hidden and half distorted, all forehead and cheeks and chin. Holding the mop, which silhouetted could be a severed head, the crinkly hair still waving about lifelike, George looked a bit like a primitive warrior after the slaughter, but Digger could hear no drums, just the cold silence. Digger thought suddenly of crickets. When had their fervent twilight communication died out? Months ago.

"You, too, Professor Diggerson," said the student-turned-custodian, and under the cricket-less night, the two men bid adieu, nodding a final farewell, each heading in opposite directions toward his own light.

Driving home, Digger pulled his mind off of resurrected ghosts by realizing that the fridge was just about empty, so he pulled into the local Stop & Shop for some sliced turkey and bread, maybe some other stuff. Did Simba and Snodo have dog treats? Thoughts like this kept him from noticing the trailing car lights that turned whenever he did, that slid into a parking space in the row behind Digger's. A form, darkly dressed, followed well behind him into the brightly lit store, where Digger went first to the deli and then up and down various rows. In the juice aisle, he passed an attractive middle-aged woman who was looking at the very bottles of cranberry juice that Digger wanted to select.

"I like that brand," he told her, and the woman turned green eyes on him and smiled.

"This one?" she said, pointing to cranberry with a hint of lime. He hadn't exactly been flirting, just connecting, since the George North talk had had almost the opposite effect, a cooling one, a separation with humanity. This woman's smile warmed Digger up.

"Well, that one when I'm feeling bold, but I really meant just that brand. The Stop & Shop brand's less expensive, but it tastes just like the other ones. I really like their cranberry juice."

The woman had black hair, fairly long, and with those green eyes, she looked Irish. She wasn't young, Digger realized, but he was close to fifty himself. And she was thin, too, looked energetic, attractive. Why not? Why not flirt with a strange woman in the aisles of Stop & Shop?

Digger reached forward, selected a bottle of cranberry juice with a hint of lime, and then smiled at the woman. She reached up and took another of the same.

"I guess I'm feeling bold," she said. Then she rummaged in her black purse, wrote something on a piece of paper, and handed it to Digger. The note contained seven numbers, a hyphen after the first three. "I don't search through Stop & Shop's looking for men, you know!" she said, probably because Digger looked surprised at the telephone number. Maybe his eyes had widened. "My name's Valerie," she said, holding out her hand.

"Digger," said Digger, adding "I mean Matt, my friends call me Digger. My last name's Diggerson." He was sort of stumbling.

"Well, Digger," smiled the Irish-looking woman as she wrote 'Matt' on another note, then 'Digger.' "Maybe I should get your number, just in case you lose mine." Digger felt reluctant, yet foolish. *Anna!* Anna. *Why not?* He gave her the seven numbers.

"This was quite a trip to the grocery store," said Valerie. "A great bottle of juice and a nice-looking date!"

"And I still have more things to get!" said Digger, immediately feeling dumb, but the Valerie woman laughed, said "Bye, Matt," as she strode away, and finally, "Call me!" when she was about to turn at the aisle's end. She made that 'calling' motion with her outstretched thumb and pinky, and Digger mirrored it. When he was alone again, he looked down at his hand, which was still stuck that way, so he released the three middle fingers and lowered his arm, again feeling a bit dumb, juvenile, but a little excited, too.

With all these feelings vying for supremacy, Digger had not noticed the watcher at the row's apex, the dark figure that had disappeared upon the cranberry-loving woman's approach.

He followed her through the night, stayed far enough behind the white two-door sedan to seem innocuous, but *my god, what a lot of turns!* This was getting annoying! When was the woman going to pull over and let him bonk her on the head? Wherever this Digger-chasing hussy was going, she had to have a more direct route, yet he had to admit to himself that this chase was exciting. Insane but fun! Could she possibly know that he was on her heels? Should he break off, make a run for it? Maybe drive up and off the Bay Bridge. Fly and scream and flip his finger at the universe! Well, wasn't that what he was doing now?

*Bang, bang, Digger's little club came down upon her head. Squeeze, squeeze, Digger's fingers made sure that she was dead.*

Now wasn't that a nice little ditty, centering, and *where's the bitch going now?*

She was home at last, and after she drove into the fairly secluded driveway (about as private as a homeowner could find in the overdeveloped southern end of Ocean View), hoisted her big paper bag full of groceries into her arms, and turned from the car, she wondered who was coming down her driveway. *Please*, not Derek, not another fight with her ex. But that wasn't Derek's pickup. *Who?*

"Hello!" said the man who popped out of the SUV. "Are you a friend of Matt Diggerson's?" He asked this as he approached her, smiling all the time.

The question confused her. Matt Diggerson? That man she had just met in Stop & Shop? What could this guy want?

"Matt wants me to give you something," the man said, and just as she was thinking, "What?" his arm fell right out of his right sleeve. At least, that's what she thought, her last one before the silver pain exploded above her eyes and left nothing but black.

*Bang, bang, squeeze, squeeze*, he hummed to himself while the woman's face grew darker and darker. *My god, faces really can go blue!* He looked about him. *Nice house!* Nice quiet neighborhood. Maybe he should move here. After all, he knew of one house opening up. Unless, of course, her family was inside, but it didn't look that way. Just one little hall light on, one little outside light that barely even reached them over here. *C'mon now, woman!* Hurry up and float away. Here was another woman who would be adding no more joy to Diggerson's life.

Ironically, Digger had been thinking the same thing as he drove home from the grocery store. Should this unknown woman, this Valerie, be the one to follow Anna? *No one should follow Anna!* But why not? Why this loyalty to an illusion? What's life but an illusion? *Stupid! Stubborn! Sap!* Yet still? And what about Dark Anna? Jean or Joan or Jane? Maybe George North had given him the answer; maybe it was 'Johna.' The whole "J" thing was ironic. Digger smiled and shook his head. He knew Officer Zorn's last name but not her first, and he knew this grocery-store woman's first name but not her last. Leaning forward, he looked up at the sky and saw the Seven Sisters, dim, though, maybe just five of them. He knew none of the twinkling siblings' names. He looked back at the road, thought of his dogs, of his past without them, of Anna. In two minutes, he would be home.

Digger rummaged in his left pocket for the slip of paper with those seven numbers, the Valerie woman's introduction to her life, and when he found the crumpled square, he held it in his fingers for a moment, felt absolutely nothing, thought of Anna's annual Christmas card, felt almost nothing, and then buzzed the side window down an inch, held the note up to the opening, and let it slip out into the breeze, into the night.

## Chapter 10: To Flow

Note: To create coherent prose, you do not want to begin every sentence with a noun or pronoun, because such choppy starts will stop your flow of information after each period, causing the reader to start again with another subject. Thus, begin some sentences (definitely one in three, even every other) with subordinate word groups, such as "Although ...," "To ...," or "By —ing ..." Then listen to these flowing beginnings for comma needs at each word group's ending. Mumford and Sons can remind you what to do.

If you start a thought with a flowing word,
You will find a pause that can be heard,
So read the words aloud to find out where the comma works.

The day after classes ended offered Digger his first taste of space, of what he and Anna had called "space in time," or, in other words, not a lot to do and a lot of time to do it in. His three classes, about fifty students in all, had until the following night to submit their final papers online, and Digger's responsibilities as Chair were basically complete until next January and the spring semester. Unless something strange occurred. Something akin to students' ongoing "family emergencies," but instead having to do with his writing faculty family. *Some family!* All those colleagues who had hardly cared a rat's ass about his book. Digger thought of Billy D, of how his protagonist liked to use the phrase "rat's ass." *Billy D Wilder.* For over a month, Digger would have time to bring his alter-ego back to life, this time to solve a Tobias-like murder. By next spring, maybe the summer, Digger would be the author of a murder mystery series, not just one lonely book.

All throughout the summer and fall semester, he had been gathering ideas, jotting down notes, possibilities, snatches of dialogue, descriptive sketches. Tentatively deciding on the title *Murderous Mistakes*, the composition teacher had also jotted down errors that could loosely guide the chapters, such as "Fragments," which could reflect the killer's mind or perhaps even Billy D's, and "Run-ons," which could highlight a chapter full of plot, one event running on into the next, or maybe show a series of conversations, each relating to the first murder and suggesting suspects. While Digger had not decided on a killer or even an ending, he knew how he would begin this story—with his victim's scheduling for the spring semester, for he himself would be the model for the first killing. He couldn't use Tobias, since that would not be appropriate, to use a colleague's death for entertainment purposes. But he could use himself as Chair, and in that first chapter, he would be thinking about each person (as he contemplated his or her schedule), each possible suspect, and then the killer would strike, probably with a gun, not with a knife, not like Paul Smith's family heirloom. Digger didn't like remembering those silver teeth, the way the long knife had flashed in reflected light, as though it had been alive and eager.

He would have this entire day—what his school called Study Day, a buffer between the end of classes and beginning of final exams—to putter about and feel the earth's turning, to exist. Exerting her own presence, Snodo made a yearning noise, a long falling note of concern, and Digger saw that the white beagle was at the back door, watching the birds perhaps or maybe hearing something beyond man's reach. "You want to go out, Snodo!" he said, and the funny and somewhat small dog shined her eyes at him and patted the kitchen floor with her feet. Sometimes, such as when Digger mentioned the word "walk," Snodo would launch herself straight up into the sky with glee, but today she just shot out the open door and raced to the gate. She must have spotted something out in the sea grass or maybe on the strip of beach. Normally, Simba would be following the white dog, her bigger shadow, but the old girl had not yet appeared in the kitchen. Simba slept in the living room now, on the floor. Digger could hardly remember the last time she had even tried to get on the couch, must have been early in November maybe. Back then, Simba had launched herself about a foot and landed half on and half off the couch, the same couch that he and Anna had bought so long ago (*pretty lumpy now!*), and then just dangled there, her back legs churning at air and then giving up. Digger had hoisted her up, but before long he had helped her back down again. She had been unsettled. For weeks now, Simba had not seemed to care about the couch or about much of anything. At least she still liked her food, for if a dog stopped eating, then his or her end was near.

Digger stood and watched his other dog, who still seemed "new" after eight years, and Snodo mirrored him at the back gate, standing and staring. *At what?*

"What do you see, Snodo?" The air felt just a little past cool, more cold than refreshing this almost mid-December morning, so Digger closed the door but continued to watch the white dog's vigil. After about a minute, Snodo turned and investigated the bottom of the fence line, looking into the abandoned dog crate that had once housed two feral cats, and then peeing close to a holly bush. When Digger opened the door a crack, Snodo trotted right in and looked up into his eyes. Hers were light, magical marbles. "Good girl!" said Digger, a sentiment he uttered a dozen times a day, at least. As he closed the door, a movement caught his peripheral vision, so he looked back out at the gate. *A black cat!* A big black cat sat just beyond the gate and stared back at him, as calm as can be. *How about that!* Digger had not had a feline visitor since Shyla and Skittles, probably because of his dogs, but this cat seemed completely unafraid of anything. Looked sort of mystical, in fact, as it sat like a bowling pin and faced his back door. *Must want some food.*

Digger fed his pups just dry kibble, healthy stuff, so he had no cans available. Maybe some sliced turkey. Snodo liked that idea, and she waltzed around him as Digger went to the refrigerator, got the bag of cold cuts, and tore up a piece, which he then put in an old water bowl. He gave one ragged piece of turkey to Snodo and thought about Simba, leaving her a turkey portion on the counter. When he opened the door, Snodo wanted to go out again (her greatest joy was to go out when she was in and to go in when she was out), but Digger said, "Not this time, Snodo. You'll scare that cat away." The big black cat just sat perfectly still, though, until Digger got about a dozen feet away, whereupon it turned, took a dozen steps itself, and then turned back and sat again.

"Hi, there, cat," said Digger. "You're a pretty fellow, jet black, and look at your big golden eyes. Where did you get those huge eyes?" Digger talked to the cat and held out the food, but the animal didn't take the bait, just sat and waited.

"Okay, Inky," said Digger, who had just decided on the name because the cat was black black, jet black, as black as the color got. "I'm going to call you Inky, and here's some turkey. You like turkey, right?" He put the bowl down through an opening in the rickety gate, which he had made long ago and which could do with repair—replacement, really—and then backed away, still talking, cooing at the cat. Inky just watched him. In fact, Digger never saw whether the black Tom cat (he had a very big head!) ate the offering or not, but the meat was gone later that afternoon, the cat, too. Digger hoped that Inky would return.

The feline presence had reminded him of his and Anna's old feral cats, Shyla and Skittles, and Digger contemplated mailing Anna another note about this new cat. Would a second December card make him seem needy? *Probably*. Digger got Anna's Christmas card out of his briefcase and propped it up with the salt-and-pepper shakers on this kitchen table. The two golden retrievers smiled at him and perhaps at their own silly hats. Golden retrievers always looked old and happy, like ninety-year-old Tibetan men on mountaintops. Digger didn't read the card again; he knew its contents verbatim. Anna's *gift*. At least her dog cards had not yet transitioned to one of those family post cards showing four pictures, three of a baby in various states of silence and sound and one of Anna and some guy, no personal notes and not even a damn signature, just that guy and perhaps behind his grinning face a cavalcade of Niagara Falls water or Grand Canyon stone. Just the thought of that potential closed door ended Digger's thought about mailing Anna again.

That night, he half watched the news while taking notes on his second book, *Murderous Mistakes*, linking more grammar errors with possible chapter titles: Dangling Modifiers, Faulty Predication, Faulty Agreement, Faulty Parallelism (*too much 'faulty'!*). Running out of terms, Digger decided to branch out to punctuation errors, too, so he was paying little attention to the television and only superficially saw that another Ocean View woman had been murdered. Her picture reminded Digger of Johna since the second victim looked middle-aged yet attractive. But this one had really short black hair and a very open smile. The picture showed beach behind the now dead woman's face. Apparently a happy day. Beneath the picture ran the caption "Another Ocean View Murder." When he reached for the remote and raised the volume, the story changed to a fire in the next town, Bayside, and when Digger switched channels to learn more about this new murder, he found that those stations had covered the story already. It would have been the lead story, of course. Ocean View murders were fairly rare. Digger knew that this death had nothing to do with Johna's, but that picture, a bit fuzzy, a summer haze, had awakened the sleuth in him again. For at least a month, Digger had not thought much about Johna Adams' murder, being more preoccupied with his own bitter thoughts toward his narrow-minded colleagues, but now he wondered about this second woman, un-named at this point. *Probably identifying next of kin.* Digger thought about going online for more information, but the computer was off already, seemed like too much work to turn it on, wait, and then type away, most likely finding no details anyway. He decided to watch the late news for updates, but then he fell asleep on the couch early, both dogs laid out below him, Simba with her mouth open. The old dog snored, stiff as a log, but the white one's legs were moving, pedaling. *Running in her dreams.*

The blare of the phone yanked Digger from his slumbers. *Anna?* What the hell time was it? What year? Digger stumbled into the kitchen, saw "7:12" on the microwave's clock, and wondered who would be calling him this early. *His mother?* Could something have happened to her? The kitchen phone yelled twice more as Digger tried to clear his mind, and as he staggered about, Snodo accompanied him, seemed pretty happy about matters, too. Simba hadn't heard, apparently.

"Hello." Digger didn't bother sounding friendly.

"Matt?" said a female voice, one that Digger couldn't quite place. *Not Anna.*

"Uh," said Digger.

"Digger?" tried the voice again.

"Yes," said Digger tentatively, trying to place that voice.

"Is this Professor Matthew Diggerson?"

It sounded like Officer Zorn, Dark Anna, Jean or Jen or Jezebel, but who would name her child Jezebel Zorn?

"Matthew Diggerson!" said J. Zorn again, a little louder perhaps, more a statement now than a question.

"Yes, yes," said Digger. "I'm a little sleepy, I haven't had coffee yet. Is this Officer Zorn? Do you have information about Johna's murder?" Then Digger remembered the new murder from the news. *Coincidence?* He suddenly realized that Zorn's call was not a social one, not that he had thought that even once anyway.

"I am calling about the murder of Valerie Walt," said the policewoman, as direct as always, but Digger had trouble understanding the statement.

"Valerie who?" Snodo made a noise.

"Valerie Walt."

"Walt?" Digger needed coffee, and Snodo needed something. To go out, most likely. It sounded as though Zorn had said, "Valerie, What?" sort of like a Cockney accent. Didn't some British people add "what?" after statements, sort of like adding "Right?" Or was that Canadians or maybe Australians? Was Officer Zorn British, Canadian, or Australian?

"I'm sorry, Officer Zorn. I'm not sure who you mean. Does this have something to do with Johna Adams?"

"That would seem to be the case, Professor Diggerson. Valerie Walt was murdered with the same MO, and your name and number was found in her handbag. The name 'Matt' and the name 'Digger.' That means that you have a connection to both victims."

"But I don't even know a Valerie … Wart? What is her last name?"

"Walt, and I used her note with your name, both 'Matt' and 'Digger,' to call you right now, so clearly she knew you."

Digger's mind was racing now, thoughts stumbling, and, of course, he soon remembered the woman from Stop & Shop, the note that he had tossed out his window on the way home.

"Last night, on my way home from work, I met a woman in Stop & Shop, and she gave me her number. I'm just now remembering that her name was Valerie, but she never told me her last name. That's why I didn't know who you meant. She gave me her number, too, but I threw it away."

"Why did you discard her number?"

*Why?* Digger thought of Anna's card, of Time's long yet sudden passage. How could he explain 'why' to this cop when he couldn't even understand it himself?

"I don't know. It just seemed odd, sort of cheap, to meet someone in a grocery store." He regretted saying 'cheap,' which made the Valerie woman sound promiscuous. "I don't mean that Valerie was promiscuous," he continued. "She seemed very nice. We talked about cranberry juice." Digger decided that he had said enough. What was there to say? Only that Anna was his reason for everything, still. Muddleheaded, he thought again of the black-haired woman from Stop & Shop. Now dead? *How could that be!*

"Officer Zorn, do you mean to tell me that the woman I met at Stop & Shop was murdered afterwards?"

"That sums up about all we know right now, Professor Diggerson, and most of those facts we just discovered."

"But how can that be? It has to be a fantastic coincidence. You can't …" Digger had been about to say that the she couldn't think that he had killed her.

"We cannot assume anything, but you had better make a statement this time, an official one at the station, because we do not like coincidences." Hadn't Detective Doyle made that same comment several years in the past? Where was the little policeman? He would have known that Digger could not be to blame.

"I can be at the station in half an hour. I just need some coffee and to take care of my dogs."

"Half an hour," concluded the woman, making it sound like an order more than an invitation, and then clicking off without salutation. So much for Dark Anna. Not only was she uninterested in him, but she now thought him to be a double murderer. A smoothly flowing December had suddenly slammed into a brick wall.

Outside the station, Digger parked in the same spot, as though the cops had kept it just for Matthew Diggerson for eight years. The same gull swooped screaming overhead, the same cold sun beat down, the same maple tree waved its bony fingers at him. It was all the same, except for the cops inside. The greeter was different, younger and more polite, less personable somehow than that grumpy guy before. *What was his name?* This new one actually escorted Digger to Zorn's door. "J. Zorn" actually had Doyle's old office, the second closet on the left. As in a dream, he knocked again on that door, wondering where Doyle's old nameplate had gone, probably with the man himself, and then heard a voice call out "Yes!" But unlike the short cop, Doyle, Officer Zorn actually opened the door herself. She then returned to her chair, squeezing by the desk to reach it, and then turned to her computer, no doubt opening his file. *A file at the cops!* How did he ever get here? Digger thought of making a joke about the small office, more space deprived even than his own, yet he said nothing.

"Professor Diggerson," said the female cop, either reading from his file or just opening the conversation, or both, and Digger waited for more, for the interrogation. Again, he was perched on the edge of the chair, but probably that's what everyone sitting in this chair did. It wasn't exactly the place to recline back and breathe peacefully. Digger wanted to move his legs and look for wear marks at the front of the cushion, but he realized how odd that would look.

"Let's just review the facts," said the woman, focusing the composition teacher. "You met Valerie Walt when and where?"

"At Stop & Shop, last night, that is Wednesday night, after my last classes of the semester. It must have been about five-thirty. My office hour ended at five, but then I talked to an old student after that, so it must have been about five-thirty at the grocery store."

"And Valerie Walt initiated the conversation?"

Digger thought for a bit, his mind going to 'cranberry juice.' Who had talked first?

"I'm not sure who talked first. We were both looking at cranberry juice, and one of us—I think it was me—said something about Stop & Shop's having a good brand. Then before I knew it, she was giving me her phone number, and she asked for mine. The whole thing was strange. I hardly ever talk to people at the grocery store, maybe just the check-out person. I don't go trolling for women there, Officer. And I didn't even keep her number. I tossed it out the window on my way home." *Oops*. He had just admitted to a cop that he had littered, but then he realized that the small crime would be overlooked under the circumstances.

"You went straight home from the grocery store?"

"Yes." Could Zorn's first name be 'Jackie'? *Jackie Zorn?* That didn't sound right. Kind of cool, though. *Concentrate!*

"And could someone at your house corroborate what you are saying, this timeline?"

*Corroborate?* Dark Anna had dark suspicions.

"Only if you can communicate with dogs." Digger didn't mean for that to sound flippant, but then again perhaps he did. He didn't enjoy needing *corroboration.* "I live alone, Officer Zorn. My wife and I are divorced, and I have two dogs. I just went home and fixed dinner. I didn't see any neighbor, although maybe my next-door neighbors, Graham and Donna, saw me. I don't know. I don't think that I even talked to anyone on the phone last night." Then he thought of Inky. Too bad that the cat couldn't vouch for his presence. Almost seemed to have that ability, yet bringing the feline up here and now would be foolish. Instead, he asked Officer Zorn, "Do you know when the woman, Valerie, was murdered? I mean, the exact time?"

"Yet to be determined, Professor Diggerson, but let's return to last night. Did you see which way Valerie Walt went?"

"Do you mean when she left me or the store? I actually don't know either answer. I didn't see her again in the store, and I walked about for another fifteen minutes or so. I never saw her again, never saw her leave. I don't even know what kind of car she drove."

"Why do you say 'car'?"

"Everyone in Ocean View drives cars, or, actually, SUVs now."

"Let's go back a bit. You say that Valerie Walt gave you her number, is that correct?"

"She wrote it on a piece of paper, a little notebook, that she got from her pocketbook. She wrote only her number, she told me her name, just her first name. I never knew that her last name was 'Walt.'"

"And what about her note with your name?"

"What about it? You must have it. She asked for my number and then wrote it down. She must have written my name, which I told her, and I also remember telling her my nickname, 'Digger.' You must have that note since you said that you used it to call me."

"Just checking," said Officer Zorn, who typed into her computer, just as Detective Doyle had done long ago.

"Detective Doyle did what you're doing, back after my chairperson had been murdered. I was a suspect then, too. But Doyle ended up trusting me, and I helped him, I think. The murderer turned out to be another writing teacher, Paul Smith. He's in jail now."

"I know about Paul Smith, and I know Detective Doyle."

"How is he?" said Digger, repressing the urge to ask "And how tall is he?"

Officer Zorn ignored both questions, the one asked, the one unstated. "Johna Adams," she said instead. "From my notes, you had talked to her the night she was strangled, too. (Digger didn't like the sound of that!) You talked to her and to a Jay Moore before their classes, their night classes, and then you did not see or talk to her again, is that correct?"

"Correct," said Digger, who had decided to stop chattering.

"You did not see Johna Adams outside of your professional relationship?"

"No. I hardly even knew her. I saw her maybe twice before that last conversation. When I hired her and at the summer meeting."

"You talked at the summer meeting?"

"I try to talk with all my faculty, especially with the new people because they have a lot of questions. And Johna asked me about my book. I recently published a murder mystery." Digger stopped, recognizing chatter, not to mention the fact that *fact* and *fiction* seemed to be merging, a fact that did not cast Matthew Diggerson in an innocent light.

"You just published a murder mystery? What is it called?"

"*Composition Murder*," said Digger, realizing that her question was not a casual one, that she was enquiring so that she could read it over to find some proof that he was a serial killer. At least someone would read his book! "I wrote it loosely based on an experience I had with a boy, an OVC student, who killed himself by jumping off the Bay Bridge. Danny Jones was his name."

"I am not familiar with Danny Jones," said Officer Zorn, but Digger had a feeling that she soon would be. The skeletons all seemed to be clacking.

"My story's all fabrication. Danny wasn't murdered, at least not by any other person. He had schizophrenia. The voices in his head told him to jump, but I created a fictional murderer, a group of them really, other students."

"And do you get along with your students?"

"Well, yes, mostly. With almost all of them." Digger thought of Psych majors, their un-coachability, and then he pictured the personable Twitch, so unlike the stereotypical Psycho. "Every once in a while, you come across a strange young person, of course, but I certainly don't think that any of my students hate me enough to kill off women who ask me about my book and who give me their numbers." Digger thought of Twitch again, his lurching shoulders, his interest in Johna's murder. Then he began to picture his full-time colleagues, once again wondering if one could be a murderer. Jeff was so quiet and scholarly that it was hard to picture him anywhere but on campus. Todd seemed too short to throttle a woman, let alone two, and somehow his Midwestern accent made him seem friendly, less assuming maybe. The women, Mary, Diana, Jolie, they were too old.

Maybe not Jolie, but she liked women, right? Why would she kill non-lesbians, or lesbians, for that matter? The Blinker, the Breather, the Lip Licker. *Strange, but no! Impossible!* On humanity's grand stage, the earth, history could often repeat, but not on a relatively small New England campus. *Not again!*

"Do you know anyone who might resent your being an author or being attractive to women, who might hate you enough to kill women you know, or who might even have come on to you in the past?"

That was an awkward question, both syntactically and mentally. Quite a mouthful of interrogatives! Digger had not thought about the gender angle, at least not in relation to male homosexuality. Who would resent a woman's being attractive to him? Again, he thought of breathing, blinking, lip licking, and even twitching. Physical oddness, but those patterns had nothing to do with homosexuality. Maybe the lip licking? Digger thought of Lou Knightly, of his student's accusation ("hates females"?) and of the man's outward friendliness. A façade? In his mind, Digger recited that famous poem: "We wear the mask that grins and lies." Lou certainly grinned a lot, much more so than any other faculty members. The thin man could turn his body and possibly disappear into a crack, too. No, *impossible!* Paul Smith and his family heirloom knife were unique, one of a kind, not to be repeated. But then again the knife was *not* repeated, was it. Johna Adams had been strangled.

"Was Valerie also strangled?" asked Digger, and Dark Anna seemed surprised by the question. Her hands on the keyboard, she looked back at him. Jesse or Jordan or Juanita had very nice eyes, but Digger blinked away that thought.

Finally, Zorn's eyes blinked and she spoke: "We are making no details available to the public at this time."

And that was about the end of Digger's third trip to the Ocean View Police Department, for Officer Zorn had no more questions, no more answers, no more use for Digger at all. He was summarily dismissed.

Digger drove home numbly, not noticing the outer world except for superficially so that he wouldn't crash into it. Inside, he replayed the mantra "I'm a suspect." Officer Juliet or Whatever Zorn thought he was a killer, a two-time strangler, a scummy sort who picked up women in grocery stores and then throttled them. *A murderer!* And then there was the fact that Digger was connected to both women. How could that be anything but a coincidence? And that question made him think of Detective Doyle, who had moved to California a few years earlier. Digger had learned that apparent fact from the cop at the front desk on his stumbling way out, when the recent suspect had desired to make a connection with humanity, but the officer hadn't known whether Doyle had retired or taken a position out west. "Why don't you know!" Digger had wanted to ask, but maybe this cop had never known Doyle, had never been his "colleague." *Piss-poor peers everywhere!* Or maybe all the cops, even this friendly greeter, considered Matthew Diggerson to be Suspect Number One and thus unworthy of information.

Driving, Digger realized that he himself was very much on edge, still angry at his own faculty and now shocked at being labeled a villain, a Kevin Bacon connection between two dead bodies. Two steps? The game had an actual name, but Digger couldn't label it, something to do with "steps," anyway. Since Kevin Bacon had appeared in so many movies, or maybe just because he was charismatic or had been in many types of films, some pretty wacky ones (Digger remembered something about a giant worm), film lovers had created that game dealing with his co-stars. One step to Kevin Bacon meant...Digger couldn't remember, and suddenly he felt stupid for even trying. He thought of Valerie, now vanished from the planet, remembered the way she had smiled and taken down his name and number. Although he had not planned to pursue that option, Valerie was yet another loss, a dead end, a no exit. No return.

Matthew Diggerson didn't want to think of holes, so he turned back to the little detecitve, Doyle, who would have known that the teacher was innocent, right? *Just another hole there*. Digger wondered why Doyle had left the OVPD, whether the little detective had had a breakdown or sudden loss, whether the front-desk cop even knew the facts, whether his knowledge was second hand, third, whatever. Digger remembered a high school lesson on hearsay: half the class had been lined up on each side, about ten students per line, and one end had been told something like "Picture the gulls gliding above the blue sea and the beach." He or she had then turned and whispered that to the next person, and then the next, all down the line, until the last person had announced what was communicated, saying something like "Purchase the dumb bells at the store and some bleach," the statement rising at the end to indicate a question instead. In short, who knows what happened to the little detective? The fact was that Detective Doyle was gone.

Digger made it home, heard the driveway's little stones crunch beneath his tires, recognized Snodo's excited barking, and felt peace descend and squeeze out his mind's chaos. So what if Zorn suspected him! He was no murderer, and they would not be able to link him in any way to Valerie *Whatever*. He felt sorry for the woman, the sorrow seeping up from the shock of her death. Evaporating sadness. Could her murder possibly be his fault? Could Paul Smith have escaped his prison?

On his way to the back door, Digger glanced at the sea, and just beyond the gate, seated non-chalantly without a flicker of movement, like a big shadowed bowling pin, the black cat gazed across the yard at Digger, who almost *felt* the stare, an x-ray, an MRI searching for his soul. *Inky!* Doesn't look like a stray, seems like the kind of cat that if called would come trotting over and look up into *your* face, like a dog.

"Hi, Inky," Digger called. "Can you tell the cops that I'm not a murderer!" In response, Digger thought he saw the big eyes blink once. He would get the strange cat more food pretty soon.

When he unlocked and opened the back door, Snodo whizzed past and came to a hurtling stop right before the back gate, but the black figure beyond it hardly flinched, just turned away almost non-chalantly and disappeared into the sea grass. Almost a mythical departure. Like a dream. Snodo made a rising, urping noise, a question, but before Digger could call to her, he saw that Simba was standing inside the door and wanting to go out. He bent down and stroked her soft triangular ears, the hairs gone a silvery white, and his old friend looked up at him, the greenish sheen lifting for just a moment, a spark or two escaping. "Simba!" said Digger. "I see my beautiful girl! I see you!" And the Lion Dog's tail swayed a bit, so Digger petted her head a few more times and then watched her amble past. She went down the steps slowly, deliberately, awkwardly, and then squatted a yard or so into the grass. When Simba peed these days, her body was more flattened to the earth, as though she were losing strength, being forced down. When finished, the old girl moved over to the gate, where Snodo still searched for the magically vanishing cat, the black Tom. Suddenly, Digger realized that he had forgotten all about the cops and corpses, about being the Kevin Bacon connection to an ongoing crime, about a possible reason for that connection. And with that realization, another thought arose, simple yet shocking. *My book?* Did the answer to two lost lives exist in his peers' cold reaction to Digger's life dream?

## Chapter 11: To Connect

Coherence often involves combining sentences, thus showing readers how two ideas relate. However, connecting requires re-punctuating, as this melody from P.F. Sloan (and made famous by Barry McGuire) illustrates.

Well, your sentences sound so choppy.
They make your thoughts and skills seem sloppy.
All those statements come at a cost.
Communication with your reader's lost.
You need to connect some of those thoughts.
So use subordination, words like "since" and "when,"
Comma "who," or just a colon, then do it again.

As December passed, so did Digger's anxiety, mainly because he spent most of his time at home, and thus nothing popped up to remind him of cops or murders or even resentment. And he had work to do. The students' papers flowed in, some surprising him with the writers' improvements, others disappointing him with their seeming lack of caring about learning. The ebb and flow of teaching. Experiencing an "A" paper, a teacher couldn't take too many bows, or the next paper would flatten him. A week before Christmas, he submitted final grades, happy that he had not had to fail a single student. *Merry Christmas!* Happy, too, that he now had time for his second book, to bring Billy D back to life, and more than anything, it was focusing on that second mystery that made Officer Zorn and her suspicions disappear. Besides, no cop had contacted him for more than two weeks. No sudden banging on his front door, no more summonses to the station for grilling. *How could there be!* Digger was innocent. Inky appeared every morning, and Digger sometimes imagined seeing the cat just beyond the gate at night. Maybe that's what his neighbor had seen months ago, *Inky*, not some stalker, some shadow. *Just a cat.* Although Inky would not pass beyond the gate, he did accept food, or at least the food was gone whenever Digger retrieved the bowls he placed beyond the gate. Of course, you could never trust or underestimate the gulls, but if sea gulls had eaten the food, Digger would have noticed, would have heard them screaming and seen them flocking and fighting over the scraps.

When the phone rang one early evening, Digger thought first of his mother, wondering why she was calling again when his Christmas visit to her house (his family home) was all set up already, but on the second ring, his mind switched to Officer Zorn, to the possibility of new evidence, new proof of his guilt. *But how could that be?* He let the phone ring a third time, but then snatched it up. It was neither woman.

"Digger? Is this Matthew Diggerson?"

"Gwena? Is this Gwena Schmidt?"

"It is," laughed his old chair and colleague, once affectionately labeled the Grammar Nazi by students who lamented the professor's iron rules against sentencing errors. Digger laughed, too, and then looked down to see Snodo peering up, her mouth panting. *Laughing with me!*

"What a nice surprise," he said.

"You might not think so when you hear why I called. I'm inviting you over for dinner. Short notice, too. Tomorrow night. Richard's feeling well, so hopefully he will be up for company. If not, we can call it a short night, is that all right?"

"Works for me," said Digger.

"I don't cook much these days, never really did. Richard did most of the cooking, but those days are gone. I wouldn't let Richard near the stove now." Gwena laughed again, but no warmth accompanied the sound.

"I don't cook much either," said Digger.

"How about some baked chicken, potatoes, salad, maybe a little white wine."

"I can bring the wine."

"Agreed! Then tomorrow night, right?"

"You don't wait around, Gwena!"

"I'm too old, Digger, too old to wait."

"You know, Gwena, I can't remember the last time I was invited to dinner, other than at my mother's, and that's a long ride for a nice meal."

"Well, I want to talk about that book of yours."

"That will be a nice change," said Digger, but Gwena didn't ask him why. They said good bye, see you tomorrow, and then Digger hung up the living room landline phone and looked back down at Snodo, bending and stroking the thick hair-like mane.

"I'm going to dinner tomorrow, you little pony, but I'm afraid that you can't come. You'll have to keep an eye on Simba."

Snodo barked and leaped straight into the air, almost bumping into Digger's head. Apparently, the little horse had thought she heard the word "walk."

The next night, Digger drove his little Toyota through the "rich part" of Ocean View, right past Tobias Mann's old house (more like a little mansion), and thought of Amy Mann. Did she still live there? Had she remarried? Somebody had decorated all of the Mann bushes with white Christmas lights, and Digger couldn't imagine the bouffant-haired older woman out wrestling with those lines and the shrubs. The window to the far right showed a tree all trimmed with white lights, too. *Somebody sure likes white lights*. The Schmidt's house waited a few streets further on, and somebody (*Gwena?*) had wrapped green lights around a small arborvitae alongside the driveway. Digger approved of minimalism. As he pulled into the Schmidt's driveway, a car passed by behind him, and Digger thought of the police. For weeks he had been suspicious of cars and car lights in his rearview mirror, and each time he would tell himself that he was obviously innocent, that the police would find nothing, that if they wanted to follow him to PetCo, *then have at it!* Forgetting the car (had it slowed to a stop a couple houses up the street?), Digger tucked the bottle of white wine beneath his left arm, locked his own car (no use letting the cops slip listening devices under the dashboard), and then used the Schmidt's lion's head knocker three times. The summonses sounded a bit tinny out in the open air. As he waited, Digger thought of Simba, asleep on the floor back at home. How much longer did she have? He would have to sit on the floor with her more often, try to find the old connection, even if just for a second here or there. The shadow of Time glided by on its immense wings.

When the door swung open, an old woman appeared, but then she smiled, the years falling away to reveal Gwena Schmidt, his past department chairperson. Time had heavily frosted her, but nothing to the extent that it had marked her husband, the ex-stock broker, for Richard looked almost encased in ice. The Iceman cometh and melted. Digger sat with him in the dining room as Gwena went to the kitchen to open the wine, and the two men grinned at each other.

"Yur'n ahtur now?" said Richard Schmidt, his words slurred, but his mind clear, for the moment, anyway.

"Yes," smiled Digger. "One shot and one more in the barrel." He wasn't sure why he had just said that, why he had used a gun analogy, but the old fellow seemed to like it."

"Gwns redih. Thawt admnstr di't." Richard smiled non-stop and didn't seem to mind or even notice his speech trouble.

"We faculty like to blame the administrators," laughed Digger, but he was relieved when Gwena returned.

"I was hoping it was him," she said, "and you obviously were using Omar Johns as a model, right?"

"No, Gwena. I used nobody as a model, except maybe the poor boy who jumped off the Bay Bridge. Danny Jones. Do you remember him?"

"Not really, Digger," said Gwena.

"Noumph," said Richard.

"Richard's in fine form tonight, aren't you, my love?" The two old people locked eyes and smiles, and Digger thought of Anna and felt the tennis ball that never really left his gut, that was always waiting to rise, expand, and burst.

"However, I do remember Omar Johns pontificating at his memorial. Typical of an administrator, advertising at every opportunity. Like car salesmen! Here, Digger, let me fill your wine glass. And tell us about your second book. As Richard said, I really did enjoy the first one, and I'm not a fan of the genre, either. Not since I was a girl with Agatha Christie. We don't read murder mysteries around here, but yours flowed well. I enjoyed the narrative. And I often read parts to Richard before bed."

"It worked well to put him to sleep, no doubt!"

"Everything does, these days, isn't that right, Richard?"

"S'righ."

"We're happy to see you, Digger, so what's the next book going to be called? Will it be about Tobias?"

"Well, sort of, but not quite. Just as with Danny Jones, I don't want to use the exact person. That would be sort of tacky, exploitive, but I do use my experiences, sort of. You know, being alone, and teaching, and empty office hours. You know what I mean."

"I'm beginning to forget it all, Digger, even those office hours. Everything begins to take on a romantic air after you're no longer a part of it. Even all those student papers. I miss them, can you believe that?"

"Don Domberg would be glad to have a volunteer at Tutorial Services."

"Now, Digger, I don't miss them that much! But tell us about book two. Are you going to use the same sort of beginnings, composition terms?"

"This time I'm focusing just on grammar beginnings and guides because the book will be called, unless I decide to change things, *Murderous Mistakes*."

"Oh, I like that, fragments, run-ons, all of that," said Gwena.

"Fra, ra, ra," said her husband of sixty years.

"Yes, Richard, fragments," said his wife of six decades.

"I don't know," said Digger, adding, "I might make the murder a 'mistake,' you know, the wrong person killed. I was thinking of having the chair knocked off, with me as the chair, more or less."

"Oh, don't do some strange form of self-punishment, Matthew Diggerson, or you'll have that psycho-nut Watkins contacting you."

"Oh, I talked with William recently. In fact, I wanted to talk to you about this problem. You see, none of our peers ever mentions my book, almost none, and after telling the whole faculty about it during the summer meeting and then mentioning it to individuals throughout September, I've basically just shut up about the book. And that seems fine with everyone else since none of them bring it up, almost none. Lou Knightly has mentioned it, but mainly in connection with his own book. That was the typical response, in fact. Instead of asking about my actually published book, our colleagues just went off on a tangent to announce their own efforts."

"Digger, Digger, that's just human nature. You must know that. These people, these writing teachers, lovers of writing, they're simply jealous of your accomplishment. You're an author. You're what every writing teacher wants to be, as well as a reminder of what they are not."

"Nobody wants that reminding, I'm sure."

"N'bee, n'bee." Digger and Gwena looked at the smiling old man.

"Do I know that Lou Knight fellow?" asked Gwena, turning back to the younger man.

"Lou, no, you wouldn't. He came after you. Lou Knightly. He's a lip licker."

"What's a lip licker?"

"He licks his upper lip a lot, sort of freaky. But he's about the only one who even mentions my book, even if it's just to hype his own, which as of now doesn't even exist."

"Human nature," repeated the old chair. "And you cannot hide your success, Matt. You cannot hide."

"I suppose I should credit Eliot, too."

"Eliot! He hasn't retired yet? How is old Eliot, still trying to catch his breath?"

Digger laughed. "He's all right, Eliot. He once told me an interesting story about David Reed Winslow, about his, Eliot's, jealousy over who he called David Two Last Names' great success."

"Oh, that," said Gwena. "He told me, too. He told everyone back then."

"He did? Eliot told me that he had never mentioned his great jealousy to anyone."

"That's Eliot, Digger, just trying to live, to cling to his own importance. Like all of us."

"Gwena, I don't like feeling resentful, don't like just sitting in my office, being alone."

"Then don't do it, Digger. Next semester, walk around with a copy of your book and stick it right in people's hands. Talk about it. Let your heart show. People will thaw. I loved the book. It was entertaining, fun, really interesting. I'm not that spinster old-timer who haunts the halls like Mary Tyrone, now, am I?"

"If I made you into a character, you wouldn't be a spinster or old, or drug-addicted, for that matter."

"That's kind, Digger, but I am one—old, that is—and will no doubt before long be the other. Not a druggie, though." The two looked again at Richard, who was spilling his wine down both sides of his mouth. The old man grinned, looking like a decrepit vampire. He had stopped trying to talk.

"He has good days and bad, good hours and bad, even just good moments."

The Ancient Mariner just smiled and nodded, smiled and nodded, reminding Digger of Johna Adams' students, a macabre parody. Ironically, though, Richard looked much happier than those bobble-head teens had. Maybe, Digger concluded, the key to happiness involved turning off the brain.

"He looks happy," Digger said to Gwena.

"He can explode with anger and frustration, at any moment, just explode." And the volatile fellow nodded agreement, still quite pleasantly, as though they were all discussing an upcoming trip, perhaps a drive up to Canada to experience the Northern Lights dance.

"Maybe he rages when his mind clears," says Digger, and this time Gwena nodded, not smiling, though. "Maybe he's better off with a clouded mind. That's really what I did, Gwena, when Anna left, I mean. I just turned off part of my brain, and I've kept that part off all these years. I've put up fences, those walls, for so long that I don't have to even try any longer."

"Good fences make good neighbors," she said, as though to herself, and Richard laughed heartily. "You've reset your brain, Digger."

"I have," he said and felt good in the saying, the acceptance.

"But you made that choice, Digger, I mean, when you come right down to it. *You* chose to be a Tibetan monk, to live on a mountaintop. *You* made the mountain. For Richard, the mountain just landed on him."

"True," said Digger, and the two conversationalists looked over at Richard, who suddenly stopped smiling and nodding.

"Who?" he asked, quite coherently, but nothing more.

Digger had made the choice to live with an ideal, even if it narrowed his life quite severely, but for Richard Schmidt, the choice came from somewhere else, from severed synapses and darkened nerve fibers, from the shadows of Time.

The sad image of a smiling, nodding ghoul was one of two that Digger took with him from the Schmidt's, the other being Gwena's joyful urging of him to continue promoting his book at OVC. Gwena and Richard, one-time lions laid low now. Sprinkled in confectioner's sugar, the seasoning of Time. Simba was like the Schmidts, too, sort of, but more Richard than Gwena, who still had all of her faculties. Simba would sometimes walk in circles now, not a tight twirl like an excited pooch, but more in the shape of a hoola hoop, and as she traversed that little world, slowly, methodically, a wild animal in a zoo, she would say "Hoot, hoot, hoot," as though calling for help, over and over. As he had promised himself, Digger would get right down on the floor with her and say, "I'm right here, Simba, right here," but his words and his petting did not seem to reach the lion dog, who was clearly lost, walking in other worlds, very narrow ones. Even Snodo began to shy away from her sister and friend, who would often stop before the white dog's face and just breath, totally still, consuming Snodo's space and making her growl, a little sound that rose and grew, reminding Digger of his hidden black river of negative pathos. If his black river had a voice, it would be Snodo's loss of patience, as well as perhaps Simba's lost hooting.

This would be Simba's last Christmas, that much was sure. Probably Richard Schmidt's, too. Maybe Digger would contact Gwena more. If the two were about to lose great friends, maybe they could help each other. *No*, Digger realized that he would not make the connection. Billy D would, but his creator would just live on, taking life's punches, turning to avoid others. The King of Ignorance, that was Digger, and he sat on the throne himself, willingly. No one put him there. He had never even told Gwena that the OVPD considered him a murder suspect. Gwena had made one comment about Johna Adams' murder and had not even seen the connection to the second woman's. Why would she? She was oblivious of the link, and why should Digger shine a light into those shadows?

Mainly, though, from the Schmidt's dinner, Digger took away (with Gwena's help) a decision to change his department's attitude: he vowed to himself to get his faculty members to share their dreams, their writings, perhaps by having a push board installed in the hallway to display poems, articles, blogs, book ideas, anything that would get those peers to open up and be positive about each other's written works. The board could go right outside his "corner" office. In fact, Professor Diggerson had already emailed Maintenance a request for the board, a big one, to be installed at the end of the Humanities corridor, where nothing but wall existed right now anyway. *Tangible action.* Digger already felt renewed, but maybe that had more to do with space in time, with being alone. After all, what did Sartre say, that "Hell is other people"?

Digger wrote the first chapter for *Murderous Mistakes*, calling it "Fragments" because as the chair (this character based loosely on himself) filled in his faculty's spring semester schedule, he thought of each person briefly—basically envisioned negative or odd fragmented judgments about each teacher—thus creating suspects for his own pending murder. Billy D was one of those suspects, but Digger changed the murder location, didn't want to mimic Tobias' end too much. Digger's fictional killer used a gun, one that the hooded madman referred to as Betty, Black Betty. At this point, the writing teacher had not chosen a killer, yet his second chapter yielded an interesting possibility, the Humanities Building's custodian, whom Digger tentatively named Bradley. The writer liked the image of Bradley's swooshing his broom through the halls of an empty building, whistling and plotting. Yes, Bradley could be a good killer, but wouldn't he be obvious? Not if the chair's murder took place away from Humanities. Digger planned and wrote, finishing Chapter Three, "Dangling Modifiers," and then jumping to the last chapter, which for the moment defied a title but which ended with Bradley's failed attempt to kill Billy D (in a car chase) and with the killer's plunge into the Bay, his disappearance.

The next day, Digger drove for three hours with Simba and Snodo to his mother's house for Christmas. He felt calm, peaceful, fulfilled. The book was going well, a full beginning and an end, as well as a pathway to that end. After Christmas, he would try to finish the story before the spring semester started. That would take a lot of writing, along with no faculty emergencies. And no more murders and police interrogations!

Jean Diggerson's side door was, as usual, not locked, and Snodo (as usual) poured in when Digger opened it. Simba used to rush in, too, but now she stood uncertainly on the porch. Maybe she was still groggy, for she had slept on the long drive.

"Hello, Snodo," Digger heard his mother say, followed by, "Where's my Simba?"

"Right here," said Digger through the door, which the lion dog eventually ambled through.

"Hello, Simba," Jean said, seated at the family table in her chair near the back window, but the old dog just stood there, panting.

"She's old, mom," said Digger, kissing his mother on the forehead and then sitting across from her, "and I think she's a bit demented."

"We're all old, Matthew, and I'm feeling a bit demented, too."

"That will be the day," laughed the old woman's son.

"I'm doing pretty well for an eighty-one year-old woman!"

"Very well," agreed Digger.

"I just read your book again. I just love it! When I finished it the first time, I just went back to Chapter One and started over. I just love that Yusef. Was he real, I mean, an actual student of yours?"

"Sort of. I based him on a black boy named Danny Jones. You remember him. He committed suicide by jumping off a big bridge by my school."

"Oh, that's terrible, that poor boy. But I don't remember that name, Matthew. You know, I'm eighty-one, I'm not a young woman!"

"Young at heart."

"Yes! Young at heart. And how about your colleagues? How do they like the book? They must be excited about it."

"Oh," laughed Digger, "they're just beside themselves with joy and glee!" Then he added, "Almost none of them have read it, and none ever talk to me about it. In fact, the book seems to have made me disconnected with my peers. I'm an outcast."

"They're just busy and maybe a bit jealous, Matthew. They'll come around. People get focused on themselves and then they come to their senses. When you're my age, you will understand people better."

"I don't even understand myself," laughed Digger.

"Oh, nonsense! And what about your hero, Billy D? You said that you were planning a second book. Have you started it?"

Then the two remaining Diggersons on the family tree's last multi-twigged branch talked about *Murderous Mistakes*. His mother liked to talk, liked to complain about her age, but she was a great listener, interested and responsive. She loved the Wilder name for Billy D, and after saying that, she picked up the book, which had been laying prominently on the kitchen table (*for visitors to see*, Digger thought!), and hugged it, saying, "I just love this book, Matthew!" That was a nice image, one that Digger decided to store away.

"Speaking of Wilder," he said, "how are your siblings?"

"Deaf and crazy, same as always! You know that John. When I showed him your book, he just said 'Huh?' I said, 'Huh what? I'm trying to show you Matthew's book,' and of course he just said, 'What?' He could get a better hearing aid, you know."

"But he's happy?"

"Oh, he's happy, living in that little tunneled world of his." Digger thought of his own narrow world.

"I'll visit him, maybe tomorrow. You can come …"

"Oh, I don't want to see that old fogey so soon."

"Okay, I'll go with Snodo, and you can keep Simba company."

"An old woman and an old dog with dementia. That will be quite a scene." Digger laughed, but Jean didn't. She had her chin raised in a way that Digger had always thought of as "New England," sort of a British thick-upper lip.

"Family roots are strong," he said, transitioning the topic onto a well-worn path.

"You and those roots, Matthew. Yes, blood is thick. Your father and Emma, even your grandparents, whom you never met. They're all still here, all with me." The old woman touched her chest, patted it a few times.

"You're really talking about Time."

"Time?"

"Time is the real enemy, but strong roots can conquer even it. At least for a good long while. You know, you always ask why I don't remarry, and it's just like what you say about Dad, that you're already married. I feel that way with Anna. I can't kill those roots, I won't! They nourish my dreams."

"Hmph! Now you've lost me, Matthew. You had better save ideas like that for your second book. And you had better finish it soon! I'm eighty-one, you know!"

Throughout his three-day trip home, Digger counted the number of times that he heard Jean Diggerson make that statement: eleven times total. Eighty-one was not a number he would soon forget.

It was a pretty nice holiday visit, all things considered, and Digger replayed various scenes on the long drive home. At the nursing home, Uncle John hadn't known who he was, at first, but Digger had kept pointing to himself and then to his book, which his mother had demanded he take and leave with John to read ("since the old fool can still read!"), so that the eldest male

Diggerson finally announced "Matt!" At his mother's house, Aunt Carol and Aunt Mary came to Christmas dinner, each entering through the side door with casseroles in their hands ("I'm so tired of casseroles!") and smiles on their ancient faces. Later, alone with his mother and once again talking about Digger's use of the Wilder name in his books, he had said, "After Dad's death, did you ever think of going back to your maiden name, back to Wilder?" And his mother had said, "Never," explaining that his father's car accident and death had changed nothing. She was still married to him, always would be, and Digger thought of Anna again. That conversation had just been an extension of the "strong roots" one. And that was exactly the way he felt, *still married*, as illogical as that emotion might be.

Thinking of that conversation as he drove home through the night, Digger wondered if Anna had changed her name back from Diggerson. On her envelopes, she always put just "Anna" and then her address. Maybe she didn't know who she was anymore? Probably she was just trying to spare him, to prevent ink pain, the slash of words. As he drove, still an hour away from his cottage, he glanced at Snodo on the front seat. The little horse was curled up and deep in sleep, snoring slightly upon each exhale. *That dog even sleeps hard!* Then he swiveled his head and looked quickly at Simba, laid out on the back seat as though jumping through a hoop, but the Lion Dog would jump no more. She was fast asleep, too, and silent.

Every other house on the long but familiar journey glittered with lights, and Digger felt that little lump that puffed up upon occasion, *too often*, just below his heart. The world was just so beautiful, and so sad.

Winter break played out smoothly except for one incident, one faculty emergency: Patricia Pauley resigned, temporarily. Midway through January, she sent Digger an abrupt email announcing that she could not teach the two night courses slotted for her, that she needed to help her husband. Her husband, good old *Bob*, the gumshoe. *Help Bobby do what?* Patricia didn't say, but she did add that she was sorry and that she would contact him about next fall. When this responsibility arose, Digger had been 30,000 words into his second book, which had completely blocked out the OVPD and Officer Zorn and her suspicions, and even tempered Simba's slow descent from his world. Damn life sometimes! After responding to Patricia that she should take care of herself and that she shouldn't worry about the last-minute cancellations, Digger thought immediately of the Blinker, Jay Moore. He could probably take the Tuesday night class, but he already had a Wednesday night one again. Who could take that? Of the remaining adjuncts, Digger landed on Dave Jepson and Liz Lawson, each of whom had just two courses, three being the mandatory number for adjuncts (otherwise, college administrators would hire no full-timers, just populating faculty with cheap part-timers!). Whom should he ask first, Dave or Liz? He decided on Liz since she currently had Wednesday open, so he sent Liz and Jay emails, offering them an extra course each. By the next day, he had received replies, both accepting the extra class. Faculty emergency averted!

That night at twilight, Digger stood with a Bud Light and looked out his back door at his favorite scene, his own back yard. His accent spruce tree wore the Christmas mantle of blue LED lights, which shivered in the breeze, making the image even more magical, and stars shone behind swiftly passing, low hanging pieces of cumulous clouds, Digger's favorite sky. *Life was all right!* His visit to his mother had been nice, his second book was half finished, his spring semester was still close to two weeks away, and his decision to change the Humanities Department, to make its members more open to sharing their works, buoyed him, made him feel closer to his colleagues than he had since last August—even though none of them had yet earned that comaraderie. He felt like a writer, he was one, an author, one with a pair of books, soon anyway. Shifting from that positive vision, Digger wondered how he would feel if Lou Knightly, for instance, had published a book and was about to release a second story. Envious, small, guilty. *Probably*, but not to the extent that he would ignore the Lip Licker. Then Digger thought of Eliot's jealousy anecdote about David Reed Winslow, a man who had conquered the literary world, who knew life so deeply that he could no longer stand to live within it. Digger thought of Danny Jones then, the Boy Who Flew. The Man Who Flew! Digger admitted to himself how close he had come after Anna's departure and his sister's death to taking the path laid out by so many before him. *To fly!* Outside the professor's back window, twilight, too, had fallen. The world had grown dark, but the black just made the blue Christmas lights out back and the celestial ones above glow even more magnificently.

Due to the hooding of the night, Digger didn't notice when the black cat arrived, couldn't see even its shape, especially since "Inky" stood so still. And Digger had long since retired to his couch and to some TV viewing when the other shape appeared, the taller one. Digger didn't see how each shape, tall and short, contemplated the other and then turned back to its solitary vigil, keeping an eye on the cottage, turning patiently with the earth, waiting.

## Chapter 12: To Point

Besides functioning to introduce, a colon can be pictured as a mark that points—i.e., what comes after the colon is what you pointed to before that mark. The following melody, made famous by the deep voice of Eric Burdon and The Animals, will help you to use colons correctly.

Well, there is a way to hear if you
Have used a colon right.
Just listen for a subject-verb
A statement that sounds tight.
Now the question you must ask yourself
For a colon used quite well
Are you pointing to what you just said
Showing what you tell?

On the morning of the first day of Ocean View College's spring semester classes, Digger discovered that Maintenance had in fact installed the push board just as he had requested, right outside his office door at the end of the Humanities corridor. Three-foot wide by three-foot tall, the top at head level, the board even sported a dozen brightly colored pins. Since he had received an email from Maintenance a week prior about the board, Digger had known that it was up, but seeing it in physical form filled the chair with happy resolve. Immediately, from his briefcase, he extracted a few pieces of paper, one being a Xeroxed copy of his first book's cover, and pinned each onto the board. Centered across the top were three cut-out words, each in size 48 print: 'Share,' 'Your,' and 'Dreams.' A foot below and on the left, he tacked his book's cover, which depicted a cobalt blue murder scene where the poor Yusef had met his end off a jetty into the swirling waters of the Bay. The Whirlpool. Indeed, Hell *is* other people *when they form into gangs,* thought Digger. Above the blue and merging into the book's black top, the words *Composition Murder* dripped just a bit in stark white print, and beneath the scene, his name appeared in small but bold white letters across the cover's bottom. *Matthew Diggerson.* Beneath that, below the cover, Digger had typed, "Available on Amazon.com." *There!* If that advertisement weren't enough, then Digger would start hooting like Simba.

Having arrived on the half hour, ninety minutes before his first class, at eleven, Digger had met nobody yet, and even Gloria had not been at her desk. However, unlike the emptiness of last semester, Digger felt strong and determined. *Things were going to change!*

Within ten minutes, Digger caught his first fish, for John George, the stately retired secondary-education teacher, appeared before the board and studied Digger's book cover.

"That's a nice cover," said the older man. "Good dark tone."

"Thanks," said Digger, seated at his desk. "I described what I wanted to my publisher, and she sent that back, along with a few other alternatives, but I liked that best. Dark but not too dark."

John nodded, then said, "I like your idea here, Digger. 'Share your dreams.' That's a good idea. I once wrote an article about peer reviews, but I never found a publisher for it, so I gave up. Maybe I will pin it here with a note asking for advice."

"Do that, John, and we'll get something started here. We're a writing department, so we need to write and share our writing!"

"I will, Digger, on Friday. If I can find that article in my filing cabinet."

"I look forward to reading it, John, and I know a few places to send scholarly articles, so if your piece fits, I'll give you contact info."

"Good, thank you," said John George, adding, "and I'll read your book, see if I can find myself in there."

"You're the first person I killed," laughed Digger, and the other teacher caught the mirth.

After the older man left, though, Digger wondered about his article. *Peer Review?* Was John for or against it? Digger had discovered that most of his peers were dedicated peer reviewists, yet students had told him repeatedly that they didn't care for that activity, citing the discomfort at giving criticism—and at getting it from peers! Especially when they couldn't really understand their fellow teens' critiques. *Probably John was for it.* Digger would just have to keep an open mind. At least, the piece would start a dialogue, would get peers to share, as long as he were careful with his own words. Age didn't really change people, for adult professionals could also feel discomfort. Digger remembered again Eliot's graduate-school story, the power of jealousy, and he wondered for the thousandth time about Johna's and Valerie's murders, about being the Kevin Bacon connection. Just a single link—him—to both victims. *Well, coincidences do occur*, no matter what the little detective had said. If they didn't exist, then the word would not appear in the dictionary.

A few minutes before ten, Digger heard voices, and soon Lou Knightly appeared before the pin board, studying the dark cover and thinking who knows what? Lou had to stoop to peruse it.

"Has anybody read your book yet?" he asked, not exactly pleasantly.

"Not that I know of," Digger answered, not exactly pleasantly, either, so he switched tones, remembering his spring-semester vow. "Professor Watkins says it's because none of you like me."

"What a toad!" Lou responded, or he might have said 'turd.' "Bunch of psychos! Everybody loves you, Digger. We're all just busy with our own little problems. I'm going to read it, I planned to this month, but you know what happens. Life. Life happens."

Digger knew all about life's happenings, or at least up until he somewhat stopped existence after Anna's departure. Along with Simba, nature, Snodo, and even Paul Smith, his book had started the clock ticking again, loud and strong, especially now that the second novel was moving toward completion. *Two Billy D Wilder tales!* One more in the chamber, too! Digger decided not to mention these gun images to Lou Knightly, who seemed a little down. Digger thought of Officer Zorn's question implying some homosexual murder motivation and dismissed it immediately. He had never gotten any vibe like that from any male colleague, not even the tall Lip Licker.

"You okay?" Digger asked.

"Yeah, just a tough first class. You know when you get a couple students who you know will be pains in the ass all semester?"

"Yeah, Psych students!"

"Exactly! Right! And I have three in one class!"

"Ouch," said Digger, grimacing to match the word. "But maybe they'll surprise you."

"Do students like that ever surprise you?"

"No," Digger had to admit, adding, "Or at least not often."

"Not ever!" said Knightly, who then turned on his heels and marched off down the corridor. *Share your screams.* Digger pictured Lou's long steps, thought of Paul Smith, the Stork. Smith was unique, one of a kind, right?

Well, at least Lou was open, honest. The thin man appeared to hide little! Digger pondered the one colleague, besides Johna Adams, who had talked about *Composition Murder* last semester. Talked but *not read.* A salesman, a seller of half-truths, of lies? Could the Lip Licker harbor such envy and anger that another's success could push him beyond reason? *No way*. A false analogy. Not reading and leaving a path of corpses were too different to compare. Twisted logic. *Twisted?* Lou's tongue had not appeared during the entire conversation. Maybe he was hiding it?

Within the hour, two more composition teachers had scanned the Dream Board and commented on it. Jolie had complimented Digger on the idea and vowed to pin up one of her songs ("I write songs, you know," she had said.), and Bill Jacobs had looked quickly at the wall and laughed. At what, Digger was not sure. "Composition Murder!" Bill had said, dramatically, and then followed up the veiled statement with a question: "Are you making any money yet?" Digger had said that he was pulling in reams of cash, too many checks to count. "Sure," Bill had laughed. "Each one for seventy-two cents." Unfortunately, the son of a bitch was just about spot on. After Bill had left, Digger vowed to stay positive, not to sink into solitude and silence as he had done the previous semester. Growth took change, and change was difficult. Hadn't he voiced the same mantra repeatedly to students about their grammatical skills!

With that resolve, Digger decided on another connection, so he accessed his email and typed 'jlambmann@svcc.edu' into the computer. What to say after close to twenty years? An excuse or two or a hundred seemed appropriate, but what? *My wife left me, and a colleague tried to knife me*, thought Digger, somewhat humorously. Instead, he typed this: "Johnny, long time! Johna talked about you this summer, before her tragic death. I miss her and still can't believe she was killed. Several years ago, another colleague was murdered, and the killer turned out to be another writing teacher (but you probably know all about that). Strange times. I often think back to SVCC. Simpler times then. I miss our talks. We definitely need to get a cup of coffee or a beer sometime, old friend. I have two dogs now. What does your family look like?" Then he signed his name (Digger), read the little paragraph once, thought it jumped around a bit too much, but clicked "send" before he got too pedantic over an email. Connecting felt good, like having money in the bank. Maybe it would grow.

When he sat back in his chair, Digger suddenly felt a presence, startling him. It was Diana Pell, the Reluctant Smiler, standing before the push-pin board, reading. She must have emerged unseen from her office, or maybe she was heading that way.

"Diana," said Digger, "why don't you add your latest poem to the board?"

The former State Poet swiveled her old head his way, and her face held no expression, making Digger think of a box turtle again. Then the lip ends started to rise, as though two strings were attached, and Digger witnessed that miraculous sun coming out from behind those thunder clouds. He couldn't help but smile back even though Pell had said nothing yet.

"My muse seems to have dried up, Digger," the old poet said. "I have not written a poem in five years."

"I'm sorry to hear that," said Digger, adding, "Maybe you've just said already what you wanted to say. All those past poems. Maybe your creativity has drifted to other areas. I know that I'm like that. Creativity travels."

"Yes, I have been painting. My words have become colors, paint slashes." *Slashes?* The word made Digger think of Paul Smith and his *family heirloom*, a long, jagged knife.

"You will get your words back, Diana, and in the meantime, why don't you add one of your last poems to the board? It would inspire others to do the same. It would show how much we care about and need writing."

"In a way, Digger, it is a relief not to write, not to feel that obsession. I'm not sure I even want words again."

At this conclusion, Pell's smile had succumbed to gravity, and Digger wasn't sure how to respond. The darkness was enveloping. "Does your son, Michael, write?"

"Nary a word. Michael would say that his concentrations are better spent on reality."

"He sounds like a businessman."

"That would be an accurate representation." The sides of Diana Pell's mouth twitched but settled down, making Matthew Diggerson think of Simba, of gravity. "Digger, I like this board. I like your cover, even though that title is pedestrian."

"It's the genre," Digger said, trying not to feel defensive. "I wanted it to be corny but to relate to teaching writing."

Pell seemed not to hear, continuing, "I think that I *will* add some 'dreams' to your board. We all need to fly a little, do we not? Especially as we get older and more rooted to the ground."

*As the ground calls out to us!* The morbid atmosphere was catching. Digger tried to turn the dark energy: "I like that, Diana. Writing as flying. I've actually used that analogy on student papers."

"Most of those fly like Icarus. They don't make it." Again, the lip sides twitched but gave up.

"Icarus," Digger laughed. "Now there's a poem right there, some verse about students' essays. You see, you still have the words, Diana!"

"Perhaps," the wise old box turtle said, turning, unlocking the door opposite Digger's, and making her slow way into the darkness of her office.

Digger looked at his watch. Still more than half an hour before his first class at eleven. Outside his office window, he noticed a swarm of birds dragging their net dance across the sky above the library. Back and forth, up and down, like a twisting school of fish, hundreds of birds, black specks, perhaps starlings. Had they recently returned from down south? If so, they had come back too soon, smack in the middle of winter. Digger watched the celestial swirling and swaying until the choreography drifted too far north and disappeared behind the library. Here or there, a solitary bird zipped madly across the empty stage. Digger noticed that the two clock towers showed the same time for a change, the right side usually being behind reality a bit. He wanted to get going with his first class.

Most of the writing courses took place in the Classroom Building, a short walk north from the Faculty Offices Building, and soon Digger found himself in one of his usual rooms, teaching the most common spring semester composition course, EN 102, Writing about Literature. Students always seemed to be conscientious about coming to their first class ahead of time, so Digger saw twenty faces (five rows of four each) and recognized one of them: a grinning Twitch. "Hello, Professor Diggerson!" said the slightly odd fellow as though the two were all by themselves, not surrounded by all these other humans.

Digger smiled, said, "Good to see you," and decided not to add "Twitch," just in case the boy had changed his mind about that nickname. Maybe he wanted to be called Michael instead now, for that was his Christian name, just like Diana Pell's son, still a common one among students.

Digger greeted the whole class and then turned to the white board, where a previous professor had actually left a blue gel pen. In big blue letters, he wrote his name, the course name, and his email address, all of which were on the syllabus, he said, which they could find on their Bridges course site. He then used the big screen to show them how to navigate their site, noticing Twitch's smiling and nodding throughout the presentation. The gangly student knew all about this. Usually, OVC dissuaded students from repeating their writing instructors in both EN 101 and 102 because administrators and the faculty both wanted the young people to learn different viewpoints, but sometimes pupils would request the same teacher. As Chair, Digger had heard their arguments, which all boiled down to this: "I like the teacher's style. I learn best with that style." Twitch must have used that argument on the Registrar, or perhaps it was just luck of the draw. *But whose luck?* If Digger were to receive one repeat student, he would *not* have chosen Twitch, despite the boy's enthusiasm, Digger's favorite quality in a student. However, Twitch's zeal often went off purpose, as illustrated by his papers, too. In short, the lad was a bit of a handfull.

That fact resurrected itself during "peer presentations," which Digger used during every course's first class. Grouped into quartets, each student would be responsible for asking the other three one or two questions, taking notes, and then presenting the answers to the class. The first question called simply for names (including how the person would like to be addressed), the second for home towns (and something interesting about their place of origin), the third for their writing experiences the previous semester (since nearly all of these 102 students would have completed EN 101 in the fall), and the fourth for their overall OVC experiences so far and any recommendations for peers. The latter question fell to (or was selected by) the lanky Twitch, whose habit of hunching his shoulders—a full-body twitch!—every couple of minutes did not seem to shock any of these 102 students and who did indeed still want to be addressed as "Twitch." Maybe today's students really were more accepting of diversity.

In preparation for his soliloquy, Twitch let his shoulders rip, or more likely the clavicles just jumped on their own. Digger wasn't sure what the boy's mental or physical problems were, but he *was* registered as a "special needs" student. Then his repeat student let go vocally: "Well, Connor here had a great first semester and he says that Tutorial Services saved him in 101, and Kendra over here agrees that Tutorial Services is a great place. She recommends that everyone go there, too, and I told her that you, Professor Diggerson, require us to go at least once, and she said 'good' to that. Kendra also recommends not living in the Bridge View dorms because the fire alarms are always going off and the water takes too long to get hot. Connor lives there too, and he says that his dorm didn't have those problems but the dorms are pretty old, he says. Micah over here just transferred in from Sea View Community College, and she thinks that OVC is beautiful and she wants to get a degree in Criminal Justice. I told her that she's come to the right school since the teachers are always being murdered. I mean, not always, but sometimes, and I told her that our teacher, you, Professor Diggerson, always seem to be involved in the killings, that you actually fought off a killer ten years or so ago, and that you knew the woman who was killed last semester. Actually, that you knew another woman who was killed just last December, too. I suggested to Micah that she interview you, Professor Diggerson, because you're always connected to murder."

Digger's mind had slumbered a bit until Twitch had gotten to his Micah answers, at which point he woke up fast. The word 'murder' had a way of catching his attention, and how did Twitch know that that Valerie woman's murder had been connected to him? How could he have known that?

Twitch was done now, and twenty faces faced their teacher, who seemed to be asleep, despite the fact that he was standing with his eyes opened. In the silence, Digger realized that some response to Twitch's presentation was required.

"Mine is a perilous occupation," he began, and the students all laughed at that. "Twitch is right. I did fight off a killer eight years ago, a person who murdered my department chair and one of our janitors. But he was caught long ago and is now still in jail. He won't ever get out. And I did know the teacher killed last September, Johna Adams, who is sadly missed. So, Micah, Twitch is right. When your classes cover homicide, come see me for help. I do have some experience!"

"What about the woman murdered last December?" said Twitch, smiling.

Digger had wanted to cover up that juicy tidbit, to hide it behind all his other words. *Damn, Twitch!* "Well, I didn't really know her," said the composition teacher, reluctant to tell these teens how she had "picked him up" in Stop & Shop. "But I have talked to the Ocean View police all about the killings. Eight years ago, in fact, you might say that I sort of worked with the lead detective on the twin killings."

"And now there have been *twin* twin killings," said Twitch, the little bastard!

"I don't know what's going on now," admitted Professor Matthew Diggerson, adding, "But it has nothing to do with Ocean View College this time."

"You're like Kevin Bacon," said Micah suddenly, and several other students nodded and some verbally agreed.

"Who's Kevin Bacon?" asked another student.

Micah took the reigns: "He's that old actor who's been in so many films with so many other actors that a game was created connecting them all. It's called Six Degrees of Kevin Bacon. If someone says an actor's name, then you need to figure out the steps to Kevin Bacon. In other words, you need to link the actors who played with Kevin Bacon to find one that wasn't in a movie with him but who was in one with an actor who was in one with Kevin Bacon."

"Huh?" said the student who didn't know Kevin Bacon.

"My parents play the game sometimes," said Micah in summary, adding, "It's all about *steps.* Whoever can find the steps to Kevin Bacon soonest wins."

Digger had gotten a little lost in Micah's explanation, so he said, "Kevin Bacon's a good actor, but he's been in some lousy movies, and he's been in many genres. Horror, comedy, drama. That's why the game Micah described was created. He's come across so many other actors, many of whom work just in certain genres. I remember one B-movie about giant worms, which was actually very entertaining. Horror-comedy, if I remember correctly."

"He was in *Flat Liners,*" responded Micah, and heads nodded again. Then she said, "You're Kevin Bacon with one degree of separation, Professor." The link to two corpses smiled at that, a grin that slipped into a frown, making Micah and the rest of the class laugh.

At that point, Digger decided to transition away from this murder subject to another quartet's presentations, but as these other students introduced each other, he couldn't stop wondering how Twitch knew about his connection with the second victim, Valerie, *what was her last name?* Something odd, like Wart? *Valerie Wart?* The local news having moved on to other tragedies, Digger no longer heard or saw her name. *Walt?* A man's name? *Twitch!* He would have to question his strange student.

Thus, as the rest of the students were filing out, some actually saying *good bye*, Digger stopped Twitch by saying, "Twitch, I'm glad that you're in my class again, but did you want a different teacher this time, maybe to get a different angle on writing, some different lesson plans maybe?"

"Oh, no," said the grinning fellow. "I requested to be in this class. I talked with the Registrar about it. I like how you get us in groups and how we move around a lot. Most of my teachers just put us in circles and have us *engage* in class discussions. I like what you do."

"That's good, and I like your enthusiasm. You're a leader. You gave a good presentation today, for instance, but I was wondering how you heard about my connection with the second victim, the woman this past December."

"Oh, that," said Twitch. "That's no secret. One of your friends told me."

*What friends?* Digger thought of Simba illogically. "Who?" he asked the boy.

"One of your teacher friends. I asked where you were, and he said that you were probably talking with the cops about the recent killing. He even said 'recent killing.' I remember that phrase because I hadn't heard about any recent killing. This was back in December, during finals. I stopped by to let you know that I was taking your 102 class. Warning you!"

"You didn't need to do that," said Digger. "I'm happy to see you again, but this friend of mine, was he...did he...did he, sort of, lick his lip?"

"Lick his lips? No, not that I noticed."

"That's a weird question, but I'd like to know who told you about me having a Kevin Bacon connection. Did he blink a lot?"

"Not that I noticed," said Twitch, who was frowning now in concentration, thinking back. "He smiled a lot," concluded the boy.

"Was he old?"

"Professor Diggerson, you all look old to me!" Twitch laughed again. *Fair enough*. Digger remembered thinking how old his sister Emma had seemed when he was still in high school. She had always appeared to be so far ahead of him in life, but now he had passed her long ago. *Strange*.

"Fair enough," Digger smiled, adding, "But how did you know that he was one of my friends, you know, a writing teacher?"

"He was down by your office."

*Oh*. Digger thought about that, didn't particularly enjoy some of his conclusions.

"Well, Twitch," he said in order to release the boy. "If you hear anything else about those murders, let me know, okay? I can pass the info on to the police."

"They don't know what's going on!" the boy laughed.

"Yeah, they could use some help. Do you think you could help them, tell them about the man you talked to? Could you describe him or pick him out in a lineup?"

Twitch laughed. "A lineup! You mean like on TV?"

Digger pictured the cops rounding up all his male colleagues, yanking them to the station, and lining them up for Twitch. "Well, not exactly like on TV. More like if you saw his photo, could you remember the man?"

"I don't think so, Professor Diggerson. "You know, he was old, like you, like all you teachers, and he was a white guy, I think. I only saw him for a minute, and I wasn't really paying attention. I was excited to tell you the news."

"The news?"

"That I was taking your class again!"

"Oh, of course, that good news," said Digger, continuing, "If you see the man you talked to again, could you tell me, and maybe memorize what he looks like? That could help me and the cops a lot."

"I will, but I don't think I'll see him again, Professor Diggerson."

"Why's that, Twitch?"

"I just don't remember faces at all. I forget who people are all the time. Even my own cousins sometimes." Yet last semester the lad had remembered Johna's face, not to mention Digger's. Selective memory?

Digger nodded and told his student to be careful, remembering Dan Pinsky's blabbering on and getting himself stabbed by a listening Paul Smith. After Twitch left, Digger got up and looked down the hallway. His odd student was just turning the corner, moving his arms somewhat robotically. He took long leg strides, too, like a cartoon insect, maybe a praying mantis. *Walks a bit like the Lip Licker*. But Digger was mainly watching all the closed doors down either side of the corridor. Were they empty? Was a Paul Smith clone crouched behind one, his hand cupped to the inside of his door? Which of his peers had been hanging out near Digger's office at the end of last semester?

In his cottage that night, Digger forgot about reality and worked on *Murderous Mistakes*, deciding to get a student involved as a suspect, a student who resembled Twitch but without the same muscle spasms. Digger's fictional student had multiple sclerosis, an early case of it, so the determined lad had to pull himself through life, grind away at it. Having noticed that disabled students often seemed to be alone on campus, Digger made his student character a lonely, mysterious figure, sympathetic but suspicious. Digger decided to call him 'Tim.' The one-book author had now completed about three-quarters of his second story, which came more easily than the first, probably because the fictional people and places were already established so that Digger had just to place himself in a scene and look around for ideas, for dialogue and descriptions. He decided to make the swooping gulls a sinister motif. Having killed off the chair in an earlier chapter, Digger had chosen not to mimic the custodian Dan Pinsky's death, especially since the killer in this second tale was, in fact, a janitor (a "maintenance engineer," Bradley would say in his book), so he created an administrator for his second victim, a bipolar pencil pusher named James Jameson, enjoying the repetitive moniker. This administrator had a connection to Tim, and since Digger's fictional killer used a handgun, even a disabled student could have been the culprit.

Digger wrote deep into the night, having no classes the next day and, of course, no papers yet, and beside him on the couch slumbered Snodo, who not only lived hard but even slept that way, continually dreaming, emitting muffled woofs and twitching her legs, all four usually, as though she were running. Usually, the white pony would awaken startled, raise her head, and stare at Digger, catching her bearings, no doubt. "Did you have a little dream?" Digger would say. "Were you chasing rabbits?" Then Snodo would lay her head down and within a minute, close her big eyes again.

On the floor, Simba slept still and silent, like the proverbial log. Earlier that night, when he had gone out back with his dogs to have them relieve themselves for the night, the lion dog had slipped as she squatted and then stayed slumped over as she relieved herself. It was another step, Digger realized, in his beloved friend's exit from the world. From now on, he would have to hold her up with her leash and harness as she peed.

## Chapter 13: To Fix

Note: About 75% of the time, students use semicolons incorrectly, and approximately 50% of their colons are misused. Comma inconsistency runs rampant, and most students don't even attempt dashes. In short, punctuation often requires fixing. This beautiful melody from Coldplay provides helpful editing tips.

When you use a comma where you hear no pause,
When you put a semicolon after a subordinate clause,
When you fear that a dash or colon will make a flaw,
Could you edit worse?
Read aloud to hear the spot,
Where a mark belongs and where it does not,
And edit right, to fix it.

Midway through February, Digger discovered two additions to the Dream Board outside his office. One was the peer-review article written by John George, the other a sweet poem by Diana Pell. John used too many weak verbs, Diana nary a one, but both facts reflected the writings' genres, the somewhat laborious style of scholarly articles, the precise, even pedantic word choice for poems. Standing at the hallway's end and reading each piece, Professor Matthew Diggerson smiled.

And while writing his book, he also discovered a new killer. Because of Paul Smith, Digger had not wanted to mimic reality, so he had not immediately chosen a colleague, a composition teacher, as the villain, but as *Murderous Mistakes* progressed, the writer kept coming to the same dark place, the same white face: a disgruntled adjunct. His first "killer" choice, Bradley the custodian, began to seem more like a strong suspect, but not a realistic murderer. Why not mirror reality, especially since his fictional characters resembled none of his present or past peers? But what was wrong with this part-timer? Digger couldn't have a dead wife as the catalyst, as had happened to Smith. Back before then, Digger had actually met Debra Smith, who had seemed mousy to him, and in his mind he had labeled the couple the Morbids. Thus, Digger decided to refer to his fictional killer as Mr. Morbid (in Billy D Wilder's mind), and he chose to use jealousy and unfulfilled dreams as the catalyst for the killings. He decided to introduce the wife, too, and to make her quite bitchy—that Mrs. Morbid, quite a nag. He decided to call his villain Ned Dunlap, for no real reason other than that he liked the name. The "Dunlap" implied tires, of course, and poor Ned had been run over repeatedly in life, daily by his wife alone, adding some subtle symbolism.

With the birth of Ned, the second book took wings and obsessed its author, and on mornings before school and early evenings after it, Digger poured out his tale, with Snodo's snoring showing her acceptance of her human's focused task and Simba's slumbers sinking deeper and deeper into rest. By February's end, over sixty-three thousand words later, he had a completed first draft. Digger wanted some space from the book so that he could revise it with a more objective angle, and the downpour of student papers through his Bridges sites helped him to escape his "Murderous" obsession, at least for a couple of weeks. As March began, the Humanities Chair was targeting Spring Break, two weeks off, as the perfect time to reread and revise *Murderous Mistakes*. Before the month was out, he would be able to submit the manuscript for review and probable publication. Digger pictured holding two books in his hands.

One night, a cold and breezy one reminding New Englanders that winter still had teeth, Simba walked away from her dinner with half the food still in her bowl, which Snodo pounced on before Digger could intervene.

Dogs, who engulfed every speck in their dish as fast as possible, had very different eating habits than cats, who often left food for later visits, so this new behavior occupied Matthew Diggerson's thoughts as March progressed. Now, when he fed his pups, he kept the two dogs more separated, and when Simba left kibble in her bowl (more and more), he snatched it out of the way and offered it to her later. At that time, the lion dog would usually finish the offering, somewhat listlessly, sometimes just one kibble at a time, by hand, but at least her physical nourishment continued.

She was losing weight, though, and—thinking of cancer—Digger took Simba to the vet's. Doctor Palmer had been the only veterinarian Digger had ever known, and in response to his cancer worry, she said, "Nothing's wrong with Simba accept a bit of cataracts, a touch of arthritis, and plain old age."

*Plain old age*. Digger had never really had to deal with that eventuality, because his father had died relatively young, his sister, too, and because Simba was his first dog. Certainly, his aunts and uncle were old, but they had always seemed that way and never appeared to change much. Simba's plain old age reminded Digger to give his first dog more attention, even though she didn't soak in his words or his touch as she once had. Dementia had broken her fierce connection to him, and when he petted her now, Simba either froze up and moved away or simply failed to react at all. Mostly, she slept, and Digger thought that perhaps that was a blessing, that perhaps in her dreams Simba ran on the beach and bounced off of Snodo and laughed up at her human, still tethered to him by love, need, and concern. These days, when the three would take walks on the beach, Simba would stray behind and sometimes wander down near the water, worrying Digger by making him think of Virginia Wolf, who had left life by striding off into the sea, a fact known by every teacher of literature in America. Simba's apathy contrasted with Snodo's verve as clearly as January and June, and looking at the old Corgi-shepherd mix, her once-black muzzle completedly frosted now, dipped in milk, Digger could hear the ripple and roll of his black river, the darkness that never slept and never stopped and that existed in the shadows just beneath consciousness, occasionally lifting an iceberg periscope into reality.

Changes, positive ones this time, were taking place down the Humanities corridor of Ocean View College. With a week to go before Spring Break, two more teachers had added their *dreams* to Digger's pin board outside his office. Jolie presented a song (three stanzas) about being gay, the chorus repeating "Just like you, just more blue." He asked her to sing it, and she did. *Catchy*. Eliot and Mary had been attracted by Jolie's singing voice, and they had both clapped.

"You have a nice voice, Jolie," Mary had said, sounding and looking like a grandmother, and Eliot had nodded and replied that he had once written a song.

"About what?" Jolie had asked, but Eliot had not been able to remember. "Probably love, lost love" he had decided.

The other contributor was Jay Moore, who pinned up the first few pages of a play, seemingly a family drama involving two sons, a mother, a father, and a living room. The arguments and tension made Digger think of O'Neil's Tyrone family, but he wasn't captivated by the Blinker's foursome. Moore had titled the work *The Dying Room*, which seemed a little melodramatic, too, but Digger kept all criticisms to himself. He didn't want to sever any roots. Often, he would find a pair of teachers reading something from the board and talking, and before he unlocked and entered his office, he would join the discussion and thus start his working day off in sunshine.

On the last Friday before Spring Break, Digger found Eliot Gladstone alone at the board and then discovered that Diana Pell had added another poem.

"Diana's poems have gotten darker," Eliot said, not looking at Digger, glancing instead at the poet's closed office door.

"Has she added another?"

Eliot turned his gray head and gave Digger a hollow-eyed stare; then the odd fellow exhaled deeply. Digger had rarely witnessed a teacher who needed Spring Break more than this one. He thought of his fictional villain, Ned Dunlap. Maybe Digger would make his second book's killer a little older so that he could describe his features the way that Eliot looked now.

Then Mr. Happyrock returned his attention to the pinned up poem. "Time calls, the shadow crawls," he read, and turning back to Digger said, "That's pretty bleak. 'The shadow crawls'! That's downright melodramatic, Digger. Your 'dream board' has turned Diana sentimental and trite."

"Maybe she's just exploring different views," said Digger. "Why don't you ask her?"

"You don't *think* that I would be honest with her, do you? You *think* that I would just congratulate her on her poetic brilliance."

"Eliot, I would hope that you wouldn't tell her that her poem's 'trite'! I know that you wouldn't do that! You wouldn't want to hurt Diana."

"Like anything could hurt that old toad," said Eliot, adding "leathery skin" and something else that Digger couldn't hear. Digger tried to laugh off his colleague's words. Then Gladstone said, "She's probably unhappy about the return of the prodigal son. Disappointing children can turn a sunny outlook blue."

Digger wondered how Eliot knew about disappointing kids since the Breather had never married. Maybe he had disappointed his own parents.

Thinking of Anna, of her saying, "How's Mr. Happyrock?," Digger said, "You don't sound quite like yourself, Eliot. Spring Break's coming at a good time. Are you doing anything fun next week, anything out of the ordinary?"

"The shadow crawls," Eliot repeated, frowning, but then he turned back to Digger and said, "Nothing out of the ordinary." Then he smiled, making Digger think that teeth could be more frightening than attractive, especially when the grinner's gums were receding. Eliot exhaled his mirth and asked, "What about you, Professor Diggerson? Are you done with your second book? Have you killed off a couple more writing professors? Am I one of the victims?"

Digger again pictured Ned Dunlap, his angry fictional adjunct, but he smiled back at Gladstone, who was non-fictionally full-time and seemed pretty non-fictionally angry, too. "You're not a victim, you're the killer," he decided to say, and both men laughed. Then Digger continued, "I'm done with the first main draft. Over Spring Break, after I grade about a hundred papers, I'm going to revise the draft. If I have time, I'll then edit and proofread. With luck, I can send it off to the publisher by the end of the month."

"Then I wish you luck," said Eliot, actually bowing slightly and then swiveling away and disappearing. Digger heard him say melodramatically, "The shadow crawls," and then a door opened and closed.

*That was strange*. To dispell the image of Eliot's breathing smile, Digger read Diana Pell's poem, which *was* in fact dark. The words resonated, though, and Digger looked at the whole Dream Board and felt a sense of pride, of accomplishment. Perhaps Spring Break would lead to several more additions.

Later that day, Digger was alone in his office, everyone else's having left the Humanities corridor, even Gloria Swanson, who an hour past had bid him a "happy and productive break!" *Gloria!* Thank God that she no longer tried to set him up with every middle-aged female! His secretary had apparently given up on him. *About time!*

Upon leaving the Faculty Offices Building, the professor noted that the campus, too, seemed deserted. Just a flock of seagulls bickering and dive bombing the earth. Digger watched them for a minute but failed to determine what they were up to. Nature was beautiful yet brutal. The gulls were no doubt eating something. Violently! Digger felt an overwhelming sense of emptiness, one that not even this spring-like mid-March early evening could temper. Turning back to his office building, he saw all dark windows, no lights on in any of the narrow openings, and in the background the Bay Bridge loomed, reminding the composition teacher of Danny Jones, the Boy who Flew so long ago, the model for his first book. *Thank you, Danny*. Walking forward again, Matthew Diggerson saw that the gazebo was empty. All the smokers, the cafeteria workers and international students, mainly Middle Eastern, were gone. The Psychology Building exuded no life, either, and Digger thought of William Watkins, of his assertion that maybe Digger had no friends, just enemies, and the tone of emptiness thickened even more, so much so that Digger almost would have welcomed Watkins' entrance into the scene. *Almost*.

Then, as he passed by the Administration Building, Digger finally saw another human being. *George North!* The student-turned-janitor was cleaning the floor, faced away from the windows. George was wearing headphones, swiveling his head back and forth. To the beat of a tune or of the repetitive task? *Probably both.* Digger sort of wanted to talk to the young man, to connect, but North never noticed him walking by. Digger left the campus having uttered not a single word, accompanied by only the gulls' disagreements.

On the drive home, Digger realized suddenly that Johnny Lambmann had never emailed him back. *No reply*. His and Johna's old friend must be pretty busy, or maybe the email had got lost in space. Digger glanced at the sky as though to find his endlessly traveling message, but instead he found a beautiful crimson twilight descending on the western horizon, and on a spur he decided to stop at the Ocean View Police Department to talk to Officer Zorn. To talk and hopefully to listen. To do something anyway, to hear something. For months, Digger had suspected that the OVPD was keeping tabs on him, following his car, watching the cottage at night. Frequently, Snodo would look out the back door and occasionally bark at the shadows, or at something concealed within them. She never barked at Inky during the day, either, so her attention couldn't be on a mysterious black nightly feline guest.

Driving west now, Digger watched the horizon's darkening, like a monstrous eye closing, the crimson turning dark grey and then almost black, like old blood. The scenery did nothing to elevate his mood. Determined, defiant even, the composition instructor turned into the OVPD lot and parked in back again, right where he had both three months and eight years earlier to discuss other murders. *Life is a circle*, he thought, and as he exited his car, he noticed that night had now almost fallen, making the hour seem late. Perhaps Officer Zorn had gone home already. Digger tried to picture what that would be like, couldn't muster up an image of the dark cop's standing before the stove with a dish of lasagna or reclining before the television with a glass of white wine. Like his old pal Detective Doyle, this female seemed like a cop only. Perhaps he was not being fair.

At the front desk, a young guy told Digger where to find Zorn (he already knew but listened to the fellow anyway), and suddenly there he was again, standing before some detective's door, poised to knock. Why did he always hesitate like this? He rapped the windowless door three times, trying to sound decisive but grimacing at the little tapping noise, the heavy object seeming to absorb most of the sound. A voice told him to "come in."

Well, she didn't look surprised, that was for sure. Neither frowning nor smiling, Officer Zorn just stared at him in the doorway, and Digger realized that she was waiting to see what the hell he wanted.

"I wanted to talk with you," he said.

"I gathered that," the woman said without a hint of warmth, but Digger laughed anyway, partly because he just wanted to release a little anxiety.

"Yes, and that's why you're the detective," he said, immediately feeling stupid. "Actually," he continued, "I wanted to talk about some suspicions, maybe a motive, and then to find out how your investigation is progressing."

Zorn looked tired. She had lines around the outsides of both eyes, lines that sloped down a bit, and Digger saw dark half circles beneath her oval eyes, too. While the policewoman still looked pretty, she lacked Anna's inner glow. Officer Zorn looked a bit frozen, but at least her pretty black eyes blinked regularly.

"Proceed," she said, turning to her computer and typing at her keyboard. *Switching screens, files*. Digger decided that cops didn't have the typical problem found in student papers: wordiness. After staring at the screen, Zorn turned back to Digger. "You have a theory?"

"Well, yes, I do." Digger hesitated. "I'm basically living the theory. You know, several years back, when I talked to Detective Doyle, we came to the conclusion that Paul Smith was the killer, and we ended up being right. We didn't know that Paul's wife, Debra, had died, causing him to go unhinged. I just knew that he was unhinged, and Doyle believed me. Now, all these years later, it's all happening again. Murders. Suspicions. Just like then, I suspect some of my colleagues. I know that sounds horrible, and I know that you cops suspect me even, because I knew the two victims, or sort of knew them. I actually hardly knew either woman, had just met the second one. But Doyle didn't believe in coincidences, and neither do you, I'm sure. Neither do I. I'm thinking that one of my colleagues might be murdering women who seem interested in, or attracted to, me."

There it was, the red meat on the rug, as the author Donald Barthelme had once written about unappetizing facts glistening in the light of reality.

"Do you mean that one of your colleagues does not wish you to be happy?"

"Yes, I think so. I think that's it."

"Why is that, Professor Diggerson? Why would you be so important to one of your colleagues? Is it your position? Does a colleague covet your position?"

"No, he covets my book."

"Your book?" said Zorn, looking back to her screen. "You mean your murder mystery, *Composition Murder*?"

"I know that it sounds impossible, implausible, but that's what I now believe."

"And you have suspects?"

"Many!" But now that the time had come, Digger felt reluctant to reveal his accusations. Hadn't this happened with Doyle? Hadn't he told the other detective about Bill

Jacobs, for instance? That had not been fair, and Digger decided to leave the curmudgeon adjunct off the list this time.

"Who?"

"Well, a number of my peers, most of them, almost all of them, didn't react with what I would call interest or pleasure at the news of my book. Johna did, and then she was killed. When Johna was asking about *Composition Murder*, another teacher was there, Lou Knightly, but I don't really suspect him. Maybe just a little bit. Lou's a full-timer, and another full-timer told me a story about jealousy, his jealousy over a peer's publishing of a book. His name's Eliot Gladstone. He's older than I am, Lou's younger. Neither man's married, for that matter. No kids. I don't know why I mention those facts, maybe just that nobody would be around to see what either man's doing. I don't know. I have no evidence, Officer Zorn, just that jealousy theory, really, and I do feel as though my cottage is being watched. Of course, that could be you police."

"We lack the resources to 'watch' all our suspects, Professor Diggerson." Was that a whisp of a smile?

"I didn't kill Johna or that Valerie woman," said Digger, suddenly wanting this cold cop to believe him.

But Officer Zorn remained closed mouthed. Then she said, "Do you have other suspects?"

"Dozens!" said Digger, "One less likely than the next. Like Jay Moore, an adjunct, but he seems suspicious mainly because he blinks a lot." He stopped to let that absurdity sink in.

"And you do not trust people who blink?"

"Not like that, not rapid-fire blinking," laughed Digger, and then he continued. "One of our faculty was once State Poet, and she has a son who just returned from Switzerland. Some sort of problem, I don't know what. Maybe it's him, doing it for his mother. His name's

Michael Pell. And then another faculty member—another adjunct—has a husband who's a private investigator, and she's had black eyes. Not just sleepless shadows but actual injuries, at least it looked that way. I don't know, Officer Zorn, but that private-eye vocation seems suspicious to me. Her name's Patricia Pauley, but I don't remember his name. Oh, wait! I do. It's Bob. Bob Pauley. I know I'm rambling, and I know that these people might all be innocent, that most must be, but I believe my theory now. I believe that extreme jealousy could be, *is*, the motive. I believe that both women were killed to keep me from more success. From feeling happy, basically. Oh, and I forgot a piece of tangible proof! I do have some evidence! One of my students, Twitch, knew about the second victim's knowing me, and when I asked him how he knew, he told me that one of my *teacher friends* had told him during final exams last semester. In other words, the middle of December! Right when the Valerie woman was murdered! So how could he—the unknown man—have known that fact? You guys never released that information to the public, right?"

"Twitch?" asked Officer Zorn.

"That's his nickname. He has a sort of hitch in his shoulders, sort of a twitch, but that's what he wants to be called," Digger added, seeing the confused frown on the officer's face and feeling a little embarrassed, maybe guilty about using the name.

"What is his actual name?"

Digger had to think for a minute, the "Michael" coming immediately (everybody seemed to be named *Michael*), but the last name not so fast since Digger never called students by their last name. "Michael Whitman," he answered, and the lady cop typed into the computer.

Then Zorn nodded and looked back at the professor, apparently requesting more information, so Digger said,

"I already talked to Twitch about the man, and he just said that he was old like me, like all his teachers, and that he wouldn't be able to identify him, because he has facial-recognition issues. Still, that's proof, right? Somebody outside my office knew about my knowing the second victim, who had just been murdered—what––a couple nights earlier?"

Zorn just stared and nodded.

"I know that sounds egotistical, like why would someone care about me that much? But I don't think it's really me. I think it's some deep-seated disappointment and self-loathing, some despair at not succeeding. You see, all us writing teachers want to be authors. Just like all you cops must want to be, I don't know, FBI agents or something like that."

Zorn smiled at that comparison, and her aura changed completely. She looked like a human. She looked again like Anna.

Soon after, resuming his drive home, Digger felt transformed, light, happy even. He had convinced Officer Zorn of his innocence and given her a new path to hunt. *Even made her smile!* On TV, murderers who had done what he did, gone to the cops, had been attempting to redirect the investigation, to create a red herring, but Zorn had known that Digger was not doing that, that he was, in fact, trying to help. *And he had!* For the past few months, he had been more caught up in his own fictional murders to worry much about the two non-fictional ones, but now he had dealt with both. And his second book had spawned that jealousy theory, the one that seemed to cement coincidence, that Kevin Bacon connection. One Degree of Separation. Digger clicked on the radio, heard the chorus to "Creep," and thought first of Ned Dunlap, then of Paul Smith, of Lou the Lick Lipper, Jay the Blinker, Eliot the Breather, and then of his student Twitch, for some reason, maybe just that the boy was different, a little awkward, off center just a bit. How could Twitch have remembered Johna's face from last summer but not a man's from last December, just a couple months later? A man who had supposedly talked to him, too. If the boy had made up the "teacher friend," then only one conclusion arose, an impossible one. *No way!*

Outside the car, night had firmly clamped down on Ocean View, yet Digger's little Toyota glowed internally with golden dashboard lights, creating a haven in the darkness, and the writer knew that his cottage home would do the same. Snodo was there, patrolling against the night, and Simba was still there, too, drifting further into shadow but still clinging on, still giving the present a future, rather than another corpse for the past.

## Chapter 14: To Divide

To balance, to compare, to divide—think of a semicolon in each of these ways. And once again think of the Beatles, whose melodies work well to inspire grammar-helping lyrical reminders. Can you hear Paul McCartney's lament to lost love?

Comma splice, if you read aloud they don't sound nice.
They make your readers read your sentence twice,
So end your first statement right.
You must edit so, your punctuation shows what you want to say.
A semicolon divides two thoughts the right way.

For the first three days of Spring Break, that Saturday, Sunday, and Monday, Digger graded papers, his EN 102 students' second main project, a comparison of symbolism in two works, Hemingway's "Hills Like White Elephants" and Obreht's "Blue Water Djinn." On the surface, the two short stories could not seem less similar due to the stark landscape and minimalistic descriptions in the former compared to the layered richness of the latter's seaside scenes, but both tales breathed double meanings. Digger liked to use these stories, too, because his students enjoyed them. Their compositions reflected that fact, too, since most of the students offered at least good (i.e., B level) content, what Digger liked to call 'paragraphing control,' the ability to organize, focus, and develop each block of information, as well as to stay on task, to maintain the assignment's purpose. Of course, many of the students had sentencing-control issues due to grammatical problems, such as wordiness, comma needs, run-ons, dangling modifiers—all the usual culprits that divided readers from the writer's message. Students historically and logically gave English teachers a negative label as 'hard graders' due to their critiquing of everything about an essay, not only what the student said, but how he or she delivered the information. However, Digger always told students to look at his grades as *friends*, as *guides* to what they needed in order to strengthen their skills.

With the wave of papers met and turned, the responsibilities completed, Digger spent the next three days revising, petting Simba, revising, playing with Snodo, revising, looking out at his blue spruce (no blue LED lights now) and at the birds, revising and then editing and finally proofreading, finishing *Murderous Mistakes* late on Thursday night, or more specifically, very early on that Friday morning. *65,464 words!* In the final chapter, which Digger had actually written earlier but with a different killer, Ned Dunlap had met his end after trying to knock off Billy D Wilder in a reckless car chase through the midnight streets of Ocean Side, the quasi-fictional town. Billy D would live to teach and sleuth again, perhaps in a third book tentatively titled *The Dart of Persuasion*, but Matthew Diggerson was too spent to give a future text too much consideration yet.

That morning he woke feeling a warm, rough washcloth on his face, but it was just Snodo's tongue. Digger had fallen asleep on his couch, his face within easy range of the white pony, who was now doing her little dragon dance, pulling her front feet a few inches off the ground and plopping them down in unison, then repeating the move, again and again. She was emitting a cooing growl, too, and Digger knew that tune: "Take Me Out!"

Digger raised himself into a seated position, stretched his arms, thought of rich, black coffee, and said, "Want to go out?" to Snodo. Then he glanced down at Simba, curled up and still unconscious, a few feet away from her cushioned rug bed. "Simba!" he called, and when he shook the lion dog gently, Simba froze suddenly, her eyes opening, and then her muscles settled back, her eyelids closing, her mind slipping slowly into slumber again. She stayed curled up, so Digger dug his hands beneath her belly, feeling the thick fur, the baggy body, *like an old punched-out pillow*, and hoisted the sagging animal into a standing position, into consciousness. She felt like a big bean bag that had lost half its beans. "C'mon, Simba!" The three went out back to find a cool but dry morning, the sun sharp but weak. When Simba fell into a squat, Digger grabbed the top of her harness and held her up a bit as the old Corgi mix peed and peed. When she was done, Digger plucked a few handfuls of Simba's double-coated fur off her shanks, white tufts tipped in gold and brown, and tossed them to the wind and to the sparrows, who seemed to be waiting just for those soft clumps. Snodo chased the little birds into hopping flights. Digger could hear the slapping of the ever-moving bay against the earth, and then a gull called, "Eyutt, yut, yut. Eyutt, yut, yut." Beyond the wooden gate, which Digger noticed needed painting again (*those damn sea breezes!*), no cat appeared this morning. Where was Inky? *Who was Inky!*

At nine, Digger put both dogs' breakfast bowls down, Simba's in the kitchen, Snodo's in the living room, but Simba showed no interest in the food. Feeling cold, sad, recognizing the sudden weight of Time, Digger put her bowl on the counter, *for later*, and then looked out the back door. The black cat, Inky, was still not present, but a dozen sparrows were busy bickering over Simba's fur. He watched the little flighty battles for a minute or two, his mind distracted. Digger wanted to start reading and revising his "Murderous" completed draft right away again, because a piece of writing was never really finished, but since he knew that *space* would make him more objective, he worked on Project Three lesson plans instead. He called this next project the "Connections Essay" because students had to find some comparison between one of the short stories read so far and their own lives, perhaps a plot connection, a character similarity (with themselves or a loved one), or even some element of fiction linkage, such as similar symbols or ironies. Most students found some meaningful connection between a character and someone they knew, quite often a sibling or a friend who had died. Digger was always surprised at how many young people had already faced death. At their age, he had been naïve, he realized.

At eleven, Simba refused the food, and at two she didn't even seem to notice the proffered bowl, which now included tempting turkey slices. At four, the lion just slept, and she did not eat with her rambunctious little sister at five. That night, Digger decided to call Sarah Palmer, the veterinarian, if Simba wouldn't eat in the morning. He knew that she worked on Saturdays, which was often when he would make his appointments, and he also knew that she would make housecalls, that she would be willing to travel to help an animal, to ease a pet's pain, to put the lion dog down.

On the couch again the next morning, Digger woke and immediately thought of Simba. Both dogs were three sheets to the wind below him on the floor, but Snodo felt either his consciousness or a ripple in the turning earth (or maybe both) and raised her head, the white mane sticking out in all directions. She looked like a hungover Billy Idol. Simba's tongue was hanging out, and for a moment Digger thought that she had slipped off during and into the night. When he stroked her ear, though, the old dog's eyelids fluttered, and then she pulled herself onto her chest, like a cow relaxing in a field. Simba's tongue continued to hang out, though, making Digger think of Lou Knightly. Digger remembered going to the police station and offering Officer Zorn Lou's name. Maybe the cops were checking out the Lip Licker right now. Jay, Eliot, and who else? Could his jealousy theory actually be true? Nothing else connected the two victims, nothing but a vendetta against him. Still, the accusations prickled at Digger, the bubblings of guilt. *Things to do*, though.

The three beings at 111 Cottage Street made their way to the back door, Snodo capering in the lead, Simba tottering at the rear. The mid-March air was cool, but the bite-less sea breezes spoke of spring. A gaggle of sparrows complained about Snodo's charging presence, or perhaps they were demanding more of Simba's fur. Today would be the lion dog's last probably, for if she refused to eat again, then Simba would just waste away. Picturing his first dog's getting thinner and more decrepit, Digger felt a resolve to phone his vet. It all depended on breakfast. One word, *breakfast*, a thin line dividing life from death.

Back inside, Digger made coffee, clicked on his computer, and then checked email. No new messages. During vacations and between semesters, OVC sent out few emails, so quite often Digger would find just the previous day's last one, which these days tended to be from himself: whenever he worked on his book, he would email the text to himself just in case his computer died overnight. Perhaps it would have been better if Simba had done that, just slipped away without awakening. The aura of emptiness that had gripped Digger as he left school the previous week began to grow beneath his chest. To take his mind off Simba, off the pending breakfast, the judgment, Digger went back to the computer and checked a couple sports sites to see how the Celtics had done last night (he had decided not to watch the game) and to discover any news. Since the NBA trade deadline had passed a month earlier, Digger would probably find no real news, but the sportswriters had to say something, right? *Good!* The C's had won, beaten the Hawks, so Digger checked the Box Score and then read about other games. Snodo spent the time moping at his feet, lifting her head suddenly every time her human so much as twitched, thinking of her food bowl, no doubt. The minutes snailed along for everyone.

It was time for breakfast.

Snodo engulfed hers, as usual (Digger added a little water to the mix so that it would slow her down), but Simba could not even be bothered to enter the kitchen. When Digger put the bowl before her in the living room and stroked her velvet ears, the old girl just lay her head back down, her gums and tongue prominent again. Time had claimed his dog, his beautiful Simba. Digger put her bowl on the kitchen counter and called the vet's office. Doctor Palmer was not now available, so Digger told the receptionist what he wanted and then waited, drinking coffee and watching the backyard view, for her to call him back. After a few minutes or hours or days, the phone rang.

"I'm so sorry about Simba," said Doctor Sarah Palmer, who had known the lion dog longer than almost anyone.

"She's ready," said Digger, "but I don't want her to … to pass away anywhere but here, at home. I don't want to drive her somewhere else and then have her put down."

"I understand, Matt. I'll bring a tech and come after work, around five-thirty."

"I'll be here, Sarah, probably in the back yard. Just come around back down the driveway. Simba always loved the back yard, so that's where we'll do it, okay?"

"It's sunny now, but it's supposed to storm later. Maybe we'll get lucky."

After the vet returned the phone to her receptionist, Digger read off his credit-card number to pay for the home visit. It would cost twice the usual amount. *Who cared!*

That Saturday ground by, yet every time Digger looked at the clock, an hour had passed. Digger began to count down Simba's life. *Six hours to go. Five hours to go.* He spent the last four hours out back with both pups, Snodo's enjoying the extended outing. Simba lay in the grass, but Digger noticed that her eyes continually opened and rotated. She was taking it all in, peaceful and relaxed.

He dug a hole before the back fence, halfway across, and for about a foot down he had no problems. The dirt came out easily, but then Digger hit sand. Every time he shoveled some out, more slipped in from the hole's sides, so Digger went to his garage and found some old plastic storage crate covers. They would do. He jammed the lids into his two-foot wide hole and pushed them down into the sand. Then he kept up the process, pushing down the plastic covers every time he scooped out more sand (it was easier to use a coffee can than the shovel). As he scooped, Digger wondered what funeral directors did in desert countries and then remembered mummies. But did all citizens get that treatment? Was the average person from an Arab state simply cremated rather than wrapped? Cremation would be an appropriate end for any man, he decided. *Ashes to ashes*. Then Digger thought about life's holes and how they didn't usually fill themselves in like this, how they usually just stayed holes. Then he thought of Simba and how the lion dog had helped to plug a bit of the crater left by Anna's leaving. These conclusions slipped in and out of Digger's mind as he knelt and scooped, the big hole getting deeper and colder. Using the crate lids, he made the grave wider at the bottom, comfortable. He would pull the lids out after lowering the body and covering it with her blanket. Against the sand.

An hour after he had started, Digger had a cool, dry grave, and at its base he stretched out Simba's rug-bed. He placed her little blanket just beyond the hole, keeping it clean. *Three hours to go.*

Simba wasn't the only one not to eat that day, which turned into a harbinger of spring and even summer. Digging had made Digger sweat, and as he lay in the grass alongside his aged dog, the composition instructor felt the warm breezes dry out each hair follicle. Gulls flew out to sea, one after another, as though late to a meeting, and inland an immense swarm of black birds, probably starlings, zigged and zagged above the treeline. What was their purpose in creating such chaotic beauty in the sky? The flock looked like tangible air, *Van Gogh wind*, and as he watched the birds dance, the sun's glare made him blink and shut his eyes, turning Digger's closed eyelids orange. *Two hours to go.*

Simba's harness looked a little bulky now, as she lay in the grass, like a horse stretched out with its saddle still strapped on. Digger unclicked it on top and eased the harness from beneath his old friend. "There you go, Simba. You're free." She looked sort of naked, and without the harness, her long Corgi body seemed even longer. A flowing golden, tan, and white. The black ear and muzzle hairs all turned a silvery white now, *all frosted*, as though Time had waved its wand right in the lion dog's face. Sitting in the silence and stroking Simba, Digger felt the earth moving beneath him, above him. The starlings, though, had taken their dance to distant skies.

With a single sixty-minute cycle left, Digger groomed his pup one last time, pulling tufts of fur off her sides and back legs, so that the back yard began to resemble a sheep shearing. As he brushed her thick fur, Digger told

Simba how *good* she was, how *beautiful*, how *special*, and the lion dog acknowledged none of these sentiments but didn't disagree, either. Probably, Digger didn't even need the vet, but he wanted to help Simba along now, to ease her journey. When he heard his name ("Matt!"), Digger was startled. Time had come.

Snodo seemed to recognize the two medical women, for she made herself scarce, rare for the little unicorn, who almost always wanted to be in the midst of things. She had retreated to the porch and stayed there during the entire procedure.

Doctor Sarah Palmer and her female assistant (one of the front desk women, Digger couldn't remember her name) worked quickly, attaching what looked like an IV to Simba's rear leg and removing objects from a bag. Digger didn't watch them, didn't want to see what they were doing. Cupping his dog's face, he lay right before Simba and looked into her eyes, glazed by cataracts but still alight. He could see the shape of his head in each of Simba's orbs. He could even distinguish his own mirrored eyes and oval head within them. Circles within circles within circles. Life.

"We're ready, Matt," said Sarah. "I have attached an intravenous catheter to ensure that the procedure goes smoothly. First, I will inject a sedative to put her to sleep, that is, to make Simba unconscious. It won't be at all painful, Matt. Then we'll add the other drug, the euthanasia solution, to stop Simba's heart. It will be very quick, Matt, just seconds."

"Okay," he said to the veterinarian, and then he faced his dog and told her how beautiful she was, over and over, just that mantra. "You're beautiful." *She was*. Doctor Palmer announced the sedative, and Simba's body drooped, flattened. Her neck felt as though all the muscles and most of the weight had slid right out of it, so Digger held her soft, light head up a bit and continued to say "Beautiful!" Then the vet asked him if *he* were "ready" (irony, it seemed), and after he nodded that he was, within seconds, Digger saw the light disappear from Simba's eyes, which lost their depth just like that, leaving a greenish haze, like moonlight on a pond. Digger noticed that the two women were cleaning up and then standing. He looked up at them.

"I have never done this outside," said Sarah Palmer. "It was really beautiful." The tech nodded. She had hardly said a word, but her eyes told Digger how she felt about Simba.

"Thank you," he told the two women, who each bent down, petted Simba one last time, said "good bye, Simba," and then the same to Digger, who suddenly found himself alone under an immense blue sky, bright and happy, a robin's egg. *Yin and yang*, thought the grieving man. Sometimes life's juxtapositions were easy to see. Only later would the storm move in from the ocean, bringing the appropriate tone, moody and mysterious, to end Simba's last day on earth. Yes, Digger had been *lucky*.

That night, Snodo stayed especially close to Digger, and the next morning, she ran right to the spot where Simba had lain and released her soul. Digger had sat with her body for an hour, *Simba's wake*, and only once had he been disturbed. Graham had stuck his head over the fence and said, "Your dog?" and then "That's too bad." During the vigil, the storm's first clouds had moved in, and the breezes had grown cold. Only in New England could the seasons shift as a person watched the sky. As the storm moved in from the sea, Digger had worried—just a bit—about rain interrupting Simba's wake. Then he knew that it wouldn't, that the sky would hold off for the hour in recognition of the beautiful energy just released. For the wait, Snodo had joined him eventually, after making sure that the vet and her assistant were actually gone. She had walked around the prone body and sniffed at Simba, and Digger had waved a fly off her earthly remains, then again, again. When the hour had passed and Digger picked up Simba to carry her to her grave, he had noticed that her body was already stiffening. Simba was really dead. After he had knelt and placed her on the rug-bed and wiped off some fallen sand, Digger had told his first dog good bye, covered her with the little gray blanket (it had black paw prints as a design), pulled the plastic tops one by one from the hole's sides, and then filled in the remaining grave with sand and then dirt. Snodo had skirted the hole repeatedly, smelling the deep earth and the other dog's place in it. When the ground was all flat and Simba farther away than ever, Digger had still felt the hole's presence. *Sometimes there just wasn't enough dirt*, he thought, and he decided to find a big pretty stone for a marker.

As he sat out back the next morning, Digger thought of that stone again. Where could he get some nice quartz? Maybe he should purchase an actual tombstone, a small one, like those white tablets for children hundreds of years ago. The old cemeteries always displayed rows of little white rectangles, whole generations lost it seemed, and the balanced lines of stones had always reminded Digger of teeth. *Here Lies Simba, my friend.* The tail of the previous day's storm still held the scene in a gloomy grip, but Digger didn't care, didn't want bright, blinding sun. He liked clouds, anyway, enjoyed the varied shapes and textures and movement. The great canvas in the sky. He noticed that the bay was louder than usual, the storm's winds slapping the water around, and he heard his neighbor's flag pole dinging in earnest. That would bother Graham. Digger sipped his coffee, black, strong, *really good.* Snodo was now investigating Simba's grave. Did she know? Snodo looked back at him, seated on the porch steps, and seemed to ask, "Is this Simba?" Birds were singing, many different types. He heard "Chicka-dee-dee-dee" repeatedly from a pair of those cute black-capped flyers, and then the distinct "Cheap" of a cardinal. Sparrows added their less melodious peepings, too, and Digger saw that those little brown birds were hopping all over the place. *Simba's fur!* The sparrows were after all the fur tufts from Digger's grooming the late afternoon before. He watched a pair bounce over to a tuft and yank it from each other's beaks, the victor flying off with the white and gold softness, the loser standing confused and just a bit affronted. But there was plenty of fur to be had. Over and over, a dozen sparrows, at least, swept the yard. Over and over.

Digger closed his eyes and imagined the bay's breathing, heard the wind's flat melodies, and felt the earth's turning, turning, all while the little birds carried Simba to the sky.

## Chapter 15: To See-saw

Students love to use semicolons and more often than not fail to do so correctly, so with the help of Johnny Cash, here's one last tip for employing this mark the right way.

Two thoughts with no connecting word, show a comma splice, which can be heard.
A comma/transition and comma/pronoun, often show where run-ons can be found.
Well, I forgot to read my prose aloud.
My sentences ran on, but I didn't hear the sound.
Didn't hear the see-saw, of a semicolon, a semicolon.

May's beginning meant the spring semester's last ten days of classes, but for Digger, that conclusion brought less excitement than usual. Simba's departure hung heavily on him, yet then he would picture his second book, which the publisher had accepted and was now preparing for publication. That pending second text could not have come at a better time. Digger had requested that the cover depict a shadowy figure holding a knife and suggesting the college setting, perhaps with a blackboard and desk. The publisher had emailed a handful of options, and Digger had picked the one that most reflected his image. Anticipating a print copy arriving in the mail made the writing teacher's head float, but then he would look around and not find his sleeping lion. *Simba!* May would be especially bipolar this year.

With Simba's burial, the back yard had become a shrine, a patch where Time could no longer wield its weapons, its frozen touch, since it had already shone its only real power:  to take. Digger realized that he had been building the yard as a portrait for that very reason, giving his small patch of the world some permanence.

Been grooming the backyard atmosphere ever since Anna's departure. *AA*, After Anna. The ethereal blue tree and the way it would shiver in a breeze, the narrow passage through the sea grass to the beach and then the deep blue water, the invitation to the birds, who would then sew Heaven to his earth, repeatedly. He had created pathways for all of life's angels, and standing in his kitchen and gazing out back, Digger could sense existence ripple through his veins. And feel alive. *Simba!* Was it his imagination or were the sparrows unsettled now that they no longer had the lion dog's fur to nestle their nests? Was he also imagining Snodo's restlessness, the way she would look all around the cottage as though searching for her adopted sister? The way she continually peered out the back door?

Since spring break, Digger had been taking his remaining dog to school on both non-teaching days, and on his Monday, Wednesday, Friday schedule, he would leave a few Kongs strewn about the cottage, those heavy-rubber toys with hollow centers that could hold biscuits and other treats, keeping dogs focused and busy as they worked to unearth the happy surprises inside. The Kongs would occupy Snodo for a bit, and Digger would just have to hope that she would not be too lonely after the distractions ran out. Once a week, too, he would go without lunch on a teaching day and drive home to let Snodo out back and to fill the Kongs again, to show her that she was not alone, just as Simba had done for him so long ago.

On the next-to-last Monday, Digger sat in his kitchen, checked his lesson plan for the day, and then put a Xeroxed copy of *Murderous Mistake*'s cover (downloaded from the publisher's email) into his briefcase. The eerie cover and his own printed name made him think of Gwena Schmidt, and on the spur of the moment he called his old colleague to tell her about the new book and to ask about Richard. Surely the two were up by nine-thirty.

"Hello!" Gwena's unmistakable voice sounded harried. The greeting had almost seemed like both a question and an accusation.

"Gwena, hello, it's Matthew Diggerson. Did I catch you at a bad time?"

"Oh, Digger! It's Richard, he's gone missing again!" Gone missing? *Again?*

"Have you contacted the police, sent out a Silver Alert?"

"Yes, yes, hours ago! He always sneaks out when I'm asleep! He gets through the locks, you see!"

"Can I do anything to help?"

"Just pray, Digger, just pray. I do a lot of that these days."

"I will," said Digger, and then Gwena hung up. He had never mentioned his reason for calling, and Gwena had not asked, of course. Digger wondered where Richard Schmidt was. Could he have taken the car? He hadn't thought of asking Gwena that, and the image of a demented old man driving Ocean View's streets surfaced. How many older Americans now had Alzheimer's? That disease and the subtler one, Time, had killed off nearly all of the country's Greatest Generation, and next up were the Baby Boomers. Digger pictured demented seniors tottering about like zombies in *The Walking Dead,* and then he thought of America's youth, of Autism's explosion and spread, and everywhere was madness. That's how the great civilizations fall, he realized. *From within.* Where was Richard now, and was Paul Smith still in his cage? Who was the current killer, and how would Digger react when he first saw Eliot, Lou, and Jay Moore, all of whom he had implicated to Officer Dark Anna Zorn and all of whom he had avoided since spring break? *No*, he had seen Lou in passing, in the Humanities corridor, but only to wave in gesture. Eliot had not visited the Dream Board, not when the Chair was in his office anyway, and Digger had been going home too early to see Jay, right after his classes rather than at five, because he was worried about Snodo's being alone on those days.

No doubt to question Digger's phone call, the white unicorn had previously entered the kitchen and was now looking out the back door. Digger wondered if she were looking for Simba. *That's where Simba left, after all.* Digger looked out, too, and saw a single blue jay tear by and land in the spruce, immediately glaring down, right and left, by cocking its head repeatedly. Digger knew that another jay would soon appear because those dinosaur-like aviators traveled together, usually in trios. Yes, another jay crash landed on the fence and began its careful survey for enemies and for food, and then a third plowed right into the middle of the yard. No doubt the leader. The jays were like a well-oiled swat team. Suddenly, Digger remembered that as a child he had named blue jays 'Out-a-my-way birds' because of their violent-looking impatience and deliberation. His mother had then called them that for years, along with her son's other labels, such as 'Upside-down birds' for nuthatches and 'Hoptoe birds' for juncos. How had he forgotten this? How could Time so completely cover memories? And people, too. People like Richard Schmidt.

He looked at the clock on the microwave: 9:39. Bit too late to call his mother, he had to get to school. Maybe he would call her that night, though. Hopefully, Richard would be back home then.

"I have to go, Snodo, but I'll be back early, before dinner, okay?"

Some twenty minutes later, Digger pinned his second book's cover to the Dream Board, where he also found an editorial written by Lou Knightly, published in the

*Ocean View Weekly*. The piece, four paragraphs, was political, torching the current Washington regime, sarcastic. Digger laughed at the ending and thought of Bill Jacobs. *What would the rabid Republican Bill say?* Lou's editorial offered an introduction, two body paragraphs, and a conclusion. *Classic!* Digger glanced back at his new book cover, liking how its green aura balanced well with the cobalt look of *Composition Murder*. He was an author! *Twice! And just look at all those other offerings,* he thought, the songs and poems, the editorial, the play, and the scholarly article (even if not yet published). The three-foot by three-foot board displayed many pieces now, and they had become a source of conversation even for those people who had yet to pin their dreams.

Next fall, Digger predicted, the board would really blossom after those long summer months, yet the composition teacher had to stay focused on *this* semester, on finishing out his fourth main project, which for his EN 102 classes was a comparison of an author's life to one of his or her own short stories covered in class. With this research assignment, students discovered that Franz Kafka had endured almost as hard a life as his most famous character, the cockroach Gregor Samsa, and that other famous authors, such as Hemingway and Carver, also put a mirror on their own lives when they created iconic tales like "Hills Like White Elephants" and "Cathedral." Besides these dead white male icons, Digger stressed women and minority authors, too (Juno Diaz, Tea Obreht, Alice Walker, etc.), but for this final research paper, most students chose the white males, maybe because so much had been written about them already that research was relatively easy. As a model for this assignment, Digger had written an essay about J.R.R. Tolkien, of course, discovering that the creator of Middle Earth had been strongly influenced by World

War I. The comparison assignment interested students, and the life/fiction connection offered transferable academic writing skills since other professors' assignments often required that students compare two topics: two concepts, two arguments, two works, two options. Despite the responsibility of grading, Digger actually enjoyed reading these Project Four connections papers, which he would collect via his Bridges site in about two weeks, a couple days after the end of classes.

In his first class, the eleven o'clock 'Twitch' one, Digger created quartets, writing the students' first names high up on the white board, leaving space below for each group. Centered in the space just above the names, he wrote a practice topic sentence, using Kafka's "The Metamorphosis" since the class had recently finished that long short story and since many students were using it for their final paper. Because Digger urged students to write short topic sentences (so that readers wouldn't be confused by extra nouns), his model contained just seven words: "The Samsas resemble Kafka's own family life." This focusing idea was specific enough to construct a tight body paragraph but broad enough to give students many structural choices. Reading his topic sentence aloud, Digger then explained what he wanted the groups to do and why.

"To make sure that you understand what this paper requires, as well as to suggest a logical body paragraph structure for a two-topics assignment, I'm using this topic sentence, this TS, to have us build *part* of this paragraph. We're going to create a side-by-side plan, first the story, then the beginning to the author's life section. I could put other topics in instead of 'family life,' too, so your ideas, your research, could also fit into the compare-contrast partial paragraph that we're going to make. Do you follow me? Any questions? Remember that if you have a question, then others do, too, so always feel free to ask. Okay, then, let's get started. What I want up next, and write it high on the board, is the first ST, the first structural point, for this 'family life' TS. You all have the knowledge to build at least the first half of this paragraph since you all just finished 'The Metamorphosis.' So let's see those first structural points, and remember that I've given you tips for making ST's stand out effectively."

Since all twenty students had decided to attend this class (somewhat rare, unfortunately, not to have one or two missing), Digger had made five groups, and two of them contained animated students, talkers, while the three others seemed to be communicating only through telepathy. He aimed some help at those three groups: "Remember that an ST needs to offer a narrowed topic, a breakdown of the TS's topic, and that your ST needs to show your shift into that idea." He didn't want to give them too much help, because Digger wanted the students to teach each other. One of the silent groups woke up, but the other two appeared to contain enemies, individuals lost in their own worlds. Twitch was in one of those two groups, and even the usually non-stop jabbering fellow seemed deflated today. Probably, these eight students were all burnt out by the semester, but Digger couldn't let them slumber through this important student-centered activity, which illustrated tips that he had repeated for every assignment, such as "Be specific," "Lead readers through your ideas," "Show; don't just tell," and more.

"No telepathy, now," he urged the two quiet groups. "What are you going to say right after that topic sentence? What are you going to go into first? Lead your reader." Then he added, "A chance for free minutes, of course!"

An emissary from one of the talkative quartets was already writing on the board, so Digger said, "Okay, we're off, and if your group wants a chance at free minutes, then get your example on the board. Two minutes for a great sentence, one for a good one, and then anything else is just a helpful example for everyone." Digger had made this speech before since he often created lessons that required students to write on the board.

The first student had finished, and Digger read, "The Samsas are poor." *Nice idea, but where's the transition?* From the second communicative group, another student approached the board and started writing, then another (from the quartet that had awakened).

"Good examples appearing," said Digger to the class, especially to the two quiet groups, "so if you want a shot at minutes, get your first ST up there." A student from one of the quiet groups, Jessica, leaped up although she had not talked with her peers much—if at all. Digger read the second group's first structural point example: "First, Kafka describes Gregar as a hard worker." Has a transition, but that ST doesn't reflect the 'family' topic. *No minutes there*. Spelled the name wrong, too. The third example looked very good, though: "In the short story, the family members often disagree, such as when the sister and parents fight over what to do with Gregor." *Nice!* A clear transition from the TS into "the story" and a narrowed topic of "disagreements." So far, three great examples since they provided the class with different ST's: one great, one good, one not effective. Jessica, the girl from the quiet group, finished and sat down. She had written, "The family members have different relationships with Gregor, just as Kafka did with his family." Interesting, but too broad for an ST. *Nice topic sentence idea, though.* Twitch's group still looked disfunctional, and Digger noticed his odd student's shoulders lurch and settle. He would have to intervene with that quartet after explaining the ST's on the board to all five groups.

"Great examples," he said, "because one earns two minutes, one one, and one doesn't clearly break down its topic sentence, and one *is* a topic sentence. Can you see which example fits which critique?"

After a question like this, one, two, or even three groups would usually have a member who cried, "Ours earns two minutes," so Digger wasn't surprised to hear two students, almost in tandem, declare their examples to be "great."

"One of you is correct," he replied and then gave the class a little more time. Comparisons were fundamental for learning, adding tangible proof (the examples) to sometimes fuzzy concepts (such as "focus clearly"). If knowledge led to understanding and then to actual use, then a skill could stick and transfer to future assignments. To aid in his students' understanding, Digger narrowed his questioning by saying, "Two of the four offer transitions, but only one of those two clearly breaks down the 'family' angle of the topic sentence, so can you now see which ST is great?"

"Ours," said two members from the third example's group, and Digger nodded, adding two green ink slashes (for minutes) next to the group members' names to keep track of their total. He underlined parts of their example and said, "See this 'In the short story'? That prep phrase transitions readers from the topic sentence into the first structural point, the story itself, and this 'disagree' idea focuses the first supporting section on a shared family aspect. Nice idea, one that might work with any chosen author and story."

Then he went over to the shortest ST example. "This one has a nicely narrowed topic, 'poor,' but it offers no transition, so it earns just one point." He added a single green slash near the names. "Again," Digger continued, "this 'poor' idea might fit other authors and stories, so borrow from each other, teach each other." At that advice, he heard a strange "Urp" and realized immediately that Twitch had erupted. Digger almost looked over at the lad (others did), but maintained his balance since he wanted to keep the class focused, didn't want interruptions, especially odd seal sounds. To keep the lesson on track, Digger walked over to Jessica's ST example and said, "This example's too broad for a structural point because it points to both the story and Kafka's life, but it could be a great topic sentence, one that breaks down the family members. In fact, you might have to spend a couple body paragraphs on these different relationships. Maybe sister, mother, father in story, and then a second body paragraph on Kafka's comparisons. Or you could do a sisters comparison in one paragraph, first Gregor's and then Kafka's, if he had a sister, I can't remember that." Pointing back to the example in question, Digger concluded, "So no points for this one, but this group has provided a nice topic sentence idea, maybe even two."

That gratitude did nothing toward enlivening Jessica or her three group members. Twitch laughed. Digger remembered that he hadn't explained the ST that didn't fit his written topic sentence. "This one," he said, walking to it, "does have a transition, but you don't want to overuse 'First.' Transitions like that, including 'Furthermore' and 'Finally,' often sound rigid when used in more than one body paragraph. More importantly, though, this example refers to Gregor as being 'hard working,' but that idea doesn't clearly support the 'family' topic sentence. It could if you said something like 'the only hard working family member,' and I also like that 'hard worker' idea for a paragraph focused just on a Gregor and Kafka comparison."

"One minute for the transition?" a fellow asked from the latter example's group. Digger laughed, shook his head, and then said, "Okay, next up, an illustration for the first ST, and all you groups can use either the 'poor' or the 'disagreements' idea. I'll leave those two ST's on the board as a reminder. Okay, offer your illustration, in other words, the next sentence in this body paragraph." That's all Digger said. While he wanted a story quotation next, he waited to see if his students understood that need, so he offered no more help yet. Since students in four of the groups were looking through their short story anthology, he knew that they were on the right track, but Twitch's group was still lounging like a squashed sea star. Twitch was watching Digger, who approached the group and said, "Any questions about that ST? You see how the body paragraphs for this comparison paper will probably work? You narrow to one shared aspect and then build the paragraph around two STIR sections, the first structural point, illustration, and reasoning on the story itself, the second on the author's life. So now you need an 'I,' an illustration for one of those two ST narrowed ideas."

Twitch was nodding, fairly vigorously, and Digger wondered why his usually sociable student wouldn't open his mouth. Maybe he had some problem with another student in the quartet. Who knows what happened with these young people outside of class! Since the quietest quartet's two other boys and one girl had been somewhat listless all semester, Digger had grouped them with Twitch. The teacher had thought that the talker would be a leader, would get some words out of the silent trio, but Digger's plan clearly wasn't succeeding. Collaboration didn't always work.

Then Twitch stood up, and just as Digger was about to smile and say, "Don't you need to talk to your peers before adding an illustration?" the boy stalked off, all arms and legs, *like a sinewy old farmer*, and left the classroom, somewhat slamming the door so that everybody looked up. After watching Twitch's exit, Digger turned to face the three remaining group members, who stared back at him, eyes wide open, mouths tightly shut. "Okay," he said. "Apparently Twitch is out looking for an illustration, but in the meantime you three need to find one. Where will that illustration be?"

All three students had smiled at his "out looking" comment, and the girl, Keesha, answered Digger's question: "In the story." After that point, the quiet trio perked up and ended up creating some winning examples. As the 'family connection' paragraphs grew on the board, all five groups earned at least a few minutes for early release. But Twitch did not return.

After class, on his way back to the Faculty Offices Building for the hour between his late morning and early afternoon courses, Digger thought about his strange student and decided to email him. Then he encountered another strange human, his colleague Bill Jacobs, whom Digger rarely saw at this noon hour. Jacobs was alone in the adjunct faculty office.

"Hi, Bill," said Digger in the doorway, and the bearded man, gray speckled now, looked up as though startled and confused. Digger thought of Simba.

"It's almost over," Digger said, and this time Bill Jacobs responded.

"Thank God!"

"I didn't know you were religious, Bill," smiled Digger.

"Thank God anyway," responded the man whom Digger had once accused of possibly killing his chairperson, Tobias Mann.

"Have you had a tough semester?"

"They're all tough, aren't they?"

Digger conceded that they were, but added, "You haven't yet added anything to the Dream Board. I know that you write. Why don't you add a short story?"

Jacobs didn't answer at once, so Digger waited him out.

"I haven't written for years. I gave up. I'd sent out so many manuscripts and gotten squat back, nothing. So I quit trying."

"It's hard," said Digger. "I got lucky with my publisher. Sometimes success is just timing."

The bearded older fellow looked up at Digger, who although uninvited entered the office and took a seat. "Your book started something in me, Digger. Just a little anger at first, or maybe jealousy, envy. Anger at myself. I've never found that timing. But then I started to think about writing, and now I'm actually doing it again, writing again. Over the winter break, I wrote a lot. Of course, there's no time now during the semester with all these rotten papers to fail!"

Digger ignored the usual dig at students, along with the tired "time" excuse. "What have you started writing?"

"Literature," said Bill Jacobs so that Digger wasn't sure if his murder mysteries were being negated, but he blanketed any feelings of defensiveness.

"A novel, a short story?"

"Not sure yet," said the bearded man. "It started as a short story, but then it kept going. You know, I used to think that unpublished writing was a waste of time, but over the winter break, I really enjoyed the writing itself. I'm going to finish it and then see."

"You're right, Bill. That's exactly how I approached my murder mystery. It's the journey in life that matters, not the destination."

"Put that in one of your books, Diggerson."

"Too trite for yours!"

"You said it," laughed the bearded man, and for some reason Digger stuck out his hand in farewell. Bill Jacobs and Matthew Diggerson shook hands, two solid pumps. Digger would never see Bill again.

Three hours later, restless and alone in his office, Digger had just risen to leave forty-five minutes early when Twitch appeared in the doorway.

"Professor," said the boy. "I just wanted to explain why I left class."

Digger sat down again and motioned his student into the other chair. "You seemed a little upset," he said.

"I was, but not at you or your class. It's just that everything's come down on me right now. Papers and reports and tests, and I even have to do an interview this week. I was just thinking of all that work, and then my group members weren't talking, and I wasn't focused, so I just left to get some work accomplished. I'm sorry if it seemed disrespectful."

"Twitch," said Digger, "I'm too old to feel disrespected, and you've been a good student, both this semester and last. And I remember the burdens of a college workload. College is all about managing all your projects, organizing your time, and of course reading. College is still mainly reading."

"A lot of reading!" said the young fellow, and his shoulders heaved and settled. Digger wondered what his affliction was, whether it was physical or mental, or both.

"Don't worry about today, Twitch, and your workload will soon be a thing of the past. Until next semester anyway!"

"Yeah," said Twitch, and then the young man exclaimed, "Have they caught your friends' killer yet? I've seen nothing on the news." The boy could certainly use some work with transitions!

Digger didn't really want to talk about the killings, yet he had to say something. "Me neither," he responded, adding, "I have no idea, but at least there hasn't been another murder in close to half a year now."

"Yeah, it's been a long time. That's good. Do the cops have any leads?"

"Twitch, the police don't share their information with college writing teachers!"

"Yeah, especially when they're a suspect, huh?"

*Friggin' Twitch!* "Not anymore, though," said Digger. "That was just a coincidence. And you haven't seen the man you talked to again, have you?"

"No, like I said, I'm not so good with faces. Plus, if that guy was the killer, I don't really want to talk with him again. In fact, I was a little nervous coming down here again, but I saw your door open."

"You're smart to be careful, Twitch. You never know."

"Killers everywhere!" The boy sounded sort of happy about that, as though he had just said, "Have a great summer!"

"You have a great summer, Twitch," said Digger, who actually wanted to leave early, and the boy took the hint and unfolded his gangly appendages and rose. After he said, "You, too" and exited, however, the Dream Board caught the student's attention.

"Your second book!" he announced. "I like that cover. Eerie, and I like green. Green for the Boston Celtics!"

"My sentiments exactly," smiled Digger, who found both topics—his book and basketball— worth staying for, more appealing than non-fictional murders. Twitch was looking at the board's other entries now.

"This is a lot of stuff," he said. "Poems and plays and articles. I don't have time now, but I'll stop by and read some later."

Then the two males, one with most of his life ahead of him, the other with at least half his behind, thought about the long hallway leading up to the board.

"Maybe you shouldn't check it until next semester," said Digger.

"Yeah, I think I'll wait, and I'll wait till I see your door open down here again, too." At that wise decision, the teacher and his student laughed. Then Twitch disappeared down the hall and out of Digger's life. Digger couldn't hear any footsteps, and he thought of how the lad walked like a giant praying mantis. Legs unfolding and settling down, silent. Getting up from his chair again, Digger looked down the empty corridor and then closed his door, sat back at his desk, and glanced out the window. Twitch was moving away in those lunging strides toward the Psyche Building. Maybe he and William Watkins were going to discuss some case history that nobody else cared about. "Maybe your colleagues just don't like you," Digger imagined Watkins saying again, but that voice had been erased this semester, *almost*. Still, a killer still roamed Ocean View, perhaps even Ocean View College, and that person might, in fact, not like Digger one bit. The writing teacher tried to conjure the image of Twitch, right outside this door, being told about Digger's connection to the second victim. Which of his colleague's had known that fact? And how? Digger had told nobody about the cops' suspicions toward him, not even his own mother. Whom had the strange boy talked to last December? Only the killer could have known.

That conclusion, repeated yet again, still sent a ripple down Digger's spine, and he scanned the quad one more time, studying the stillness for approaching enemies. Twitch had walked out of view, but then Digger spotted a small flock of gulls circling the library's left tower. He thought of vultures. On both clock towers, the time read four twenty-two, and as usual at this time of late afternoon, shadows stretched from both lighthouse imitations, just pale lines, reaching. Thinking of a faceless killer, of Snodo's being alone, of calling his mother, and suddenly of Richard Schmidt, Digger got up and left.

At home, he thought of calling Gwena, but he didn't want to bother her in case she were resting from the ordeal of a wandering spouse. So after going out back with Snodo and then feeding her, Digger called his mother, who answered after the third ring. "Hello!" She sounded a little put out.

"Did I catch you at a bad time?"

"No, no. No, Matthew. I was just indisposed."

"You were in the bathroom," Digger laughed.

"Maybe I was," said Jean Diggerson, adding, "So what's so important? To what do I owe this call?"

"Nothing really," said Digger, and, in fact, he couldn't remember why he had wanted to connect with her. Then he thought of the blue jays. "Oh, yeah! I thought of something today that made me think of you. Remember when we used to watch the birds and the names I made up for them?"

"Like 'Upside-down birds' for nuthatches? Of course, Matthew. You were always so interested in nature. You were a cute little guy!"

"Do you remember 'Get-out-of-my-way birds'?"

"Of course! Blue jays! The way they charge right in and scatter all the other birds, the way they squawk so loudly."

"I saw a trio of them do just that this morning, and then I thought of my old name for them. I hadn't thought of that name in, I don't know, decades!" He had almost said "centuries."

"Well, you're not getting any younger, Matthew."

"When I think of names like that, from my early childhood, I feel pretty young."

"It's just that our minds, as we age, go back more easily to early in life. That's why older people remember a day fifty years ago better than yesterday."

"Yeah, but we're not that old, mom!"

"I'm eighty-one, Matthew, and you're almost fifty."

"Neither is old these days, mom. Eight-one is like the new sixty."

"Who said that?"

"Well, I just made up that number."

"That's what I thought, Matthew. How are you doing? How's that white dog? Is she a little more calm now?"

"Snodo's fine. She misses Simba. She looks and smells for her everywhere, and I see Simba everywhere still. I really miss her."

"Simba was a really good dog. Calm and always happy. Oh, Matthew, you always got so wrapped up in animals. I remember the turtles you had as a boy."

"I remember that baby box turtle. Animals taught me about death."

"Death! Matthew, you also always get so, so, serious, but maybe that's the writer in you."

"A writer of murder mysteries, serious?"

"You know I'm right, Matthew. Have you started your third one yet? Have you gotten a copy of the second? You know I don't like to order things off the computer. I just don't know how. You have to know where to click."

"I'll get you a copy, mom. As soon as I get one in the mail, and that should be this month. I'm almost done with the semester, another week and a half and then a bunch of papers. I'll visit in June and bring a copy then, or I'll order one online and have it delivered to you."

"Thank you, Matthew. That would be nice."

"And I *have* started taking notes on book three. I'm thinking of calling it *The Dart of Persuasion*."

"The Dart? That's a strange name!"

"Aristotle called rhetoric the 'art of persuasion,' so my 'dart' would suggest murder. I'd start each chapter with a rhetorical topic, like ethos or pathos or a logical fallacy, and then use that topic to loosely guide the chapter, same as I've done in the other two books with composition terms."

"Well, you've lost me now. Remember that I didn't go to college like you did. Your readers will not all be educated, Matthew."

"Mom, college *is* reading, so you're about the most educated person I know!"

Jean Diggerson gave a "humph" to that assertion, and then Digger imitated that sound and laughed. He said that she would see him *soon* and see his book even *sooner*. Both sounded good to the eighty-one-year-old mother, so the two strongly rooted Diggersons said good bye.

After hanging up, Digger felt the cottage's silence and called for Snodo, who appeared from the living room, her eyes bright, expecting a treat or maybe a walk. "I just wanted to say 'hello,'" said Digger, and the small white horse wagged her tail in response, said "Urp, urp," like a performing seal. Digger smiled and thought about Simba, her wide, goofy grin, and then about his mother. That had been a nice conversation, mostly positive, except for that 'age' talk. Sans Simba, sans Anna, how many people in the world actually loved him? If Jean Diggerson were to be swept away, too, by that dedicated custodian Time, then what would the last twig on the branch do? Let gravity take over and just float, drift a bit, then steer into a star, become light? But what of Snodo? Digger could not leave the little white dog. The living unicorn would tether him, albeit precariously, to the earth.

Maybe he should get Snodo another companion. *Yes, but not yet,* not while Simba still walked so tangibly through the cottage, where he could still see her everywhere—on the couch where she once twitched in her dreams, in the back yard where the little lion played tag with the sparrows, even almost below his consciousness where she frolicked alongside the black river, a shadow herself there, a dark silhouette.

After his phone conversation, Digger had forgotten about Richard Schmidt, so he was startled to see the distinguished old man's picture on the local news at six. Richard had been found after a Silver Alert lasting three hours. He had been discovered by a neighbor on a back road more than a mile from his and Gwena's home. Gwena and the police had mobilized her neighborhood, and the story's end was a good one. This time, anyway, but Digger wondered about the Schmidts' future. If Richard could escape locked doors, then what was Gwena to do? Digger thought of Anna. He had not tried to lock the doors on her. That was a silly thought.

At around midnight, he fell asleep on the couch, but Snodo was not by his side. The white unicorn was crouched in vigil at the back door, keeping an eye on the darkness because something hid within it, something out of harmony, twisted, waiting. Snodo could hear it breathe.

## Chapter 16: To End

Note: Nobody needs lyrics about periods, except perhaps one of my dear cousins, Penelope Wilder, who in her missives used dashes instead of end marks, so that her letters were like wild roller-coaster rides of plots and emotions, slashed statement after statement. Memorable but exhausting. For everyone but my cousin, a period simply announces the end.

Diggerson wasn't home, and neither was that pesky white beagle, who always seemed to know he was there, watching. He was sure the little bitch could see through the dark. *Loud yapper, too!* Why did the littlest dogs have the loudest barks? Maybe he'd ask Digger that, right before he shot him, two or three times, just to make sure. He should have done it last month, before that damn second book was finished. *That hurt!* Two damn books! He planned to have gotten the prolific bastard during Spring Break, but then Diggerson's other dog, the nice quiet one, died. He had seen the Chair burying it and then sitting near the hole, and he had felt bad for the man. *How couldn't he?* It was like Diggerson was burying a child. Now *that* really would be sad, *that* would be worth taking a walk out into the bay or off the Bay Bridge or perhaps smack into one of those OVC commuter buses. But if he did any of those things, then he couldn't taste the rippling sweetness of revenge.

That damn cat was back at the gate, though. What was it doing? It never varied its routine. Every time, there it would be, sitting with its four black legs all together, just peacefully looking at Diggerson's cottage. It was maddening! Was it even real? Maybe he was just imagining the animal.

"Scram! Go away!" He waved at the black cat with his left arm, the one closest to the animal, but it just stared up at him, didn't take him seriously.

"If I had my trusty little club, you'd scram! Right into Hell with a huge dent in your head!" He kicked at the cat with his left leg, and this time the animal jumped back. "See! Don't like that, do you!" And he swung his leg over again, causing Inky to back away along the fence line and then to turn nonchalantly and amble off, disappearing over the stone jetty that marked a curve south in the bay.

"Good!" he said, suddenly noticing that he had been talking aloud to the cat, not just in his head. He was visible, too, because night had yet to fall. Why was he taking these chances? Didn't they say that people like him, the ones who went against society's flow, wanted to be caught? *I'd rather just be dead!* he thought, happy that he hadn't voiced that conclusion out loud. He was back in control. Time to take a *big step*, though, and Eliot Gladstone gulped at the air twice, opened the back gate, and walked directly across the yard toward Matthew Diggerson's cottage. He was happy. Just like his name.

Digger had just about finished the last office hour of the spring semester, his three classes having ended the previous day. Now he just had to sit in his office waiting for problems to appear in his doorway, but luckily none so far had. Digger thought about that girl from Lou's class, the one who had called the Lip Licker a "female hater," or something like that. She had never followed up on her complaint, had not even replied to Digger's email. Problem solved, apparently. Johnny Lambmann had never emailed him back either, so apparently that connection was indeed severed for good. Time had already done so a couple decades ago. Un-nurtured roots, of course, shrivel and die, especially thin ones. However, on a positive note, several OVC teachers had commented favorably on his second book's cover, mostly full-timers, quite a change from the previous semester's reticence. Digger wondered how Bill was getting along with his "literature." The Chair had enjoyed his semester-ending talk with Bill, quite a character, but a good one to have experienced. Maybe Digger would model a teacher after Bill in *The Dart of Persuasion*. Making a Republican the killer. Not a bad idea! So far, though, Digger had made few notes about this third Billy D Wilder tale, mainly having just chapter title ideas: Pathos, Ethos, Logos, along with the dark side of the latter, such as Generalizations, Faulty Emotional Appeal, Slippery Slope, etc. All those fallacies in logic. Since human beings commonly twisted logic in manipulative ways, creating whole categories of fallacies, Digger would have no shortage of chapter titles.

Endings always felt a little sad, happy and sad, the yin and yang. While some of his students had made great strides, others continued to repeat the same problems, some of them superficial, like putting a colon after verbs (like "states" or "includes"), others much more important, like offering only a single sentence of broad explanation after quotations. *Well*, he had done his best, had offered students many examples and lots of tips, most of which had hit their targets—*hopefully!* Now, he was completing his third year as Department Chair. Maybe that was enough. Maybe he should devote more time to writing, but how many murders could possibly occur on one college campus? Could Billy D do some traveling perhaps? Maybe he could find love?

If he did, though, would some killer take it from him, snatch away even the possibility? Had that happened last year? Twice! Could Digger really be the Kevin-Bacon connection to murder? Digger had begun to disbelieve his own jealousy theory, for none of his colleagues seemed capable, even the weird ones who breathed, licked, and blinked too much! Patricia Pauley had emailed him again, too, requesting fall courses, so whatever work she had done with her Private Dick husband Bob must have reached a satisfactory conclusion. A happy ending? Digger could hear a retort to that question: "No such thing as happy endings, Diggerson!" Now whose voice was that? Of course, Mr. Morbid, Paul Smith. He might have said that very statement when he and Digger had squared off in Digger's kitchen eight years past. After that experience, Digger probably should have purchased a home-alarm system. *Oh, well.* Just ten minutes left to this final office hour.

As though reading his thoughts, Snodo popped out from beneath Digger's desk and stared up at him, her mouth and tail both smiling. "Not quite yet!" Digger said into the white beagle's face, and Snodo took those words as an invitation to dance about the office. Digger laughed. Outside, the OVC quad looked absolutely deserted. All the good little students in their dorms studying for final exams? Somehow, Digger didn't think so, but maybe they were. Probably the library was full of focused pupils, all pouring over their notes, finding research on the computers, and staying away from their iPhones. *Yeah, right!* After five, the sidewalks would ring with their laughter and footsteps all headed for the cafeteria. Not yet, though.

What was it about endings that seemed so sad? The end of possibilities perhaps. With the stamp of a period, a sentence could offer no more words or images or proof. That was it, over! This semester wouldn't be over until Digger graded all those papers, and who knows what other problems might arise and need his attention? He had already completed the fall schedule, basically just copying last fall's but changing a few names, such as

Johna Adams'. Who had killed Johna? Digger tried to picture her face, but nothing much would materialize. Time had started to take even his more recent memories. *Simba!* When he glanced down, he saw Snodo still staring up alertly. She was a very smart dog! Snodo didn't need Digger the way that Simba had, not the same somewhat desperate connection, the thick tether between the two broken beings. The connection that dementia had severed. Digger pictured Simba walking into his office and saying "Woof!" the way she always had. *Woof, woof!* Not a jarring sound at all, almost muffled in fact. Digger had known what that word meant: love.

Maybe that's how he would end his Christmas card to Anna next year: With "Woof." Fatigue wrapped in goofiness. Maybe simple tiredness made endings sorrowful. Digger checked the library towers' clocks. One said four-fifty-two, the other four-forty-nine, so Digger decided to believe the first one. "Just eight minutes early. Let's go, Snodo!"

On the way to his car, Digger let the white dog run free, but little on the campus presented itself for investigation. Just bushes, old smells. Nobody exited a door or called out in greeting. The buildings all seemed to have called it a day, and not even George North, mop in hand, appeared in the Administration Building's windows. Thinking of Christ, for some reason, Digger made the long straight walk to his little Toyota Yaris, and Snodo hopped right into the passenger seat and sat waiting. What a good girl! *So long, OVC.*

He had broken into the cottage easily, through the side window directly into Diggerson's living room. That side had no neighbors, just a garage and the bay's elbow turn to the south. Would be a nice view if not for the garage, which was a piece of *junk* anyway. He wondered why Diggerson hadn't torn it down. *People are pretty wacky,* he thought and then laughed at that. After all, he had to admit that it was *pretty wacky* to break into a colleague's house and then shoot him!

He had already checked out all the rooms, such that they were, being careful to avoid the windows on the north side, where nosy neighbors possibly lurked. He had looked first for silent alarms, of course, but Diggerson seemed pretty trusting. No cameras or complicated locks or surveillance systems of any kind. No hardware or wires anyway. That made things easier. No dog, either, not that that little white yapper would have been any problem, other than the noise. But he had not wanted to kill the dog, he was not a monster, after all! Anyone who would kill a dog should be locked up or put down. Hadn't he just shooed that black cat away? He hadn't actually kicked or hit it?

Thinking of that cat, he moved into the kitchen and looked out back. It was back at the gate, resuming its vigil. *Son-of-a-bitch!* That cat was a bit unnerving! What the hell was it doing, anyway? Was it really real? He now wanted to go out back and shoot the creature, but that would be crazy. The neighbors would surely hear him and probably see him and then the jig would be up. He didn't plan on spending any time in a jail cell. Being incarcerated, a person might as well be dead, for *freedom* was all that made life tolerable. He would have laughed had he known how uncomfortable the word "freedom" made Matthew Diggerson.

"C'mon, Digger, my boy, my two-time author, my old friend, my new enemy," chanted Eliot Gladstone. "Come to your destiny. After all, dead authors sell more books!"

Digger wasn't used to coming home in daylight, but since five-o'clock in May didn't even hint at twilight, he immediately saw Inky out back. When he opened the driver's side door, Snodo leaped across his lap and ran across the back yard, no doubt to charge up to the cat, but then suddenly the white dog stopped and looked toward the house. Digger laughed because her right arm seemed stuck in the air so that she looked like an unconventional hunting dog.

"Yes, yes, Snodo," laughed her human. "You're going to eat soon, but let's just say hello to Inky first."

Digger walked slowly up to the black cat, not wanting to scare the feral animal, expecting Inky to back away nonchalantly and maintain some distance, but this time she (he?) just watched him approach. Maybe Inky *was* somebody's cat, not feral at all. When the composition instructor reached down a hand, the animal just looked up until fingers met head, and then the great golden eyes closed happily, and Digger actually heard that rumbling ripple that meant cat rapture. *Purring!* Inky was purring away like a little engine.

"Why, you're quite something!" Digger said to the cat, but apparently Snodo didn't share his enthusiasm. Frozen comically, she was still poised and staring at the back door, totally ignoring the scene at the gate. "Okay, Snodo, food soon, and this time we're going to give a little more to Inky." Turning back to the black feline, he said, "Do you mind a little dog kibble? I have some turkey slices, too, I think, so maybe that will have to do. I'll get some cat chow for you tomorrow."

The big cat just blinked at him again (*cat kisses!*) and then pushed her head right into his palm. "That's quite a bump!" he laughed at Inky, adding, "Maybe I'll change your name to Bumper. No? *No*, you're already Inky."

Digger straightened up. He thought about his neighbors, Graham and Donna. If they saw him talking to the cat like this, they'd probably have a good laugh. *Let 'em!* They didn't seem to be home, anyway. With a glance back at Inky, Digger passed Snodo and beckoned for her to follow. *The little nut!* He went up the back steps and stuck his key into the door, and the sound seemed to unlock his remaining dog, who suddenly dashed up the porch steps. When he entered the kitchen, Snodo stayed behind him for a change, but Digger thought nothing of that.

The apartment was dark, as though somebody had closed all the shades, and even when Snodo barked, Digger didn't recognize the warning. He still had the outside sun in his eyes, so he entered his living room blinded. And in the darkness, a man's shape stepped forward and worlds merged like currents in deep water, light from reality refracting into prisms of imagination, dreams, and consciousness, life and death, fantasy and reality, and "who knows which is which, and who is who?" And Digger wondered if that Pink Floyd music were coming into his ears or out of his soul. Past into present, fiction into fact. From the darkness, it came, with bad intent, Aqualung, quite bad intent, for its eyes blazed and its teeth gleamed, big canines gleaming, impossibly long and pointed (*family heirlooms!*). And its white skin said death, and its smile held back no joke. Was it a man, a woman, a vampire, an illusion? One second the face was Paul Smith's, then it looked like Lou, like Jay, even like Twitch, and then like a stranger. Michael Pell? Bob Pauley? Breathing, it came out of the dark, hovering toward Billy D Digger (whom?) of the Wilder clan as though riding an invisible horizontal escalator. Arms raised, of course, with long fingers out and flexing.

*Why are people always trying to kill me?* Digger thought, and he almost laughed. *They've gotten almost all of us: my sister, my father, my colleagues, my dog and cats, and Danny, too. This must be how Jewish people feel!*

That's what Digger thought, but when the spots faded from his eyes to reveal a recognizable face, what he said was, "Hi, Eliot. Fancy meeting you here." Digger nodded at the gun in Eliot Gladstone's right hand, a simple looking revolver, short barreled, an ugly snub. "You've changed your MO," he said to the double murderer.

"Oh, this?" said the aging killer. "Well, Digger. I didn't think that you would let me walk up and throttle you. I'm old, you know, and somehow I don't think that strangulation—that's a strange word, isn't it, Digger? It actually sounds the way it feels! Anyway, I didn't think that would work. At the least, I'd end up with bruises, and how would I explain that to my friends and neighbors?" Eliot laughed at the impracticality and then choked, coughed, breathed. "You know, Digger," he continued, "this is ironic. You once said that fighting for your life against that nutter Paul Smith made you want to live again, to live after your wife dumped you. For me, it's fighting against life, it's killing, that makes me want to live. Regular life makes me want to blow my brains out! Isn't that jux-ta-po-si-tion funny?" For that penultimate word, Gladstone puffed out each syllable, making Digger think of an old train beginning to chug up the tracks.

"If you mean 'odd' funny, then, yeah, I see your point, Eliot."

"Oh, I think it's a bit 'ha-ha' funny, too! Come now, Professor Diggerson, published author, twice even, you must laugh at life's anomalies."

Digger thought that he was looking at one of life's anomalies. Then he heard Snodo's growling, and now his remaining dog was walking bravely toward the killer. "Stop, Snodo! Stay with me!"

"Oh, Digger! Do you think that I would hurt an animal? I could, of course, but I would never do that! That would be monstrous. I didn't even hurt that black cat outside. There is a black cat out there, right?"

Digger ignored the question. Instead, he asked one himself. "So that old David Reed Winslow envy never really left you, did it? Not like you said."

The older professor's lips started moving, twisting, forming first a frown and then a sick smile, which exuded a thick exhale of emotion, a groan blending frustration, anger, and helplessness, meat and rocks. "My nemesis, Digger, my old nemesis. David Two Last Names. Please give him my regards, when you see him, soon."

Digger thought of this twisted human walking down the Humanities hallway next fall, strolling into the summer meeting in August. The Breather would have to build some thick fences, but he was obviously good at doing that. Digger thought of David Reed Winslow, then of Danny Jones, who became Johna Adams, Tobias, other faces, all shifting and merging, all pages in the book of Time. Anna's face tried to materialize, once, twice, repeatedly, but Digger found that he had forgotten her details. He thought of J. Zorn, her face, the Dark Anna, yet that comparison didn't help. Janet or Joyce or Jezebel or whatever her name was didn't really look like Anna. *My Anna!* Digger focused again on the gun, just a little thing in Eliot's hand, a dark toad. It looked like a toy.

"That's not much of a gun," he said.

Eliot turned his hand and looked down at the weapon, at the short dark-gray barrel, the opposite of Dirty Harry's 44 Magnum and its impossible length, the way it pointed at the future like the Ghost of Christmas-Yet-to-Come's skeletal finger. Compared to that image, Eliot's gun looked like it would expel only pellets, maybe even popcorn or a little white flag.

"It will do the job, Digger. A 22 caliber might not blow all the way through your head, but it will get in there and bounce around quite a bit. Later on, the pathologist will dig the bullet out. Maybe a couple of them. Depends on how I feel."

Although that image wasn't pleasant, Digger didn't feel any sense of panic. He almost guffawed at the way the older man was trying to goad him. And maybe Digger was just ready. Who would really miss him, after all? How big of a hole would he actually leave? His mother, of course, but she would still have her sisters and brother, even though John probably wouldn't be able to hear the news. "What?" he would say. Carol and Mary would commiserate with her, nodding their heads in tandem, and Jean Diggerson had handled death before. She was a pro at that. The Wilder clan would go on, at least for a couple more ticks of the turning Earth. *The Wilders*. Billy D would die, too, after only two tales. Digger pictured his pair of books alone on a shelf, and that was too bad because he was just six months or so away from completing his third story, and that would have made a real series out of Billy D Wilder. A trilogy! *No series now*. But what did that really matter anyway? It wasn't like reams of people were reading the first book, and the second had just taken flight, if you could call it that. Anna had not even read the first, not that he knew. *Anna*. She would come to his funeral, and that made dying almost worth it, being close to her again. *Death. Simba*. Maybe Simba would appear. Maybe Digger would see a white light and it would lead to Simba, her big mouth broken open into a wide smile, her eyes on him, her soul tethered to his again, not broken by dementia. That would be fantastic!

But then Simba made Digger think of Snodo, the little unicorn dog, intense and enthusiastic. Snodo could still be happy, though, without him. Unlike Simba, the white dog could thrive with anyone who simply fed her and occasionally talked into her upraised face, her light-brown eyes that fell into her soul and just kept going, all the way back to the beginnings of life, it seemed to Digger. Her glow. Her spark. Beautiful Snodo and her Middle Earth name!

The Shire dissolved and left Eliot Gladstone standing there, like a broken Saruman, dangerous but pathetic.

"Why did you tell my student that I knew the second victim?"

"Did I?"

"Last December, right after you killed that Valerie woman. You must have followed her from Stop & Shop and killed her right then. Then you told my student about it, about my knowing her?"

"Yes, that was exciting, Digger. All of it! And I told your weird student because I had to tell someone, and I hoped that he would tell someone and get you into trouble. I was laying a trail, Digger, bread crumbs for the police pigeons."

"I did that myself, Eliot, when Valerie wrote my number down. The cops found the note, of course."

"Of course! I had hoped that *that* would happen. When I saw her talking to you at the store and then write something down, I had hoped that it was your name and number. I was excited for you, Digger. A woman after all these years!"

"I threw her number away, you know. She and I were never going to get together. You killed her for nothing."

"Oh, not for nothing, my friend! The killing is actually everything."

The Breather had once again aimed the little revolver at Digger, at his head, and Digger remembered what his demented colleague had said about those 22 caliber bullets *bouncing around.* The little gun made Digger think of that poem about the deceased baby, how the speaker had looked at the little body and thought, "How could such a small thing hold so large a thing as death!" Something like that, anyway. Then Digger again thought of Snodo, who had laid her body flat to watch this scene, her back legs frogged out tranquilly, her eyes locked on Digger's to see what was up.

"You must be lonely," Digger said to his probable killer.

"Aren't you?" responded the standing man, the Breather.

"I was, and I suppose I am."

"Of course you are," said Eliot. "Just look at this place. You're all alone in it, have been for decades. The air stinks of emptiness!"

"No," said Digger. "Anna's here." Digger didn't want to mention Snodo, didn't want Eliot to do anything to her, despite the killer's promise to spare the dog.

"You're delusional, Digger!"

"And what are you, Eliot? You're standing here, in my house, with a gun. You're going to kill me, and you've killed others, Johna, that other woman, a stranger, and how many others? What kind of a life is that?"

"You would be surprised," answered Eliot Gladstone. "I didn't want to start, you know, killing. At first I just wanted to kill myself. Because I know all about feeling lonely and useless, feeling …"

"Jealous?"

That word seemed to focus the killer, who swiveled his stare back to the seated man and then smiled, breathed, smiled.

"David Reed Winslow," he sneered at Digger. "Matthew Diggerson! I was over the other, you know. I actually felt bad about David Two Last Names. I was free from that past, free from …"

"Jealousy?"

"Yes, Digger. Jealousy. That's all and that's everything! Jealousy!" The gun-toting creature spoke this last word as though it were three. His breathing seemed to be a separate presence in the room. Digger wondered if Eliot Gladstone were about to collapse.

"Your book was just too much!" the old man said, breathed, again talking not only to Digger, but to some force within, without. "Too much! How much can any man accept? Loser! Waste of breath! *You* actually killed Adams and that other woman, Digger. *You* and your *book*!" Gladstone was throwing his arms around now, as though giving a speech, accenting words and letting some spittle fly. Digger wondered if the crazy old fool was about to shoot himself. About to commit a murder-suicide.

"Oh, I was so happy when nobody wanted to read it, when you were just ignored! I told myself that your book was junk, one step above self-publishing. In fact, I even had myself convinced that you had found no publisher, had just done the thing yourself! But I could not stay convinced. I fell at times, fell into despair, and David Reed Winslow came back. He came into my dreams, Digger, did you know that? Do you know how it feels to be mocked by a hanged man in your dreams? Digger shook his head, but the other was not paying him any attention. "No, you wouldn't know, how could you know? You wrote a book, and then another. Is it here, that second book? Does it exist? Digger shook again—no reaction. "No! Don't tell me! I don't want to see it. I don't want to know about it. I will finish my own book, do you know that, Digger? That I will finish my book?"

"Definitely," said Digger, still seated, still oddly calm, and he remembered his last dance with Paul Smith, the way that peace had settled over him when death appeared. How often did death show itself to a man? Probably just once, just at the end, and Digger thought of the end, pictured it as a shiny line of tape strung across the road ahead—life as a marathon, a long walk with a sudden conclusion, always sudden, no matter the person's age, always unexpected, no matter his or her state of health. Digger felt healthy, but that shining tape did not bother him. He could run through it.

Eliot Gladstone had gone silent, and Digger noticed now that those two slightly bloodshot eyes were again aimed at him, as was the little gun. The green-eyed monster had eaten his old colleague, devoured him from the inside out, and Digger wondered how much Eliot weighed, whether he had any substance at all, whether a strong breeze would carry him off, like a gull. He pictured Eliot crying "Eyut, yut, yut" and sailing off—a nice image, comical. The vampire man moved forward one step, another.

Our hero stood in the diminishing light, immobile, the approaching figure dragging shadows and swallowing all light. In Digger's mind, a reel was running out or perhaps being rewound for storage, and that's the way it is in the end, the big reel sputtering and flapping to a close, all wound tight, all those played-out images packed in black, just one cell showing, one remaining, Digger's face, a white oval framed in shade. Digger thought of Simba's darkening eyes.

Indeed, the last time someone had tried to murder Digger (Paul Smith with the knife handed down to the madman from his ancestors), the incident had had the opposite effect, not killing Digger but reigniting his interest in and desire for life. This time, eight years later, the would-be victim felt acceptance, but then Digger thought with guilt of his students' final papers. Who would grade them? Then that responsibility faded. *Maybe Eliot would!* Digger's death would cause his killer extra work! *Irony.*

Digger decided to sit, so he took a step toward Eliot Gladstone and then two to the side, dropping onto his couch. Snodo slinked over and burrowed under his legs.

At Digger's movement, Eliot had halted, startled, but Diggerson was up to no tricks. "I'm going to fix you forever, Digger," said the looming man holding the little gun, and Digger thought of that Coldplay song about trying and not succeeding. In his mind, he heard an old man singing it, not the Coldplay guy, because he had seen a show on PBS about a nursing-home choir, and he remembered one ancient fellow, with a respirator, seated on the stage and delivering that song, slowly, in a lower voice than the Coldplay star, the one who was married to the woman who had always reminded Digger of Tolkien because she resembled Galadriel's daughter, as though if she lifted up her arms, Christ-like, she could just float away, her hair waving all about, elfish and magical. To Digger, this woman (what was her name? *Gwena?*) had always looked like a Lothlorien princess. Was she still married to the Coldplay leader? Galadriel's daughter had probably left him, or maybe the pop-rock star had been like Billy D and left her. Digger thought about asking Eliot, who reminded him a bit of the old "Fix You" singer, but he knew that the other would not take the question seriously, would think that Digger were stalling for time. *Time!* Digger had had enough of it, had held up the fences for long enough. He suddenly remembered the name of that ancient choir: Young at Heart.

Gladstone stood just a handful of feet from Digger, the snubby gun leveled down. "You look a little pensive, Digger. Are you lost in those fantasy worlds again, trying to get away into one."

"I was just thinking of Galadriel's daughter."

"Who's that? Some Harry Potter character?"

Digger smiled. How could anyone exist without knowing Galadriel? He felt bad for Eliot Happyrock.

Eliot's tongue came out and passed across his upper lip, and Digger of course pictured Lou Knightly, felt a stab of remorse for having not trusted Lou's words, his enthusiasm. Jay Moore, too—the Blinker. And even Twitch, a lonely eighteen-year-old boy. And others, too, just about everyone Digger knew and even people he didn't, like Diana Pell's mysterious son, Michael, and Bob the Private Eye. For the past few months, he had placed them all in the defendant's chair, had judged them, at times finding each guilty, too. Guilty! No, Digger realized that Eliot had done all that, Eliot and uncontrolled emotions, an inability to accept. Eliot and his rotting corpse in the cargo, those heavy green chains of jealousy.

Then Digger pictured the Dream Board outside his office, all of those pieces of paper, so many that they overlapped. *Layers of dreams*. He imagined Anna, saw her sitting with coffee and reading one of his books, the other waiting on her kitchen table. His name printed clearly on the covers. In his mind, both books appeared again, this time in his mother's living room shelf. Cobalt blue and green. It was good. It was enough.

This time, when Digger watched death's renewed approach, he experienced no surge of defiance, no zeal to turn the tables, no fire at all, for he felt sorry for the man. This time, he offered the approaching darkness his outstretched neck, and he felt peace now—except for one whispered image, one nagging thought, the very last cell in the reel.

"Eliot," he said, looking into the approaching eyes. "Please don't hurt my dog—afterwards."

"Oh, don't worry, Digger. I could never kill a dog. But I'm a little surprised at you. I thought you'd be a little more freaked out here, maybe begging or crying. You see, this is reality, Digger, not those mysteries or Tolkien or *The Walking Dead* or Harry Potter, all those fantasy stories you're always so gaga about. This is real."

At that, Digger actually smiled broadly, showing teeth, because his mother had often said the same thing, minus the hatred and the gun. "You sound like my mother," he told the hovering figure, and he thought about the eighty-one-year-old woman again for a moment. She still had her siblings, her blood roots, and she had dealt with death before. She knew how to survive, having handled loss far more productively than he, that's for sure. Digger returned to the present: "But you're both wrong. Nothing is fantasy. Everything is reality. The orcs, the walkers, the Death Eaters, they're all in us. They're the insecurities that keep us up at night, self-abuse, guilt, ego, the cross words spoken rashly to a loved one. All the antagonists, all the obstacles. It's all right here on this earth. You should know that better than anyone, Eliot, for jealousy's just an evil shadow, the main nemesis in any so-called 'fantasy.'" Death stopped, paused in thought.

"Maybe, Digger. Maybe. But it sounds like you're calling me an orc, old friend." Out came a breath, like a sentry for that inner force that had taken over an old man, turned him young and vulnerable and oh, so angry. Digger almost expected to *see* the breath, a thought bubble perhaps, maybe an image of the inner demon, a slitted eye, flames. That image would have oozed out right at this moment in a Stephen King story, and, of course, it was actually happening here, too. Just because the beast couldn't be seen did not make it any less real. Eliot Gladstone breathed again.

"Not an orc, Eliot. Just an obstacle. We're all antagonists at times, right? And mainly to ourselves. But you can be a hero, too. You see, I need you to feed Snodo and then to let her out into the back yard. My neighbors will check on her tomorrow. Make that be your last selfless act, Eliot. To care for a little being."

It was.

That's how it ends, my friends, and don't think that any of our own periods are any different than our hero's. What follows the period? Is it empty space or just a strong pause before the next chapter? Can it be too much to hope that this story's protagonist finds Simba, follows a soft hooting and discovers her thick, double-coated fur, her wide grin? Let's hope that he meets Shyla, too, and that he puts out a hand to touch her little head, as round as a tennis ball, and that she kisses him with her eyes, that Skittles appears, too, crouched, still, the wild watching from her black, ancient eyes. And of course his father, and Emma. Let's hope that Digger connects again with them all. Let's hope that we all do.

## Epilogue

Snodo couldn't find the right smell, the right sounds, the right creatures. Nothing was *right*. The old couple was fine, warm and generous, but Snodo felt restless and lost.

"At the pound," the man said, "they called her 'Snowdoe.' What do you think of that name?"

"Sounds like a hobbit," said the woman.

"Hm," replied her husband, a retired postal worker, long retired. Remembering those long *Lord of the Rings* movies, he gazed down at the white dog who just lay quietly on the couch, her eyes open but not seeming to see much—that thousand-mile stare that dogs could shift into almost at will. "With that ruff and those big eyes, she looks more like an orc than a hobbit."

"Oh, Len, not an orc!" said his wife, who had not only loved the movies, but actually read the books! "I don't want to think of orcs when I look at her. Look how fuzzy and sweet she looks, especially when her eyes close. Let's call her Muffy!"

"You call everyone that, Annie, even me, and half of our old cats were Muffy's."

"She looks a little like your brother Mike," realized Annie, and Len laughed at that.

"With those big, deep eyes and all that white ruff, she looks like something that would emerge from a mountain in Tibet."

"So does your brother," laughed the woman, and the man laughed again, too. Snodo opened her eyes at the nice sounds, safe and promising, but she didn't turn her head. The atmosphere was good, soothing and undemanding. The dog's eyelids slowly descended.

"Look, Len. Muffy's closing her eyes!"

"Muffy or Mike," laughed the husband.

With her sight shadowed, Snodo was searching again, drifting back, yet thoughts were not senses, gave nothing to grasp, breaking apart, slipping away. One of the people was petting her now, the old man. "Soft," he said, and Snodo stretched once, twisted her body to lie flat, showing her belly.

"Oh, she likes that!" exclaimed the old woman. "Snodo? You know, Len, that name fits." Len nodded and kept petting the slumbering little animal.

Soon, very soon, the white dog could drop out of consciousness and fly in her dreams again, searching for her own couch, for the smells of the cottage and of the sea, for Simba, for Digger, for home.

The room at the end of Ward C held an air of mystery, not only because it offered no window to the outside world and displayed no identifying number to the inside one, but also due to the armed police officer who sat in a hard chair before it, barring access. Even when this official presence disappeared into Time's passage, the dark green door, always closed, still exuded a warning, almost a threat, as though the occupant had an exotic disease that waited to spring and latch onto any trespasser.

Few ignored the implied repercussions and entered the nameless room, and for those who did—doctors, nurses, aides—no greetings awaited, no movement, no trivial conversations other than the whispered remarks amongst themselves. Facts announced. Small orders given. In this somber room, designed originally as a janitor's closet, silence reigned, except for the continual beeping of a tall machine to the left of the narrow bed, a buzzing so insistent and annoying that nearly any man would have been driven howling mad. But the man in the lone bed, fair-haired, lay with one foot already off of this earth, hovering just above the sleep of the dead, perhaps three feet down, maybe four, but not six. Not yet six.

THE END

## ABOUT THE AUTHOR

After graduating from the University of Connecticut and then the University of Arizona, Dave Gillespie returned to New England to teach college composition and continues to do so. In Providence, Rhode Island, he lives happily with his wife (Elena) and two dogs (Belle and Holly). His "Simba" passed away peacefully in 2013 at the age of 16.

*Marked for Murder* is the third in his Matthew Diggerson mysteries. The first two were *Rules to Die By* and *Planning to Die.*

www.ingramcontent.com/pod-product-compliance
Lightning Source LLC
Chambersburg PA
CBHW050403260626
47156CB00003B/856

*9781946063571*